MIRIAM'S SECRET

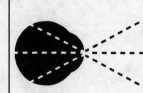

This Large Print Book carries the
Seal of Approval of N.A.V.H.

MIRIAM'S SECRET

JERRY S. EICHER

THORNDIKE PRESS
A part of Gale, Cengage Learning

GALE
CENGAGE Learning·

Farmington Hills, Mich • San Francisco • New York • Waterville, Maine
Meriden, Conn • Mason, Ohio • Chicago

GALE
CENGAGE Learning·

LIBRARY OF CONGRESS CATALOGING-IN-PUBLICATION DATA

Eicher, Jerry S.
  Miriam's secret / Jerry S. Eicher. — Large print edition.
    pages cm. — (Land of promise ; 1) (Thorndike Press large print Christian romance)
    ISBN 978-1-4104-7946-4 (hardback) — ISBN 1-4104-7946-3 (hardcover)
    1. Amish—Fiction. 2. Large type books. I. Title.
  PS3605.I34M568 2015b
  813'.6—dc23   2015012467

Published in 2015 by arrangement with Harvest House Publishers

Printed in Mexico
1 2 3 4 5 6 7 19 18 17 16 15

MIRIAM'S SECRET

CHAPTER ONE

With almost no effort, Miriam Yoder drove her buggy along the familiar road leading to Amos Bland's farm. Her horse, Mindy, needed little direction. For the past three years this journey had been part of their routine every weekday morning since Miriam had turned seventeen and answered an ad placed in the *Holmes County Budget:* "Elderly man in need of daily assistance. Excellent pay," the ad had said. And, indeed, the pay had been excellent. The *Englisha* man was a successful farmer. His well-kept farm was one of the most admired in Possum Valley. Later in life he prospered as an investor, wisely using his profits to purchase land that he was able to sell to a local developer for new tract houses.

When Miriam had showed the ad to her *mamm,* there was some reluctance to allow Miriam to even consider such a job proposal. The "excellent pay" was what had persuaded *Mamm* to let her look into it. Still, she'd hesitated when they talked about what the job might entail. Was it true that this man was old? And how old was "old"? *Mamm* said they wouldn't consider allowing her to take the job if he didn't pass inspection. And just to make certain, *Mamm* had gone along for the job interview. It was only after they'd spoken at length with Mr. Bland and his sister, Rose, that *Mamm* had grudgingly glanced at her daughter with a look that Miriam recognized as permission to accept the job if it was offered and she wished.

Rose explained that she had her own business to take care of during the week, but she'd be able to care for her brother on weekends. At night Mr. Bland would be on his own. If she wanted the job, Miriam would only need to work during daylight hours. Rose said the last person had quit three weeks ago, and they hadn't found anyone suitable until now. Rose glanced at Amos before turning to Miriam. Would she like the job?

"I'll take it!" Miriam said. She was ready to say so before the desperate reasons given by Rose.

Her answer brought pleased looks to Mr. Bland and Rose's faces.

"Wonderful!" Rose exclaimed. "When can you start?"

Miriam smiled. "I can start work whenever you want me to."

"Tomorrow then?" Rose asked.

Miriam agreed. After wrapping up the details and saying good-bye, the two Amish women drove home in their buggy. On the way, *Mamm* said there would never be an overnight stay no matter how helpless Mr. Bland might become in the years ahead. "Not under any circumstances!" she'd emphasized. "I don't care how much we need the money or if Mr. Bland's health declines. I know he appears perfectly harmless, but some things simply aren't decent."

As it turned out, the issue never came up. Mr. Bland remained well enough to tend to himself in the evenings. For most of the day when Miriam was there, he sat in his recliner and looked out the large, front window, occasionally lapsing into naps. Sometimes his mind wandered or his memory faltered, and he would forget Miriam was there. Other times while Miriam was doing household chores or fixing his lunch, she could hear him speaking to his late wife, Thelma.

As the months flew by, Mr. Bland expressed his gratitude to Miriam. He gave her occasional raises by amounts that made her blush. When she objected, Mr. Bland said, "You're doing a good job, Miriam. And I can't take it with me." He would then smile and return to gazing out the window.

Mamm raised her eyebrows at times when Miriam brought the checks that reflected the raises home on Friday nights. "What are you doing for the man, Miriam?" she'd tease.

"Mamm!" Miriam would exclaim. "I just take care of him."

And *Mamm* would say nothing more because the truth was that their family was among the poorest in Possum Valley and needed the money. There was no shame in that either. *Mamm* and *Daett* made no attempt to hide the fact. *Daett* was lame from a farming accident when he was a child, and he walked with a pronounced limp. It didn't stop him from working his farm, but he needed help. The two oldest boys, Lee and Mark, worked hard too. Even so, there were evenings when *Daett*'s face was etched with weariness from the extra efforts he had to expend.

Despite the hardship, there was much the family could be thankful for. For one thing, *Mamm* and *Daett* loved each other. That was what mattered — not how much money was in their bank account. Still, the extra money

Miriam earned was a help, especially because the Yoder family was continuing to grow. There were ten children now, and another one was on the way. Their ages stretched from Miriam's twenty years to the current youngest, Tony, who was three. When the baby arrived, there would be eleven mouths to feed.

Holmes County was one of the busiest Amish-related tourist centers in America. People came from everywhere to watch the Amish and buy their goods. *Daett* could make extra money if he'd cater to them, but he didn't believe the Amish should benefit monetarily from their faith. So he worked harder on the farm and paid the price for his convictions. *Daett* had high ideals, and *Mamm* supported him fully. So far the Lord had supplied the needs of the Yoder family, and there was no reason why He wouldn't continue to provide for them. They would make it with His help.

For one thing, Miriam's sister Shirley was seventeen now and had been out of school for three years. She too would take on a job soon, though she probably wouldn't find one as good as Miriam's.

There was the possibility that Shirley might take over Miriam's duties with Mr. Bland — if Miriam's life went in another direction. If, say, Ivan Mast asked her home some Sunday evening . . . and things progressed from there. One thing was certain: Miriam would say *yah* to dating Ivan at the drop of a hat. They had been sweet on each other all through their *rumspringa* time — if smiles and winks from Ivan counted. Even though Miriam's *rumspringa* hadn't amounted to much, her heart had taken Ivan's attention seriously. One highlight had been the three-day trip she'd taken with a group of young folks to Virginia Beach. The others had made sure Miriam and Ivan had moments alone to chat with each other. Ivan hadn't said anything then about long-term plans. No doubt he had his reasons, she figured. Surely soon he would ask her home after a hymn singing. They were both baptized now. Maybe that was why Ivan had been waiting. Surely another girl hadn't caught his eye. She would have noticed, wouldn't she?

After the turn into Mr. Bland's lane, Mindy slowed her pace and made her way toward the familiar barn. She stopped and waited patiently while Miriam climbed down the buggy steps. Miriam unhitched Mindy and led her into the barn and then a large stall. Grabbing a bucket from the barn floor, Miriam dipped it into a large bag of oats. Feed for Mindy was another thing Mr. Bland wasn't stingy about. The horse was downright spoiled with the oats she ate each day. Miriam smiled and poured the grain into the feeding trough. Mindy stuck her snout right in and began to munch happily away. Miriam walked out of the barn, pausing to close the door. She rushed across the yard and into the house. Faint noises were coming from the bedroom, so Mr. Bland must be up. He was an early riser.

"Bones can't rest no more," Mr. Bland would mutter as he came out of the bedroom on some mornings.

Miriam busied herself with the breakfast preparations. Bacon and eggs were on the menu this morning. It was Mr. Bland's favorite breakfast besides pancakes, which, if he had his way, he'd have every morning. But Rose had told Miriam, "Absolutely not!" when Miriam had mentioned Mr. Bland's preference. "One morning a week is enough!" Miriam had served pancakes just yesterday. She turned on the electric stove and studied the soft glow of the burner for a moment. She'd gotten used to the fancy *Englisha* household gadgets during her time working here. There was the electric stove, the microwave, and the electric washer and dryer. All nice conveniences she never talked about at home. *Mamm* would worry and wonder how much the convenience was affecting her daughter. Would she one day wish to forsake the Plain community's ways in favor of an easier *Englisha* life?

Miriam straightened her shoulders. That would never happen. She was Amish and would always be Amish. That's all there was to it. One day she'd become an Amish wife — hopefully Ivan's!

Miriam paused to listen. Where was Mr. Bland? He still hadn't come out of the bedroom. She turned down the burner on the stove and went down the hall to Mr. Bland's bedroom. She knocked on the bedroom door and called out, "Do you need help, Mr. Bland?"

A low groan answered her call but was quickly followed by, "I'm okay."

"Are you sure?" Miriam waited.

There was silence for a moment. "Maybe I could use some help with this shirt."

Miriam opened the door and entered to find Mr. Bland seated on the side of the bed, dressed except for his shirt that was hanging over one shoulder. A disgruntled look was on his face. "I'm having trouble this morning."

"Let me help you." Miriam lifted his arm gently and brought the shirt sleeve around.

14

Mr. Bland sighed as his arm slid in. "Maybe I should just stay in bed all day."

"And miss your bacon and eggs? I don't think so!" she teased.

He smiled. "You're awfully cheerful this morning."

"I can be a sourpuss if you prefer," she retorted.

"I doubt that!" He chuckled. "Although with me, it could happen."

"Now, come." Miriam stepped closer to button his shirt. "No reason for being downhearted. The Lord has made a beautiful day. I'll help you outside to enjoy it right after breakfast. You can put on your jacket and sit on the porch."

He seemed pleased as she finished the last button and helped him stand. "I think I'd like to go out on the porch right now."

"Before breakfast?"

"Sometimes the soul needs feeding more than the body," he explained. "It's been a long night, dear. Someday when you're old, you'll understand."

"Well, if you're sure." Miriam took Mr. Bland's arm, and the two made their way into the living room. He waited while she grabbed his jacket from the rack and slipped it on him.

"I dreamed about her last night." His

voice hung in the air for a moment.

Miriam didn't ask. She already knew. There was only one woman Mr. Bland would dream about — his beloved Thelma. There were pictures of her everywhere in the house. Thelma and Mr. Bland at their wedding. Thelma and Mr. Bland on vacation somewhere with a great range of snow-covered mountains behind them. Thelma and Mr. Bland on a beach with ocean waves rolling in at their feet. Mr. Bland had told Miriam about Thelma soon after she'd started working for him. "She was the most beautiful woman I ever knew. Right near an angel from heaven."

Miriam led him toward the front door. "What was the dream like?"

"I saw her." A smile spread across his face. "She was young again. Like when we first met, only even more beautiful. Heaven has made her radiant."

Miriam opened the front door, and they walked out. She helped Mr. Bland into the rocker. She didn't know what heaven would be like. Bishop Wagler said one wasn't supposed to have wild imaginations about such things. But if Mr. Bland dreamed about his *frau,* what could be wrong with that?

He sat down and groaned again.

"Let me get a blanket," Miriam said.

16

"That chair must be cold."

He nodded.

Miriam rushed into the house and returned with the quilt from the couch. She lifted his arm and helped Mr. Bland stand enough to slide the quilt partly under him. The rest she draped over his shoulders and arms.

He settled in with a contented look on his face. "It's a beautiful morning, Miriam. And you are beautiful too. Almost as beautiful as Thelma."

Miriam looked away. "You don't have to say that, Mr. Bland. I'm just ordinary."

"Some man will love you someday like I loved my Thelma." He beamed with pleasure.

"That's awfully nice of you to say." Miriam felt her face flush as Ivan's handsome face rose in her mind.

"It's true!" Mr. Bland's gaze settled across the open fields. "Don't ever forget that."

"Thank you," Miriam replied. "I'm going to finish cooking your breakfast now."

He said nothing more as she slipped back into the house.

CHAPTER TWO

Miriam tended to the eggs — sunny-side up as Mr. Bland liked them — and turned the bacon. Her thoughts drifted back to Mr. Bland's kind words, though she knew he'd exaggerated considerably — especially the part about being beautiful. She knew she wasn't that *gut* looking.

Her hope rested in the words *Mamm* often told her: "Beauty is the condition of the soul." *Mamm* said the same thing to Shirley, and to fourteen-year-old Naomi, and to Dana who was nine. But the truth was that Miriam's three younger sisters were beautiful in their own right. And seven-year-old Elizabeth and five-year-old Cheryl would be no different.

Daett didn't have lots of money, but he had beautiful daughters — if you disallow me, Miriam decided. Was that why Ivan hesitated to ask her home? He'd certainly smiled at her often enough, but perhaps he wanted a beautiful woman as his *frau*. And that was to be expected, wasn't it? Didn't every husband think such things about his beloved? No doubt *Daett* did of *Mamm*. Miriam could easily imagine her *daett* telling *Mamm* how *wunderbah* she appeared to him. The words would be spoken with the same tone of love and admiration Mr. Bland used for his beloved Thelma.

Miriam rubbed her neck, sure that she was flaming red at such thoughts. But Mr. Bland wouldn't notice when she went back outside. He'd be in the midst of thoughts about his Thelma and the great love he once enjoyed with her. How sweet that Mr. Bland had dreamed of his late wife last night. The Lord must have sent such thoughts to comfort him during his final lonely days on this earth.

Mr. Bland isn't dying, Miriam corrected herself at once. That wouldn't happen anytime soon. He'd had a bad night, that was all. She would make a point of cheering him up today. Maybe she'd cook something special for lunch. She'd ask him what he wanted, but she already suspected what that would be: a bowl of potato soup spiced with pinches of salt and pepper.

The first time Mr. Bland had shown her the recipe, he'd told her, "Make this for me once in a while, Miriam. Rose won't do it. I suspect the soup reminds her of what she wishes to forget — the time of great poverty in our youth. Even after I married Thelma we went through some hard times. This soup sustained us. Now the taste of it takes me back to those precious years when Thelma and I were poor but in love. That potato soup kept our bodies and souls together." His eyes twinkled at the memory.

Yah, Miriam told herself. She would go ahead and make a bowl of potato soup for lunch. From how Mr. Bland had looked when she left him on the porch, this would fit his mood exactly.

Miriam sprinkled a few grains of salt on the eggs. That was how Mr. Bland liked them. Not too much. "Just a touch," he'd say. With a smile on her face Miriam put the plate and a glass of orange juice on a tray and walked through the living room to the porch. Mr. Bland would enjoy his breakfast on the porch. If not, she would help him back inside.

"Mr. Bland!" she called as she swung open the screen door. "Breakfast is ready."

There was no response. Miriam approached him and waited for him to look up. Had he started his morning nap already? She tried again, louder this time. "Breakfast,

Mr. Bland! Just as you like it!"

When he didn't move, she laid one hand on his shoulder. His body slumped forward. Miriam gasped as she dropped the tray and grabbed for him. The tray clattered to the porch floor. She moved to the front of the rocker and fell to her knees. Her hands were on his now. "Mr. Bland! Mr. Bland!"

His head slumped lower.

She noticed he had a slight smile on his face, but the life had clearly gone out of him.

Miriam took a deep breath and forced herself to her feet. *What happened?* she wondered. Was she to blame? Should she have not encouraged him to sit on the porch? Had she done something wrong? Why would Mr. Bland die without warning? Tears stung her eyes, and she wiped them away. Now was not the time to give in to emotions. She must do something, but what? Perhaps *Englisha* doctors could still bring Mr. Bland back — if she called them quickly.

With another glance at Mr. Bland, Miriam rushed inside to the phone on the kitchen wall. What number should she call? 9-1-1? Isn't that what the *Englisha* people used in their times of trouble? *Yah,* it was. Her hand trembled as she punched in the numbers.

A woman's voice answered quickly. "What is your emergency?"

Miriam choked out, "The man I work for just passed, I think. He isn't responding. I left him on the porch while I fixed breakfast, and now he's not . . ." Miriam caught her breath. "I think he's . . . dead." A lump formed in her throat.

"What is your location?"

"County Road 135 — 2945 County Road 135," Miriam managed to get out.

A barrage of questions followed.

Yah, she could leave the phone to check Mr. Bland's pulse, but she knew there wouldn't be one.

The operator assured her paramedics were on the way. In the meantime, could she start CPR?

"I've not been taught," Miriam said almost apologetically.

"Help is on the way," the woman repeated. "Stay on the phone with me until they arrive."

"I'd rather not," Miriam responded. "I should be out there with him."

The woman seemed to understand. Miriam left the phone dangling from the cord and groped her way outside. Sirens would soon fill the air. They would spell out in a language everyone could understand that something had happened to Mr. Bland on her watch. What should she have done differently this morning that might have made a difference? Were there signs she should have recognized that would have told her to summon help sooner?

The bacon and eggs were still scattered over the porch floor. She ought to clean things up before the *Englisha* people arrived, but she was too weak to try. And they would understand. Rose would too. Miriam stopped her thoughts suddenly. She had to call Rose! Rose would want to know about her brother. Miriam headed back into the kitchen and lifted the receiver. The 9-1-1 operator was still on the line. Miriam blurted, "I need to call someone else. I need to call Mr. Bland's sister, Rose. She needs to know what's going on."

"I can make that call for you," the 9-1-1 operator said. "What's the number?"

Miriam read the number off the note on the kitchen wall where Rose had left it. Miriam had only called Rose a few times in the two years she'd been working for Mr. Bland. It had always been for minor matters. Nothing like this. Rose's brother had passed over the river, and only Miriam had been here.

The operator said, "Stay on the line . . .

or at least keep this one open, okay?"

Still dazed, Miriam agreed but said she needed to go back to Mr. Bland. She let the receiver hang from the cord and made her way back to the porch. *Maybe Mr. Bland wanted to die today.* How that was possible, she didn't know. *A man couldn't choose his day of dying, could he? Or the time?* She approached Mr. Bland and took his hand in hers. *Yah,* she supposed it seemed possible. But she would not speak such thoughts to anyone else. *Mamm* would think them terribly out of order. "Only the Lord can choose such things," *Mamm* would say.

She let go of Mr. Bland's hand and stood beside the chair. Soon the wail of a siren sounded in the distance, and moments later an ambulance turned into the driveway. Two attendants grabbed their gear and sprinted across the lawn. She stepped back, and they gave her brief nods, but their attention was on Mr. Bland. That didn't last long either.

"He's gone," one of them said. Turning to Miriam, he asked, "Is he your grandfather?"

Miriam pressed back her tears. "No, I take care of him during the daytime. His sister comes on weekends."

"Has his sister been notified?" the other man asked.

Miriam nodded even as Rose's car raced

into the driveway. The car stopped abruptly, the driver's side door flew open, and Rose jumped out and ran across the lawn. Miriam stepped back even further as Rose rushed to her brother's side.

"He's gone, I'm afraid," the paramedic repeated.

Rose nodded and turned to Miriam. She slipped an arm around the young woman's shoulder. "Were you with him, dear, when he passed on?"

"I left him on the porch while I fixed his breakfast," Miriam said, motioning toward the splatter of eggs and bacon on the floor. "I found him this way when I came out with his food."

"I'm glad you were here," Rose said. "I'm glad he wasn't alone. He was here, on his porch, looking across the farmland he loved. Really, it's the way he would have wanted it."

Miriam nodded. *Yah, it was the way he would have wanted it.* She knew him well enough to know that much.

"He loved you like a granddaughter," Rose continued.

The paramedics were on cell phones, no doubt calling in their report to the dispatcher.

Rose went on. "He was an old codger, but

you made his last days on this earth happy. For that I can't thank you enough. I know he would have worn me out, and I would have had to place him in a nursing home. How horrible that would have been. He would have died there of a broken heart years ago. Instead, he was able to pass over from his front porch, probably with Thelma on his mind, while a beautiful woman fixed breakfast for him."

Miriam wiped at the tears now flowing freely.

"Amos made arrangements for his passing long ago. I'll let you know the day and time of his memorial service. I hope you'll come."

"I'll need to check with my parents," Miriam replied, meeting Rose's gaze. "I'd like to come, of course. He meant a great deal to me. He made me feel special . . . like I was more than just the hired help." She choked on the words a bit, but they were true. *Mamm* would probably blush mightily if she heard her daughter speak them aloud though. Maybe the *Englisha* world had affected Miriam more than she'd imagined.

Rose gave her a hug. "I loved him too, Miriam."

As the paramedics approached with a clipboard and paperwork, Miriam stepped back, hoping Rose would take over. "I'll go clean up the kitchen," Miriam said.

"I wouldn't think of allowing that," Rose said. "Not after the shock you just had. Go on home and rest for the day. I'll let you know when the viewing and the funeral will be."

"You and Mr. Bland have been so kind to me," Miriam said, her smile trembling.

"Nothing you didn't deserve, dear." Rose pressed Miriam's arm.

"I'll be going then." Miriam walked through the house, out the back door, and headed toward the barn. Mindy greeted her with a loud whinny, as if surprised they were leaving so soon.

"Come. We need to go home," Miriam whispered into Mindy's ear. Miriam took Mindy out of the stall and got her harnessed. Leading the mare outside, Miriam hitched her to the buggy and climbed in. The horse set off at a steady pace. A wave of emotion swept over Miriam. Right now all she wanted was to feel *Mamm*'s arms around her in a tight hug. *Mamm* would know the right words to say to comfort her.

CHAPTER THREE

Eventually slowing Mindy down, Miriam went over the events of the morning again and again. It still seemed so . . . so impossible. And yet it was true. Mr. Bland had died. He was now in heaven with his beloved Thelma.

At the Yoder driveway, Mindy took the turn and headed for the barn, stopping short, knowing the routine. Miriam made her way down the buggy steps and unhitched Mindy. She pulled open the barn door.

"Home already?" her brother Lee greeted. "May I take Mindy for you?"

"*Yah,* that would be great."

Lee waited with his hand on Mindy's bridle. "You're home early. Did you get the day off?"

Miriam dropped her gaze. "Mr. Bland died this morning."

Lee's hand jerked as Mindy pulled forward. "While you were there?" he asked.

Miriam bit her lower lip. "*Yah.* I took him out to the front porch and went back in to fix breakfast. By the time I brought him his food, he'd passed."

"Wasn't that quite a shock?" Lee opened a stall door and led Mindy in.

"*Yah,* of course."

"So you're out of a job then?" Lee was suddenly practical.

"I suppose so." Miriam turned to go. She didn't want to think of the implications of what had happened this morning. Her sorrow over Mr. Bland's passing was still too fresh.

Lee shut the door on Mindy's stall. "Milo Miller stopped by this morning to borrow the single tree. He told me Ivan Mast took Laura Swartz home from the hymn singing last night." Lee glanced at Miriam for her reaction.

"Was I that obvious?" Miriam asked as an image of Laura Swartz rushed through her mind. Laura was young and beautiful. The Swartz family had only recently moved back to the area from the Amish community in Clarita, Oklahoma, where *Mamm*'s sister Fannie and her family lived.

Lee's hand touched Miriam's arm. "Don't worry. I doubt anyone else thought anything about it. Besides, if Ivan's not the one, there's a decent man out there for you."

Miriam mustered a smile. Lee was obviously trying to be kind. After all, *he* had noticed, so no doubt others had too.

"Don't mourn too much," Lee continued. "But then you won't. You're the stable and firm one of the family."

Miriam glanced at Lee's face. "I may not be all you think I am. Sometimes my life hurts too, just like everyone else's. Right now I can't think about Ivan. Mr. Bland is barely gone from my life. He was a kind man, and I'll miss him. He wasn't just my employer. I counted him as a friend."

"Trouble does seem to come in strong doses," Lee agreed. He shrugged as if that were the end of the matter.

"I'd better go," Miriam said. "*Mamm* will be wondering why I'm home. Thanks for your concern. That was nice of you."

"Just remember, there's bigger fish in the ocean," he chirped.

Miriam closed the barn door and walked toward the house. Despite her sorrow over Mr. Bland's death, Lee's news shocked her. Ivan Mast had taken Laura Swartz home! He'd never asked Miriam home. And even Laura's older sister, Esther, was almost as *gut* looking as Laura was. But Ivan had chosen the younger one. Pain throbbed deep inside her. How could Ivan have done that? Had she been wrong to think God was bringing them together? What about all the glances, smiles, and implied promises? Did Ivan believe he'd found someone better than her?

And who was she to say he hadn't? Did she esteem herself above another woman? *I don't want to,* Miriam told herself. But the truth was the thought of Ivan in his buggy with Laura seated beside him made her heart feel like a chunk of lead. Possum Valley suddenly felt straight and narrow, making it hard to breathe. Miriam wanted to run and never stop.

She quickened her pace toward the house. There was no place she could go, and no money to go anywhere anyway. She'd simply have to face the facts as they were. Somehow she'd get over the dreams she'd had for Ivan and herself. Laura Swartz had a perfect right to make a move for Ivan's attention, and apparently she'd won his heart fair and square. Miriam hurried on and pushed away thoughts of Ivan and Laura. *Mamm* was waiting just inside the doorway with alarm written on her face. "You're home at this hour? What's happened, Miriam?"

"Mr. Bland passed this morning after I

arrived." Miriam kept her voice matter-of-fact.

"Oh, no!" *Mamm* gave Miriam a long hug before she led her daughter to the couch and sat beside her. "Tell me what happened."

Shirley appeared from the kitchen as Miriam began to recite the story. When she got to the part where Mr. Bland slipped quietly away to join his beloved *frau,* both *Mamm* and Shirley teared up.

"The man had a *gut* heart," *Mamm* said.

"I wonder what Mr. Bland saw as he left?" Shirley said. "Do you think his *frau* came to lead him over?"

Mamm shook her head. "We'll leave those things to the Lord and not to our imaginations."

Shirley shuddered. "I'm glad I wasn't there."

"That's why Miriam had the job," *Mamm* said. "Still, you would have learned to handle the unexpected. We all do eventually. Well, now it's over and life must go on. We must pray for the family Mr. Bland has left behind. And for us too . . ."

Mamm clearly felt compassion for Mr. Bland's family, but there was also the realization that Miriam was now jobless. There would be no more paychecks until she found another one.

Miriam forced herself to her feet. "I'll look for another job right away. I can even start asking around this afternoon."

"You'll eat first," *Mamm* said. "We have lunch ready. I do agree that it would be wise if you looked for work this afternoon."

"We're always short on money," Shirley said with a shudder. "Why can't *Daett* deal with the tourists like everyone else?"

Mamm's gaze followed her second daughter as the seventeen-year-old went into the kitchen. Turning back to Miriam, she said, "I'm sorry things are the way they are, but your *daett* and I are grateful for everything both of you girls do for us. Life's not fair sometimes, but the Lord will reward you greatly for your sacrifices."

Miriam glanced away. *Mamm*'s praise might cause a burst of tears if she thought on it too long, and that wouldn't be helpful. She was the eldest daughter and had her responsibilities. Things were what they were.

Mamm gave Miriam another hug and left for the bedroom. Miriam walked into the kitchen where Shirley had set plates on the table. She didn't look up when Miriam opened the utensil drawer to help.

After a few moments Miriam said, "You shouldn't complain so much about our money problems. It's not right."

"I'm not a saint like you," Shirley snapped.

Mamm appeared in the kitchen doorway with a weary look on her face.

Miriam rushed over to slip her arm around her *mamm*'s shoulder. "You'd best sit, okay? I'll help finish lunch."

Mamm took the chair with relief on her face. "You'd think this would get easier after ten children. You're the one who should be babied right now, not me."

Miriam ignored the comment. "Are you having complications perhaps?"

Mamm shook her head. "Just the normal pains and tiredness. And now I'm wondering about . . . well, you know."

Money. There is always the money, Miriam thought.

Shirley moaned and declared, "As for me, I think I might just marry a rich man!"

"That's not a wise thing to say," *Mamm* scolded. "There's not a better man around than your *daett*. You would do well to find such a decent husband."

"I suppose," Shirley allowed, but from the look on her face Miriam knew she'd still try to find both — a husband who was decent *and* well off. With Shirley's success with men, that wasn't out of the realm of possibility. She had options Miriam didn't.

Mamm cleared her throat. "You know, Miriam, there's some other bad news you need to know about. It's been said that Ivan Mast took Laura Swartz home on Sunday evening."

Miriam looked at the floor. "*Yah,* Lee told me."

"Ivan's only a day laborer at the Beachy's store," Shirley offered before *Mamm* could respond. "That's not much of a loss, if you ask me."

"Shirley!" *Mamm* scolded again. "Ivan is a decent man, and I had hopes something serious would come of his . . . his friendship with Miriam."

"I'm only teasing," Shirley protested. "Sort of."

Miriam busied herself with placing silverware on the table. "I'll get over him, *Mamm.* Don't worry."

Mamm didn't say anything as the washroom door slammed and happy chatter crept into the kitchen.

Thankfully *Daett,* along with Lee and Mark and the younger children who weren't in school, had chosen this moment to enter the washroom. The talk about Ivan could now end. Miriam let out a sigh of relief.

Shirley opened the washroom door and hollered out, "Dinner!" Lee and Mark roared their protest at Shirley's loud greeting, and Shirley laughed heartily.

"She only does that because you jump," Mark told Lee.

"*Yah.* I'm getting a quiet wife, that's for sure." Lee came in and took his seat at the table.

"She has to be pretty, of course," Shirley chirped.

"That goes without saying." Mark made a wry face. "I wouldn't date a girl if she wasn't pretty."

"Just so she's quiet," Lee repeated with a glare at Shirley.

"That's not a nice thing to say about your sister," Shirley pouted.

Lee grinned. "I guess it would be okay if she were both pretty and quiet."

"You're so mean." Shirley made a face at him.

"Okay, enough of this talk," *Daett* interrupted. "Let's pray and bless the food." He led out in a prayer of thanksgiving for the noon meal.

Miriam peeked at her *daett* as he prayed earnestly as if there was a sumptuous fare laid out on the table when, in reality, there was only a simple beef stew served with homemade bread. That was more than enough when a person was hungry. And

Miriam had never starved a day in her life. Food, a roof over one's head, simple clothing, and love from your family. Wasn't that all a person needed? Of those there was plenty in this home. She was very thankful. *Bless You, dear Lord, for being so* gut *to us,* Miriam breathed silently.

A moment later *Daett* pronounced, "Amen."

Chapter Four

Soon after the dishes had been cleaned and put away, Miriam hitched Mindy to the buggy with Shirley's help. The two climbed in and drove out of Possum Valley toward Berlin. *Mamm* had heard there might be a job opening at the Berlin Gospel Bookstore. On the long climb up the hill into the little town, Mindy hung her head and slowed down until there was barely any forward motion at all.

"Come on, girl! We've got to get there!" Miriam called through the windshield.

The horse perked up and picked up her pace.

Shirley seemed to be in no hurry. "Miriam, let's take our time. I need to talk with you."

Miriam glanced at her sister. She'd been sober-faced ever since they left the house. It was as if a switch had been thrown since lunchtime when she'd bantered so easily with her brothers. Miriam held the reins firmly in her hands and waited.

Shirley seemed to gather her courage before she spoke. "Miriam, I've been seeing Jonas Beachy in town when I shop for *Mamm* on Tuesdays."

Miriam sat up straight on the buggy seat, turned toward Shirley, and stared. "You're seeing Jonas? *How?*"

When Shirley didn't answer, Miriam pressed on. "How did you get close enough to Jonas Beachy to start seeing him? His whole family went *Englisha* years ago. And then his *daett* made money and is now one of the richest men in Holmes County. Where did you run into him?"

"Their family was Amish way back when," Shirley countered.

"They're not *now,* so don't get any ideas," Miriam shot back. "And they attend a terrible, liberal church where Jonas's *daett* is like an elder or something. They've long forgottton Plain ways. And they live in that huge mansion between Berlin and Sugarcreek along State Road 39."

And "mansion" was a mild word to describe the house, Miriam thought. She'd never been inside the place, but her cousin Marvin Yoder had worked with the Amish crew who framed the house. He said the main ceiling in the living room was more than thirty feet high. She couldn't imagine anything like that, but the gorgeous, landscaped exterior was clearly visible from the road. Jonas's *daett* must have more money than the bank in Berlin. No wonder Shirley had been tempted. She probably dreamed of all that money. "You shouldn't even think about Jonas!" she continued. "That family doesn't live like us. And even in *rumspringa,* you shouldn't start out like this."

Shirley crinkled her nose and responded, "It's not like you think, Miriam. And when Jonas came over and spoke with me last week, he was just like an ordinary person."

Miriam jerked her head around. "You . . . you *spoke* with him?"

A smile spread across Shirley's face. "See! You *are* impressed, after all."

Miriam settled back into the buggy seat. "I'm going to calm myself now. Okay, so you spoke with Jonas Beachy. That's not a big deal, but you still shouldn't tempt yourself."

"How do you know I'm tempted?" Shirley's voice was serious.

Miriam tightened the reins a bit, and Mindy slowed down even more. Maybe they did need to take the time for a lengthy conversation. But from the sounds of things,

40

Mamm should be having this conversation with Shirley, not her.

Shirley voice was insistent. "There's nothing wrong with Jonas Beachy, Miriam. And I think he likes me."

Miriam tried to relax. "Just because a boy speaks with you, that doesn't mean anything. Why, look at Ivan and me for your example on that."

Shirley stared straight ahead. "There's more to it than that, Miriam. I'm trying to tell you — if you'll listen."

Miriam drew in her breath. "Okay. What happened?"

"I took a ride in his car." Shirley gave Miriam a quick glance. "And I didn't think I'd feel guilty about it, but I do."

"You did *what*?" Miriam heard herself shriek. She subconsciously pulled on the reins, and Mindy came to a dead stop.

"I had to tell you," Shirley admitted as she winced.

"Okay, Shirley, I'm sure there's more you're not telling me. Out with it. Like every detail!"

"Well . . ." Shirley began with a lilt in her voice.

She's a bit too animated, Miriam thought.

"Well, it happened like this. I drove into the parking lot at the German Village

Market like usual one Tuesday. And as I got out of the buggy, Jonas parked his car right near me." Shirley's eyes gleamed. "The car is a late-model convertible . . . some kind of classic sports car. Anyway, as soon as Jonas got of his car, he said, 'Hi, Shirley!' Miriam, he knew my name! And, of course, I knew his. Jonas Beachy!" Shirley spoke the last two words reverently.

"Surely you didn't say it like that to him!" Miriam exclaimed horrified.

"Hush!" Shirley chided. "It's my story."

"You're the limit!" Miriam cut in. "Remember, you're Amish even if you are in *rumspringa*. He isn't even Mennonite, he's . . ." Miriam searched for the words. "He's more like *Englisha* — but worse."

Shirley ignored her. "I said 'hi' back and complimented him on his neat car. Then he asked if I wanted a ride in it. A convertible, Miriam! I said I did, of course. I am on *rumspringa,* after all. And we were right out in plain sight where everyone could see us. There wasn't anything wrong with it."

Miriam groaned. "*Yah,* you were out where everyone could see you. And I'm sure they did."

"So he took me for a short spin," Shirley went on. "We weren't gone long. And then when we got back, Jonas came inside to help me with the groceries. That's how I made it back in time so *Mamm* didn't know I'd been doing more than shopping. I wasn't a minute late."

Miriam moaned.

"He's a nice man!" Shirley continued. "There's nothing wrong with Jonas. He had the best manners I've ever seen in a man. He even held the car door open for me — like the *Englisha* do for the people they care about."

How Shirley knew what the *Englisha* did for their loved ones was beyond Miriam. What a day this was turning out to be! First Mr. Bland's death, and now her sister had stepped way out of the boundaries of *Mamm* and *Daett*'s vision of *rumspringa* for their children. If *Mamm* found out even a whiff of this . . .

"You must forget about Jonas Beachy starting right now," Miriam stated.

Shirley gave her a long look. "Jonas asked if he could see me some evening. He said he'd pick me up at the end of the lane right after dark. I said I couldn't."

"Well, that's the first smart thing I've heard you say today," Miriam said, letting out a breath.

Shirley appeared unfazed. "Let me finish. I said I couldn't *then,* but that maybe I'd

43

change my mind. And I have changed my mind."

Miriam stared at her sister. "Shirley, before this goes any further, I think you need to talk to *Mamm.*"

Alarm was written across Shirley's face. "I hoped you'd support me in this, but . . ."

"You *have* to tell *Mamm!*" Miriam's voice was firm. "It's best if things like this are out in the open — not done in secret. And you have to think about how this would hurt *Mamm* and *Daett.*" Miriam shivered at the image of *Daett*'s shoulders bowing even lower than normal at the news.

Shirley seemed to sense the same dread and fell silent.

Miriam considered that if Jonas Beachy was a poor man, Shirley wouldn't give him a second glance. Clearly she understood where this could lead. Had Shirley entertained the thought that if this wasn't nipped in the bud, she might end up leaving the faith to marry the man? Miriam was sure Jonas would never rejoin the Amish. His *daett,* after all, was the pastor or elder or something of their church, to say nothing of that fancy house they lived in. Why did money do this to people? It would destroy Shirley's life if she didn't let go of the desire to chase it. Miriam closed her eyes for a moment. When she opened them, she clucked to get Mindy moving again.

Silence continued between Miriam and Shirley as Mindy worked her way up the final grade into Berlin. The afternoon rush of traffic had begun, but they stayed to the side streets and missed most of it. Shirley had a gleam in her eye as they approached the mall where the Berlin Gospel Bookstore was located.

Miriam parked the buggy by the long hitching rack provided for Amish customers. A few tourists stood along the street outside the mall, their cameras at the ready. If Berlin had anything, it was tourists. People flocked here in droves to see Amish life close-up. An errant thought burned through Miriam's mind: *Daett* could still make money off of them if he'd act like others in the community did. But her *daett* wasn't like the others, and she didn't wish he was.

Shirley climbed out of the buggy and waved to the tourists, who began to snap pictures at once, taking Shirley's friendliness as an invitation.

Miriam joined Shirley and whispered while she tied Mindy to the long metal rod, "You should be more reserved, Shirley!"

"I know," Shirley agreed.

As they approached the Berlin Gospel Bookstore, Shirley said, "I think this job is yours. Just think positively."

"I'll try," Miriam said, straightening her *kapp* as they entered and made their way to a woman standing behind a counter.

"I'm here to apply for the open job," Miriam said as confidently as she could. "If it's still available."

"Yes, we still need help," the woman said. "Just a minute. The manager will be right out."

Moments later, a man appeared who introduced himself as Mr. Clark.

"We're the Yoder sisters — Miriam and Shirley," Shirley said, more boldly than Miriam would have. "Eli Yoder is our *daett.*"

"The lame farmer, right?" Mr. Clark clarified.

Shirley nodded and rushed on, unfazed. "Miriam's looking for work. Her employer was Mr. Bland for three years, but he passed away this morning. And you're the first place we've stopped in to look for work."

"Yes, I've already heard about Mr. Bland. Word gets out quickly," Mr. Clark said. "Very well-off fellow. Quite a successful businessman in his day." Turning to Miriam, Mr. Clark asked, "How much were you paid a week, Miriam?"

Miriam glanced at the floor as she stated the amount.

Mr. Clark smiled. "You were well paid, indeed. Mr. Bland must have approved of your work. We can't pay that much here, I'm afraid."

"She'll take what you can give and work hard," Shirley offered.

Mr. Clark paused to consider Miriam. "So when can you begin?"

"Tomorrow." Miriam hesitated. "Is that soon enough?"

Mr. Clark nodded. "Fill out the paperwork at the front desk." Mr. Clark motioned toward the woman behind them. "You can begin on Friday — that's soon enough. I'm honored we're the first place you checked."

"Thank you! Thank you very much!" Shirley chirped with a proud grin, as if she'd gotten the job herself.

"Yes, thank you," Miriam said more softly.

Mr. Clark excused himself, and Miriam stood at the counter filling out the necessary paperwork. When that was finished, the two girls headed for the buggy.

"You did quite well in there," Miriam said.

"I'm glad I could help." Shirley was still cheerful.

Miriam changed the subject to the one they both dreaded. "You still need to tell

Mamm and *Daett* about this Jonas Beachy business. And it must be tonight before it goes any further."

Shirley was silent, her mood now subdued.

Miriam couldn't help but think of what lay ahead. *Mamm* would likely forget all about the job her eldest daughter had just acquired. There would be dark thoughts and weariness on her heart tonight, to say nothing of how *Daett* would feel. The day had begun with heavy sorrow and, except for momentary joy at getting a job, showed no change anytime soon.

CHAPTER FIVE

Once they arrived back home, Shirley climbed down to help unhitch Mindy from the buggy. She undid the tugs on her side and held the shafts while Miriam led Mindy forward. Neither girl spoke; each one was lost in her own thoughts. When Miriam disappeared into the barn with Mindy, Shirley waited. She knew she should return to the house to help *Mamm* with the household work, but she was nervous. Why had she spilled her secret to Miriam? Shirley tossed her head. There had been the guilt, of course. But now she had a bigger problem. Miriam wouldn't rest until *Mamm* and *Daett* were told.

Shirley sighed. Why couldn't she leave Jonas Beachy alone? She wanted to, and yet she didn't. She kept promising herself she'd turn up her nose the next time he walked by, but she never did. The truth was, she hadn't told Miriam all there was to tell. For several weeks now she'd been meeting Jonas on her trips to Berlin. Even now her heart beat faster at the thought of his attention. She'd always been comfortable around boys, often exchanging smiles and jokes with them. One day one of them would ask her home from a Sunday night hymn singing — once her *rumspringa* was over. But how she'd respond, she still hadn't decided. This was the normal way a man and a woman conducted themselves. *Mamm* said this was how the Lord led a young couple to fall in love and eventually share the sacred vows of marriage with each other. Marriage suitors in *Mamm* and *Daett*'s eyes did not include the likes of Jonas Beachy. That must be where her guilt was coming from. And she did want to be a decent woman in the faith, Shirley told herself. She just couldn't resist Jonas. Really, what girl could? Maybe Miriam. But I'm not Miriam, Shirley thought. Would it do any good to make stronger promises to herself? Maybe that was the reason she'd told Miriam — so her sister would help her? But Miriam planned to do what the responsible child was supposed to do — report the matter to *Mamm*. Everyone would find out now. Shirley decided she should have gone straight to *Mamm* to begin with, but she'd

50

been afraid *Mamm* might overreact. With Miriam in the middle as mediator, there was a much greater chance of resolution without regrets on either side. This was what lay behind her maneuvers, Shirley figured. She glanced toward the barn as Miriam came out. Shirley smiled slightly. "We'd best get this over with, don't you think?"

Miriam didn't answer but led the way back to the house. *Mamm* met them at the door with a worried look. "Didn't you get the job?"

"I got the job," Miriam said as she entered the house. "But something else has come up."

"Something serious?" *Mamm*'s face went pale, and she found the rocker and sat down.

If I had more wisdom, Shirley thought, I would have waited longer before bringing this up. It had been a traumatic day already for *Mamm.* But tomorrow was Tuesday again. She might see Jonas — and if she didn't do something soon, she'd agree to meet with him on the sly or otherwise. Her attraction to the man was almost scary. Had she fallen in love? Was this what love felt like? This out-of-control feeling? This breathless longing to see him again? At first she thought her attraction sprang from

51

Jonas's fancy convertible and access to his *daett*'s money. This was a personal weakness she was well aware of and must one day overcome. But she hadn't expected love — *if* this was love.

"What is it?" *Mamm*'s voice cut through her thoughts.

"Shirley's in love with Jonas Beachy." Miriam wasted no time getting to the heart of the matter, as usual.

"Jonas Beachy!" *Mamm*'s voice was filled with horror.

"It's not that bad," Shirley protested. "*I* didn't say I was in love with him." And yet perhaps she was. There was something special about Jonas. He had a confident air about him that she liked. And, she had to admit it, there was the wealth factor.

"But Jonas isn't Amish!" *Mamm* exclaimed.

"I told Miriam about Jonas so she could help me decide what to do. I made a mistake. I should have kept quiet. I'm not ready to talk about him."

Mamm stared at Shirley. "Perhaps we'd better start at the beginning."

Miriam looked away. "Shirley can tell the story."

Shirley took a deep breath. This wouldn't be easy.

"Shirley!" *Mamm*'s voice was impatient. "Tell me."

Shirley forced the words out. "Okay! I've met Jonas the past several Tuesdays in Berlin. We've talked, that's all — well, mostly all. I've taken a few rides in his car. Now he wants to see me at home." Shirley held up her hand. "But I said no, *Mamm.*"

"Exactly how long has this been going on?" *Mamm*'s voice was subdued.

Shirley bit her lip. "For a month or so. I'm sorry, *Mamm.* That's why I finally told Miriam."

"But you didn't come to me," *Mamm* said softly.

"I'm sorry." Shirley hung her head.

"It's the money, isn't it?" *Mamm* said.

"She's in love," Miriam spoke up. "It must be more than just money."

Mamm shook her head. "*Nee,* it's his access to money. Why is it always the money? Truly the love of money is the root of all evil, just as the Bible says." *Mamm* wrung her hands. "I will not lose a daughter over money!" *Mamm* turned to face Shirley. "You must know that man will never make you happy."

"He's not just 'that man'!" Shirley wished at once she hadn't said the words. Defending Jonas revealed the affection that lay in

53

her heart — a greater affection than even she dared admit.

Sorrow crept over *Mamm*'s face. "So you are in love with the man."

It was more statement than question, so Shirley kept silent.

The sound of buggy wheels turning into the driveway ended the discussion. *Mamm* slowly rose to her feet. "That will be the *kinner* home from school. We'll speak more on this tonight when *Daett* is home."

Shirley groaned silently. *Daett* would probably insist she never see Jonas again.

Miriam welcomed the four scholars home — Naomi, Aaron, Dana, and Elizabeth. "How did school go today, Elizabeth?" she asked cheerily, greeting the first child through the door.

First-grader Elizabeth's face glowed. "I got to read my first word today. All by myself!"

"That's wonderful!" Miriam exclaimed.

Shirley forced herself to join the happy conversations. The last thing she wanted was for the younger children to find out what she'd done. She didn't want to be a bad example for them. She'd have to keep her interest in Jonas a secret from younger ears. *Oh oh.* Already thoughts of Jonas and his fancy *Englisha* car were dancing in her mind again. She hurried into the kitchen. Thankfully no one but *Mamm* seemed to notice her abrupt departure. She'd gotten herself together by the time eighth-grader Naomi followed her and asked, "What's for supper tonight?"

"Still thinking on it," Shirley said as cheerfully as she could muster.

"I'm *starving*!" Naomi proclaimed. "Why not a big chicken casserole for starters? I'll help."

"You'll have to ask *Mamm.*" Shirley kept her face turned away. She would love to make a big supper tonight, but big suppers were kept as a Friday-night special. This was part of the frugality written into every area of the Yoder household. Naomi knew this, but obviously hope sprang eternal for the schoolgirl.

Moments later Shirley could hear subdued voices coming from the living room. She paused to listen. The low murmur of voices reached her ears.

"He just passed this morning."

Deducing that Miriam was telling the children the news of Mr. Bland's death, Shirley was relieved the talk wasn't about her. She busied herself with supper preparations. They would have simple potato soup and crackers tonight. That would nourish the large Yoder family, although it would be a far cry from the supper Naomi had envisioned. Naomi was like Miriam in accepting the family's state of affairs. Those two not only wanted to be good, they *were* good. She, on the other hand, still had visions of Jonas and his sporty car in her head. And, worse than that, she could envision Jonas in his *daett*'s big house in the well-to-do neighborhood between Berlin and Sugarcreek. No doubt their dinner tonight would be a roast . . . or maybe even steak. Probably mashed potatoes and gravy and dessert, such as pecan pie and homemade cherry ice cream.

Shirley stared out the kitchen window, ignoring the murmur of conversation continuing behind her. If *Daett* knew how strong her desires were, what would he do? Maybe she should make a full confession tonight. But look at the trouble the partial one had already caused! A lecture from her *daett* over what she'd already confessed wasn't something she looked forward to. But maybe if she submitted to his words and will, her soul would be washed of all her wrong desires and she'd become a *gut* girl like Miriam and Naomi. Shaking her head, Shirley tried to make herself believe she accepted difficulties — like the lack of money — as the will of the Lord for her. But she didn't, and it was an awful state to find oneself in. And apparently nothing was going to change in the near future. She decided she would listen with meekness to what *Daett* had to say tonight and go from there.

Naomi reappeared, sober-faced now from the news about Mr. Bland. She didn't comment on Shirley's supper preparations. Either *Mamm* had turned her down or Naomi had never asked. "That's sad about Mr. Bland," Naomi finally said. "I think it's harder on Miriam than she's letting on."

"She's had a hard day," Shirley offered. She almost added "in part because of me," but she'd already confessed enough for one day.

"Miriam didn't say when the funeral was." Naomi wiped a tear from her eye. "It's all so very sad." Naomi's voice took on a more cheerful tone. "One *gut* thing happened though. We have a new couple in the community. Ivan Mast took Laura Swartz home on Sunday night."

But Miriam wants him, Shirley almost said aloud. She held back. Naomi wouldn't learn of Miriam's disappointment from her.

"I'm so happy for them," Naomi shared.

Shirley forced a happy tone into her voice.

"Love is always a *gut* thing."

Naomi glowed. "I hope the Lord has such a decent man for me someday."

"I'm sure He does," Shirley said, hoping the same about herself.

CHAPTER SIX

Later that evening, after the sun had set and the gas lantern hanging from the ceiling hissed above them, Shirley sat on the couch in the living room with her hands in her lap. Supper, devotions, and the dishes were finished. The younger children and older boys were upstairs. Miriam was on the couch beside Shirley. *Daett* sat upright in his rocking chair across from the two girls. *Mamm* was sitting next to him in her rocker.

Shirley cringed inwardly, wondering what *Daett* was going to say. *Mamm* had spoken her mind earlier, so tonight the lecture would come from him. From the look on his face, he'd already been informed of her transgressions. No doubt a strong rebuke would soon begin, followed by instructions toward living a more godly life. Shirley didn't object to that — in theory. It was the unpleasantness of that kind of journey that bothered her.

Breaking the silence in the living room, *Daett* cleared his throat. "Shirley, is this true what I hear?"

"What have you heard?" Shirley wanted to ask, but she remained silent and nodded.

"I'm glad to hear that you've confessed this thing." *Daett*'s tone grew tense. "But driving around in a car with Jonas Beachy? Shirley! What were you thinking?"

"I'm sorry," Shirley whispered.

Daett grunted and fell silent.

No doubt *Daett* doesn't think much of my apology, Shirley thought. And she couldn't blame him really. She waited. More lay ahead, she was sure. And she needed all the lectures *Daett* could give her. Somehow she had to learn to obey like Miriam and Naomi did.

"Is it the money, Shirley?" *Daett* asked. "Is this why you're stretching our boundaries of a decent *rumspringa* time?"

Shirley sat up. She didn't hesitate. "Maybe. I know not having a lot of money shouldn't bother me, but it does. And I'm sorry that it does."

Daett hung his head. "At moments like this, I wish I had all the money in Berlin . . . or even in Possum Valley."

"I'm so sorry, *Daett.*" Shirley rose from the couch. "I'll forget about Jonas Beachy

60

right now. I promise!"

"I'd rather you obeyed me instead of making empty promises all the time." *Daett*'s voice was weary. "You know what's right, Shirley, but you don't get it done." He settled back in the rocker with a sigh.

Shirley almost whispered she was sorry again, but her *daett* started talking again.

"I may be tempted at times by the promises money makes, Shirley. But in my heart I know those promises aren't true. You would do well to learn the same truth. The promises of money are *always* false, and they will always be false no matter how many nice things in life one can buy with money. In the end, the Lord is glorified only when we accept our lot in life and take what He gives and doesn't give without complaint."

What if it's my lot in life to marry a rich man? she thought. She bit her lip to keep from blurting it out.

Daett went on. "If I've failed to live my life as a *gut* example before you, Shirley, I apologize from the bottom of my heart."

"And I want to say the same thing," *Mamm* said at once. "I know I'm not nearly as *gut* an example as your *daett* is, but still . . ."

"That's not true!" The words sprang from Shirley's lips. "You two are the best ex-

61

amples anyone could have." Shirley winced because the stabbing pains caused by her parents' words were cutting deep. She'd been ready for a long lecture, but their sorrow was much harder to bear.

"I'm glad to hear you say that," *Mamm* said. "Your *daett* is a father worthy of your respect."

"I know. I'll try to do better!" Shirley looked away. If only she were convinced by her own words. She wanted to obey at that moment, but what about later? How much time would pass before she forgot her resolve . . . or disregarded it and did something wrong again? She was sure one glimpse of Jonas would be all that was needed for her sincere resolution to fly out the window.

Daett seemed to be of the same opinion. "You shouldn't go into Berlin anymore, Shirley. Not for a long time. You need to stay away from the temptation to see this young man."

Alarm rushed through her. "But I have to help with the shopping! I'm the one who always makes . . ."

"Shirley!" *Mamm* cut her off. "*Daett* is right. And the way you're reacting right now is all the sign we need to know this is the way it should be. Miriam will do the shopping tomorrow, and then we'll consider what we'll do from there. No hardship on us is too much if it helps keep you safe from temptation."

Shirley swallowed hard. *Mamm* was right. If there was anything that judged where her heart lay, it was the pain running through her right now at the thought of not seeing Jonas tomorrow. *Mamm* looked at her as if she knew Shirley's thoughts. But thankfully no one said anything. They were kind to her, much more than what she deserved. Somehow she would have to get over Jonas Beachy.

Daett cleared his throat again. "And then there's the matter of our faith, Shirley. I know you're only seventeen, so perhaps you don't see the seriousness of this situation. Love will not cover the vast differences between the Beachy family and ours when it comes to what we believe. They aren't Amish anymore. They're not even of the conservative Mennonite faith. Did you know that, Shirley?" *Daett* paused, but then continued when she didn't answer. "Not that I want you to marry a Mennonite. The Beachys have left the faith of our fathers completely. Please keep that in mind. I know this can be hard in matters of the heart, but you must pay heed, Shirley. These things must be remembered even in your *rumspringa* time."

"I know." Shirley hung her head again.

Silence followed. *Am I allowed to go?* Shirley wondered. *Is Daett finished?* She took a quick glance toward her *daett.* His head was bowed and his lips were moving. *He's praying,* she realized. More pangs ran through her chest. *Daett*'s sorrow over her misdeeds was indeed great. She ought to say something that would help ease everyone's mind, but the only words she could think of would sound empty.

"You may go now, Shirley," *Mamm* said.

Shirley rose, followed by Miriam. The two girls made their way upstairs to the bedroom they shared. Once they were behind the closed bedroom door, Shirley faced Miriam and said in a low voice, "You didn't say anything."

"What could I say?" Miriam sat on her single bed with a sigh. "You know it's going to be hard for you to keep your promise."

Tears burned in Shirley's eyes. "You think I don't know that?"

"I wish there was some way it could be different. That the money situation here at home would ease." Miriam appeared genuinely concerned as she continued. "I know that bothers you much more than it does me."

"Why can't I be more like you?" Shirley's question hung in the air.

Miriam shot her a quick glance. "We're all different, and there's nothing wrong with that."

"That's kind of you to say," Shirley replied with a rueful smile. "But when 'different' involves such temptations as Jonas Beachy and money, there is a problem."

Miriam reached over and touched Shirley's shoulder. "Maybe we'd better get some sleep. A good night's rest will be good for both of us. Morning will come soon enough." She blew out the kerosene lamp and was soon in bed under the covers.

Shirley lay fully dressed on top of the quilt on her bed. The day had been a long one for all of them — Miriam especially. Long day or not, Shirley had no desire to sleep. Thoughts of Jonas wouldn't stop. And the awful truth was that she didn't want them to stop — even though she knew that in the long run the life *Mamm* and *Daett* had together was what she wanted. Yet, at the same time, she wanted what Jonas and his *daett* had. She couldn't have both, that was for sure. But making the choice still lay far ahead. Why should she have to make it right now? She was only seventeen and had just entered her *rumspringa*. What was *rumspringa* for if not to try new things and entertain thoughts that she could not after joining the church? The contradictions seemed to fill the room. She simply couldn't let go of Jonas. Not just yet. She wouldn't marry the man, of course. That was impossible. Jonas lived in a world she would never fit in with. He knew that, and she knew that. So why the guilt? If she'd simply kept her mouth shut most of the pain today would have been avoided. And . . . she hadn't been completely truthful. She hadn't given up her deepest, darkest secret. Jonas had given her his cell phone number. Not even in the midst of her promises had she been tempted to reveal such a thing.

"Call me anytime," he'd said. "I'd love to chat with you."

Jonas had given her the number after she refused his offer to pick her up some evening at home. That was a sign he must really wish to see her again. She hadn't planned to call him because she'd expected to see him tomorrow in Berlin. Now she wouldn't be there. Alarm flashed through her. She sat up in bed. What would Jonas think if she didn't show up at the usual time? Would he come to the house? That would be a disaster! *Nee,* that couldn't happen. She had to call Jonas! But how? The phone booth was down the road. She'd have to sneak out of the house, and she'd never done that. Was it even possible? Miriam would hear her, wouldn't she? And what about *Mamm?* Shirley stared into the darkness, her heart pounding. She would face this.

She looked over at Miriam, who was sound asleep. Shirley quietly got up from the bed and, with both hands outstretched, felt her way down the stairs. Her soft knock on her parents' bedroom door was followed by a soft rustle inside.

Mamm opened the door in her night-clothes. She slipped out and shut the door before moving to stand near the window. Soft moonlight revealed her concerned face. "What is it, Shirley?"

The words gushed out in a whisper. "I have to speak with Jonas. I must, *Mamm.* I have his phone number."

Mamm's fingers dug into Shirley's arm. "You can't! Not after your *daett*'s words tonight and your promises!"

A sob rose in Shirley's throat. "I can keep that promise later, but not now. Please, *Mamm.*" Shirley pushed forward with her argument. "I have to call him. I have to tell him I won't be there tomorrow. He's expecting me. If I don't show up, what if he comes to the house?"

Doubt filled *Mamm*'s face as Shirley continued. "I'll be really careful, *Mamm*. I will."

Skepticism was written large on *Mamm*'s face, but finally she consented. "Go then, if you must, but I don't approve."

Before *Mamm* could change her mind, Shirley grabbed her coat and left through the front door. *Mamm*'s shadowy figure was still by the window when Shirley glanced back. *Mamm* would, no doubt, still be there when I return, Shirley thought — and in a way she was glad. *Mamm*'s presence was comforting even in her disapproval.

Shirley ran down the side road of Possum Valley in the moonlight. Her feet kicked up pebbles along the edge of the pavement. When the headlights of an car bounced in the distance, she dove for the ditch and hid behind a bush until the vehicle passed.

The next dash brought Shirley to the phone booth. She caught her breath before she dialed the number by heart. It was as if the numbers had been burned into her brain, as had most everything about Jonas.

"Text me," Jonas had told her when he wrote down the number. He'd laughed at the perplexed look on her face. "Of course!

You don't know what that is."

"I do so," she'd protested.

"Just call," he'd said with sweetness in his voice.

Well, she hadn't planned to make the first call, let alone one at ten o'clock at night, but here she was. Jonas probably stayed up till all hours anyway. Didn't rich people live like that?

"Hello!"

Her voice squeaked when she responded, "Hi, Jonas. This is Shirley. Shirley Yoder."

"Oh, Shirley!" His voice brightened. "I didn't recognize the number. So how are you doing?"

"You can't imagine." Her breath was short, she knew, but she was in a hurry. "Look, Jonas, I can't be in Berlin tomorrow and maybe not for some time. My parents found out about us . . . and there's trouble."

"I see." He sounded troubled himself. "Is there something I can do?"

"I wish."

"You're not cutting me off, are you?"

"Of course not!" The denial rushed out of her mouth almost involuntarily. "I just don't know how to . . . well . . . keep in touch."

"We'll figure out some way." His voice was tender. "Call me when you can, and I'll see what I can do."

"Don't come by the house, okay?"

"I won't. I promise." There was a crackle on the phone. "I'll see you later, Shirley. Don't worry, okay?"

"Okay." Shirley hung up. She tried to quiet the pounding of her heart. Oh, this was such a mess, but she couldn't let Jonas go. Later she would try, but not now.

CHAPTER SEVEN

On Thursday morning the sun shone through the open upstairs bedroom window as Miriam changed into her black Sunday dress. She'd mourned for Mr. Bland often in the past few days and at the viewing last night. She missed the relationship she used to have with him. He'd been almost like a second *daett* to her, although she would never mention such a thing here at home. Mr. Bland was *Englisha.* She shouldn't have such feelings about him. Still, their relationship had grown deep and, like Shirley, she couldn't control how she felt about certain things. At least her affection for Mr. Bland hadn't been wrong like Shirley's was for Jonas.

The dark-blue drapes moved in the morning breeze as Miriam put in the last of her dress pins. Mr. Bland's sister, Rose, had said last night she'd be here at nine to pick her up for the funeral. It would be best if she was ready ahead of time. It wouldn't be decent if Rose had to wait. Thankfully, there'd been time to wash and dry the breakfast dishes downstairs. She'd also been able to help Shirley with some mending. That was one *gut* thing that had come out of her few days off this week. She had time to help catch up with the household work, which always seemed to pile up in a house with ten children.

What hadn't helped was the tension in the house over Shirley's attraction to Jonas Beachy. She'd even gone to call him on Monday night right after the lecture *Daett* had given her! So far the older ones had kept the situation from the younger *kinner,* but that surely wouldn't last long. Sometimes Miriam despaired for Shirley and her *gut* intentions that often didn't pan out. Why couldn't Shirley just do what was right? But one must not give up hope. With the Lord's help they would make it through Shirley's troubled time. At least Shirley could be kept away from Berlin until this was safely over. Miriam had taken care of the shopping on Tuesday, and she would continue to do so after she began work tomorrow in the Berlin Gospel Bookstore.

A dark cloud passed over Miriam's face. The pay at the bookstore would be considerably less than what Mr. Bland had been giving her. How would her parents deal with this drop in income? No one had said anything so far. Maybe Shirley would have to take a job earlier than they'd planned. But then the trouble with Jonas would take center court again. Shirley wasn't safe out of the house at the moment. From the looks of longing that often came into Shirley's eyes, any meeting with Jonas would lead to more meetings, more rides in cars, and more . . . well, only the Lord knew where all that might end.

Surely her sister wouldn't actually marry the man? Shirley had assured them all she had no such intention, but she wasn't known for keeping her promises. Hadn't she called Jonas the same evening she'd promised *Daett* she'd get over him once and for all?

A rattle of car tires in the driveway came through the open window. Miriam jumped. She tucked the last bit of stray hair under her *kapp* and dashed down the stairs. *Mamm* was seated on the rocking chair with a letter in her hand, so Shirley must have picked up the mail. From the smile on *Mamm*'s face the news must be *gut.* Miriam glanced at the return address on the envelope sitting on a little table by the rocker. *Mamm*'s sister

Fannie had written from the Clarita, Oklahoma, community. Fannie and her husband, William, had moved there several years ago. That was also where the Swartz family had come from. Miriam shoved that thought aside. She didn't want to think about Laura or Ivan right now.

"Fannie's first child is due soon, right?" Miriam guessed.

Mamm's smile grew larger. "*Yah!* After all these years of waiting, the Lord has finally blessed them. The midwife thinks there will be no problems." *Mamm* gazed out the living room window. "Oh, how I wish I could be there for this *wunderbah* moment! Fannie is to be a *mamm* after all."

Miriam paused by the front door as the thought hit her. "I could go to her and be her maid for a while." She'd like that better than working at the bookstore. But the idea was impossible. They had no extra money for a bus ticket to Oklahoma, and she needed work that paid. Besides, Aunt Fannie had probably arranged for one of the local Amish girls in Oklahoma to live with the family and help after the birth.

"Will you be back for lunch?" *Mamm* asked.

"I would think so." Miriam pushed open the front door. "The *Englisha* have fast services — if last night at the viewing was any indication." She'd been surprised how fast the small crowd moved through the viewing line. Miriam was glad she'd attended. Rose had asked her to be there as a "comforting presence." That was understandable with the few family members who showed up. Mr. Bland and Thelma had never been blessed with children, so mostly there were cousins, aunts, uncles, a few family friends, and some business acquaintances in attendance.

"Maybe Rose will take you out to eat afterward," *Mamm* suggested.

"I hadn't thought of that." Miriam glanced at Shirley, who was still working on the large mending pile. Shirley's eyes shone. No doubt her sister wished she had this opportunity to get out of the house.

"Well," *Mamm* continued, "either way is okay with us. If you don't show up by lunchtime, we'll eat without you."

Shirley cleared her throat. "Maybe I should go with Miriam?"

"You'll do no such thing!" *Mamm* replied.

A hurt look crossed Shirley's face, but she offered nothing more.

After giving Shirley a look of sympathy, Miriam wondered why she hadn't thought to include Shirley earlier. *Mamm* might have consented if she'd had time to think about it. The excursion would have done Shirley *gut,* and she wouldn't have gotten into trouble with so many people around.

Miriam dashed out the door. She would have to remember this in the future and include Shirley whenever possible.

Rose rolled down the car window as Miriam approached. "Good morning, dear."

"Good morning," Miriam replied as she climbed into the car. Rose was also dressed in a black dress, but it had considerably more finery than hers. Nothing inappropriate, but apparently even at funerals the *Englisha* added the extras.

"There's rain forecast for this afternoon," Rose said as she turned the car around and headed out the driveway. "I hope we get my brother buried before it starts."

Miriam didn't say anything for a second. Then she spoke in a hushed voice. "I still think of Mr. Bland as I saw him alive the last time — patiently waiting for his breakfast on the porch. It's hard to believe he's gone."

"You two did have a soft spot for each other." Rose gave Miriam a warm smile. "I'm glad you made his last years pleasant ones."

"Thank you," Miriam acknowledged as

76

Rose turned the car onto the road and headed toward Sugarcreek. "He was almost like a *daett* to me — a second father."

"I can imagine." Rose's face was pensive. "He felt the same about you . . . that you were like a daughter."

"Did he tell you this?" Miriam asked in surprise.

Rose's face softened. "He didn't have to. My brother's regard for you was obvious to us all."

Miriam watched the landscape through the car window. "I tried to be a blessing to him, that's all I know. I wish he were still here."

Rose glanced at Miriam. "I'm not sure when the best time is to tell you this, but my brother mentioned you in his will."

"What does that mean?" Miriam asked.

"Being mentioned in a will usually means the person who died wanted to give you something. We'll wait until after the funeral to discuss the details. I've set up a brief meeting with our attorney. I hope you don't mind."

"No, of course I don't mind. Whatever works best for you." Miriam took a deep breath. This sounded serious.

Moments later Rose pulled into the parking lot of Smith's Funeral Home. A few cars were already there. This would be a small funeral like the viewing had been last night. Miriam got out of the car, and Rose led the way toward the entrance. The place was familiar from last night, but Miriam stayed a few steps behind Rose. An usher took them to front row seats, and Miriam sat beside Rose. She was seated with the family, which didn't seem appropriate, but maybe they considered her like family in spirit. The service began with a hymn played by a pianist, which no one sang along to. How different this was from an Amish funeral. The place felt cold as the clanging notes rang through the large room. The music sounded hollow, Miriam thought. She preferred the a cappella sound of human voices singing in unison at their community services. She looked around discreetly. Mr. Bland deserved more than this.

When the music ended, Miriam forced herself to concentrate on the speaker, who had risen to stand behind the pulpit. Surely he must be an *Englisha* minister, she thought. He read the Twenty-Third Psalm in a slow and somber tone, and then he added a few words of commentary. How unlike Amish ministers. At Amish funerals, each minister spoke for at least thirty minutes.

Rose leaned over and whispered, "That was Amos's favorite psalm."

Miriam wiped away a tear. She hadn't known that, but then she and Mr. Bland had seldom spoken about the Lord. She'd been sure, though, that Mr. Bland was close to Him. Such awareness had passed between them. Mr. Bland had loved his *frau,* Thelma, right after the Lord Himself. And now Mr. Bland was no doubt with both of them.

The minister read Mr. Bland's obituary. It wasn't a long one. He was survived by his sister, Rose, a short list of nieces and nephews, and a few other assorted relatives. Miriam rose with the others to view Mr. Bland in his casket before it was closed for the last time. In this the *Englisha* did things like the Amish. The family didn't linger long around the coffin.

Miriam took a brief look at Mr. Bland's composed face before she moved on. He looked happy, and that comforted her.

CHAPTER EIGHT

The time wasn't twelve o'clock yet, but Miriam, Rose, and the Bland family lawyer were seated in a fancy restaurant called Dutch Valley located south of Sugarcreek. Despite the lavish-looking menu, Miriam wasn't the least bit hungry. On the way over, Rose had said again that Miriam had been mentioned in her brother's will. This time she added that she knew money was involved.

Miriam's face had gone pale. Did Rose think she'd manipulated Mr. Bland by weaseling her way into his good graces to get his money? That idea had never even occurred to her. Her face grew red at the very idea. "I hope you don't think I was nice to Mr. Bland because . . . because of. . . . I wasn't after his money, Rose. Money or anything else for that matter. I only wanted to help him and do my job."

Rose's smile was soft. "I know, dear. I'm glad you cared enough to make the last few years of my brother's life happy ones. Sometimes one is rewarded for that, and sometimes one is not. This seems to be one of those times when one is."

Miriam tried to keep her breathing even. "I . . . I don't know what to say. He paid me well, and I always felt unworthy. Beyond that, Mr. Bland never spoke to me of such things."

"I'm sure of that," Rose said. "My brother was a private man. He was very often quite generous and anonymous in supporting his favorite charities."

Miriam's heart throbbed. *Attorneys, wills, money. Money. It's come up again . . . just like with Shirley and her desire to be rich. I wish there wasn't anything like money.* If Rose only knew how much trouble money had already caused the Yoder family, she wouldn't even bring up the subject. If Mr. Bland had left her an extra paycheck or even as much as five hundred dollars, she could handle that. She'd just pass the funds straight on to *Mamm* and *Daett.* They'd understand.

Miriam hoped her face wasn't still burning red from the embarrassing conversation about money on the ride to the restaurant. Why was her family doomed to suffer from money problems? She couldn't get away from it even when she innocently did her job and took care of an elderly gentleman.

When they'd arrived at the restaurant, the lawyer had introduced himself. "Mr. Rosenberg," he'd said without a smile as he rose and shook her hand. Perhaps lawyers were stern people and never smiled? Miriam wondered. Or perhaps Mr. Rosenberg thought she'd done something wrong to get herself mentioned in Mr. Bland's will. What would *Daett* and *Mamm* say if she arrived home and had to admit that she'd become embroiled in some dispute about money? Well, she would solve all of this once she found out what was going on . . . and her voice worked again. She'd turn down the extra check or whatever it was, even though that might seem unkind or even rude. She meant no disrespect to Mr. Bland's memory, but perhaps it would be for the best so people wouldn't think she'd connived to get Mr. Bland's money.

The waitress appeared and Miriam waited until the other two had ordered before she glanced up. "I'll take the same. The buffet."

After the waitress left, Rose led the way to the buffet. All Miriam could bring herself to do was take a little bit of some of the items. She must eat something for the sake of *gut* manners, but if the knot in her stomach didn't subside soon, she'd lose anything she got down. That would be way too embarrassing.

Back at the table Miriam waited until Rose and the lawyer had seated themselves. Rose bowed her head for a short prayer, and Miriam felt relief. What would she have done if Rose hadn't prayed? Maybe a silent prayer would have sufficed, she decided.

Mr. Rosenberg frequently regarded her with a steady gaze as he ate, and Miriam felt the knot in her stomach grow tighter. When would he say something? It wasn't her place to start the conversation — even if she was up to it. The sheer tension of the moment was awful.

Thankfully Mr. Rosenberg finally cleared his throat. "Rose tells me she told you about Amos Bland including you in his will."

"She did," Miriam managed. The food had gone down whether she planned on it or not, and her stomach had settled some. Perhaps she was hungry and didn't know it. Anything seemed possible right now.

"And you weren't surprised?" Mr. Rosenberg asked, regarding Miriam openly.

"Yes, I was. I was shocked. I never expected anything like that," Miriam began. "I'm pleased that he thought of me, of course, but yes, very surprised. I didn't ask for anything and certainly never desired anything beyond my salary. And even the money Mr. Bland insisted on paying me was too generous." She smiled at the memory but then frowned. "Rose didn't say much else, but I sense your concern. You are wondering whether I influenced Mr. Bland to mention me in his will. I assure you, I did not. And please understand that if there's even the appearance of impropriety, I'll gladly forfeit whatever Mr. Bland left me. I'm content with what he set my salary at, and I was just happy I got to know him and work for him. If there is a problem with Mr. Bland leaving me something, Rose can take me home now, and that will be the end of it. I don't want any trouble or be the cause of any trouble. My family has enough of them already."

"Oh?" Mr. Rosenberg said.

The words rushed on. "My sister, well, let me start with the fact that money has caused my family untold problems. My *daett* has a lame leg from a childhood injury, but he works hard on our farm. My brothers help him, but there never seems to be enough money to go around. Yet the Lord provides for us, just as He promises in His Word. So I never asked Mr. Bland for money. Never. I didn't ask for the generous salary he paid me each week. I was thankful, and my family needed the funds, but I was more than content with what I was given." She glanced at Rose. "Maybe you should take me home now?"

Rose glanced at Mr. Rosenberg with a "See, I-told-you-so" smile. "Like I said, she's genuine."

Mr. Rosenberg shrugged. "A will's a will, but I needed to ascertain whether Amos was talked into something or not. That's part of my job, that's all."

"I don't understand," Miriam said.

"I'm sorry, Miriam." Rose smiled. "Mr. Rosenberg was my brother's attorney. It's his job to see that Amos's last wishes are carried out. But he also has to make sure there was no . . . well, no undue influence on my brother in his weakened condition. I knew Amos well, of course, and I know you, Miriam. I have no doubt about the nature of your relationship with Amos. But Mr. Rosenberg knew only Amos . . . not you. He needed to be sure that nothing untoward occurred so that the will's arrangement won't end up contested in court."

Miriam gasped. She stood up. "My people don't get involved in *Englisha* courts. I could never have my family involved in any such occurrence. That would be a disgrace.

Rose, please take me home."

Rose stood and gently held Miriam's arm. She guided her back into the chair. "Miriam, everything is okay. I can assure you that you will not be going to court."

"Let me cut to the chase then." Mr. Rosenberg wiped his brow. "Miriam, Mr. Bland left you his entire farm, including all the equipment and animals, and quite a tidy sum of money."

"He did *what*?" The world swam before Miriam's eyes. Had she heard correctly?

Rose seemed to understand. "That's right, Miriam. Amos left you his farm, debt free, along with two million dollars."

Miriam's gaze was steady, but she wasn't seeing anything. The world appeared white in front of her. The features of the restaurant, including its long bar of food, were gone, replaced by a heavy fog.

Rose's voice sounded distant and unreal. "Miriam? Are you okay, Miriam?"

"We should have chosen a better place to break this news." Mr. Rosenberg sounded irritated.

"Miriam?" Rose pulled on her arm again. "Are you still with us?"

Things came into focus again. Miriam clutched the side of the table. "Did you really say what I think you did? That Mr.

Bland left me his farm and two . . . two . . ."
Miriam couldn't complete the sentence.

Mr. Rosenberg didn't hesitate. "Yes, I did. The farm, everything on it, and two million dollars."

Miriam still couldn't breathe right. Two million dollars! She didn't even know anyone who had so much money. Right now she couldn't even remember how many thousands that was. A lot! That much she knew. Suddenly she turned to Rose. "But what about you? You're his closest relative. Shouldn't Amos have given everything to you?"

"Dear, Amos was a *very* wealthy man. I'm already well provided for, but Amos was very thoughtful. Although he left you a great deal of money, the estate was split three ways. I was given a third, you were given a third, and the other third is to be divided among several ministries he supported."

Miriam didn't know how to respond. Finally she managed to speak. "B-b-b-ut what am I to do with a farm and all this money?"

"Do you have an attorney?" Mr. Rosenberg asked.

"Of course not!" Miriam almost choked.

"If I may make a suggestion?" Rose asked.

Miriam nodded.

"I recommend you ask Mr. Rosenberg to represent you," Rose said. "You can't do better than having him look after your interests in this matter. He's very reputable, and, after all, Amos trusted him completely."

Miriam's head was still spinning. "I don't know what to do," she said. "If I need a lawyer, then *yah,* I'd like it to be you."

"I'll be happy to assist you," Mr. Rosenberg said.

"May I please go home now?" Miriam stood. "I really don't feel well."

"I'll have the papers ready for you to sign tomorrow," Mr. Rosenberg said, also rising. "There will be the property deed, bank account, tax forms, inheritance forms, and more paperwork. Can you come to my office?"

Miriam rubbed her forehead. "*Yah* . . . I think. I don't want to meet at my home. I need to think about this. I'm not sure I want my *mamm* and *daett* to know about this just yet."

"I'm not sure I understand, but that's your prerogative." Mr. Rosenberg appeared puzzled.

"I can barely grasp this news," Miriam said. "This news will be quite a shock and change a lot of things."

Mr. Rosenberg wiped his brow again.

"Whatever you deem best." He handed her his business card. "Please call me as soon as possible to set up an appointment." He looked at Rose. "I'll take care of the check, of course."

Rose also stood and took Miriam's arm. "Thank you, Mr. Rosenberg. We'll be in touch."

"Yes, of course," Mr. Rosenberg said.

As Miriam turned to leave with Rose, she glanced back at Mr. Rosenberg. He was still standing by the table. He was uncomprehending as to what this would do to her life. What this all meant for the future was so unknown. Right now, she couldn't feel anything. Would she travel through the rest of her life feeling this numb? Slowly, though, she felt a new sensation — one of deep apprehension. With this much money her life would never be the same. She knew what awful things money did to people. Wasn't that what *Daett* always warned about? Would she grow proud now? Full of herself? Trusting in great riches and forgetting all about depending on the Lord for His provision and grace?

Miriam climbed into Rose's car, fastened her seat belt, and then clutched the armrest. Rose gave her a sympathetic look as they pulled away. "I'm sorry, dear, that this is such a shock. But I think my brother knew what he was doing. He always was a good judge of character. Look at the saint of a wife he picked out. The Lord knows she did him good all the days of her life." Rose paused for a quick glance toward the sky. "Now they're together again, and he's left his farm and his money in good hands."

"Maybe I should just give it all away." Miriam's words came out in a croak. "Maybe I should go somewhere else so people won't gossip about this situation."

"That is, of course, your choice." Rose didn't appear pleased. "I wouldn't, if you ask my opinion. My brother gave you that money and farm for a reason."

"But I know nothing about managing money and very little about running a large farm!" she shrieked. The sound pierced the air in the closed car.

Rose didn't appear shocked. "I'll help you, and so will Mr. Rosenberg. He's one of the best attorneys in the area. My brother picked him carefully, I can assure you of that. Mr. Rosenberg won't steal your money."

"Steal?" Miriam clutched her hands together. Such a thought hadn't crossed her mind. She'd never owned anything that anyone might want to steal. But now . . .

Miriam pinched herself, and pain ran all the way up her arm. *Nee,* this was not a dream.

"I know this must be hard," Rose said. "And, yes, some people will misunderstand. Your godly character will win out, Miriam. Just keep a low profile, and someday you'll find the reasons for what happened today. You're a rich woman now. You shouldn't try to avoid your destiny, Miriam. God will help you, I'm sure."

Miriam took deep breaths. Then the words came out. "Do I own Mr. Bland's farm? Really? And all that money?"

"Yes." Rose took her eyes off the road for a brief glance at Miriam. "Do you want to wait a while yet before you have to face your parents?"

"No." Miriam studied the landscape outside the car window. "But I don't want them to know quite yet . . ."

"I don't think that's realistic, dear." Rose's voice was kind. "Shall I come in and help you explain it to them?"

Miriam's head spun. Maybe that would help. It might make better sense to *Mamm* and *Daett* if Rose explained. And they had to be told. Rose was right. She couldn't hide or delay this news.

Miriam turned toward Rose. "Yes, I'd like

that. But let's only tell them about the farm for now. *Daett* will know what needs to be done with that. Don't tell them about the money beyond the fact that some operating expense funds are included. I'll say something later . . . someday about the total amount." Miriam tried to think straight. "Maybe by then I'll know *why* this has happened and what to do."

"Whatever you say, dear." Rose reached over to touch her arm. "I know all of this is so sudden. Give yourself some time to adjust. Think things through, and you'll be okay. And I'll help smooth things over with your parents."

That's much easier to say than do, Miriam almost said, but that would be rude. Rose had been more than kind to her. The elderly woman believed in her and would help her. She gathered herself together as the car pulled into the Yoder driveway. The clock on the dash read a little after two. They weren't too late, so *Mamm* shouldn't be worried. At least they wouldn't start off this conversation on the wrong foot.

"Thanks for coming in with me," Miriam whispered on the walk toward the house.

She felt guilty about her decision regarding the money. How could she deceive her parents like this? Each step felt like she was walking in quicksand. *Daett* had been correct. Money was not a blessing. For now, she would simply wait and see why all this had fallen to her. She must encourage herself. Rose was right. Mr. Bland must have had his reasons for what he did.

Mamm opened the front door for them with a surprised look on her face. "Is something wrong, Miriam?"

Miriam couldn't find her voice, but Rose answered for her. "We need to speak with you and Mr. Yoder, if you have time."

"Sure." *Mamm* looked puzzled even as she attempted to smile. "Please be seated on the couch." *Mamm* hurried into the kitchen, and seconds later the washroom door slammed. Miriam glimpsed Shirley hurrying toward the barn, probably to fetch *Daett*.

Mamm reappeared and seated herself in her rocker. "*Daett* will be with us in a minute, I'm sure. May I get you something to drink, Rose?"

"No, thank you," Rose said with a smile. "This won't take too long once Mr. Yoder arrives."

"He'll be right in," *Mamm* repeated, clearly nervous.

"*Mamm,* this is good news . . . I think," Miriam said.

Silence settled over the living room.

Several minutes later Miriam saw her *daett* hurrying as fast as he could up the front steps. His awkward gait was more pronounced than usual. As he entered the room, *Daett* glanced from one face to the other.

Rose stood and nodded to him. "I'm sorry to intrude on your afternoon, Mr. Yoder. My name is Rose, and I'm Amos Bland's sister. Miriam and I thought it would best if we explained the current situation together."

Daett turned pale. "Situation? Has something bad happened? Is that why you're late?" he asked Miriam.

"Everything is okay, *Daett,*" Miriam assured him.

"Yes, everything is okay." Rose looked frustrated. "I'm sorry for the confusion. I would have called ahead if you had phone service. I made arrangements to conduct some business after the funeral, and then Miriam and I came here right after that."

"Business?" *Daett* was puzzled now. "After the . . . ?"

"There was something we needed to do," Rose said. "Because Miriam was mentioned in my brother's will, we met with his attorney, a Mr. Rosenberg. He wanted to meet Miriam before we talked about the specifics of my brother's will. I apologize again if this has caused worry for you."

"Miriam was mentioned in Mr. Bland's will?" This came from *Mamm.*

"That's correct. My brother left Miriam his farm . . . and some other things, including everything needed to run the place. It's the farm we'd like to tell you about."

Miriam tried to breathe evenly. Rose was handling the deception so well. It was almost as if the two million dollars didn't exist.

"And why did your brother do this?" *Daett*'s eyes blazed.

"Well, he was a very kindhearted and wealthy man," Rose said. "And he thought very highly of Miriam. I suppose he wanted to show his gratitude for the kindness Miriam showed him the last three years of his life. Without Miriam's help, Amos would probably have had to go to a retirement home instead of staying on his beloved farm. Miriam gave him excellent care."

Daett swallowed hard, as if overcome by what he heard.

"This was surely a wonderful gesture on your brother's part," *Mamm* said. "But surely Miriam can't accept such a gift."

Rose glanced at Miriam and then said firmly, "Mrs. Yoder, my brother gave Miriam this gift. That was what he wanted. That is the arrangement he made. I believe we should honor his last wishes."

For a moment no one spoke. Then *Daett* bowed his head. He finally looked up. "Then we thank you, Rose, since we cannot thank your brother in person. We would not wish to disrespect his kindness."

Rose smiled. "I hoped you'd feel that way. Now, I need to go. You have a good afternoon, Mr. Yoder. Miriam, there are papers you need to sign. Consider your schedule and then call me. I'm more than happy to take you to the lawyer's office and help you in any way I can. Okay?"

Rose was gone before Miriam could catch her breath. Even *Mamm* was too stunned to get up and see Rose to the front door. *Daett* stood frozen in the middle of the living room.

Miriam struggled to find her voice. "I hope you know that I had nothing to do with this."

"*Yah,* we know," *Mamm* assured her.

Still chills ran up and down Miriam's back.

CHAPTER NINE

Saturday morning dawned with rain clouds and light squalls moving across Possum Valley at steady intervals like the waving of quilts drying on a wash line on a windy day. The weather fit Miriam's mood exactly. Sorrowful, heavy thoughts swept through her heart. *Mamm* and *Daett* hadn't stopped bemoaning the idea that Mr. Bland had left her his farm. "I still can't believe this," *Daett* had said when Miriam had come home yesterday after her first day at the Berlin Gospel Bookstore. Soon the people of Possum Valley would look at her strangely and wonder what she'd done to deserve such a gift from an *Englisha* man. All things considered, though, *Daett* was taking the news better than *Mamm.* Their reactions made Miriam all the more glad she'd said nothing about also inheriting two million dollars.

Rose was scheduled to pick her up this

afternoon so she could sign the papers Mr. Rosenberg had prepared. *Daett* was still downstairs. His presence in the house this late on a Saturday morning could be explained by the weather, yet Miriam was sure there were chores in the barn he could occupy himself with — if he wanted to. But, no, she figured he wanted to talk with her before she met with the lawyer.

Well, she couldn't hide out in her room all day, Miriam thought. She'd have to face *Daett* sooner or later. She looked in the dresser mirror and straightened her *kapp*. Seconds later she stepped out of the stairwell and into the living room. *Daett* was waiting as she'd expected. He lowered the latest copy of *The Budget* when she appeared. He cleared his throat. "Your *mamm* and I wish to speak with you before you leave, Miriam."

Shirley stuck her head through the kitchen doorway. "Can I listen in?"

Daett sighed. "What we have to discuss is a serious matter, Shirley. Please be respectful and take the younger children upstairs. We don't want to be interrupted."

Shirley appeared mournful as she gathered up her siblings, and then they all clattered up the stairs. Miriam almost wished Shirley could stay and listen in. She can even have the farm and the money, she thought. But in her heart she knew Shirley would do herself great harm if she were given a lot of money. Maybe it was best this way.

Mamm appeared in the kitchen doorway and then took her seat in her rocker. She sat with clasped hands resting on her extended middle. *Daett* glanced at her. "Are the younger children all upstairs?"

"*Yah.*" *Mamm* studied the floorboards in front of her.

Daett turned to face Miriam. "Please sit. This may take a while."

Miriam moved toward the couch and sat on the end closest to *Mamm*'s rocker. The comforting presence of *Mamm* reached across the space between them. *Mamm* clearly felt deeply for her plight. Probably *Daett* did too, even if neither of them had found the words to express themselves that way.

Daett cleared his throat. "*Mamm* and I have spoken at length about this matter, Miriam. You know how we feel about money, so you can imagine our feelings on Mr. Bland leaving you his large farm."

"I didn't know he was going to do such a thing," Miriam said. "Rose assured you of that. And the lawyer questioned me at the restaurant about it too. They are satisfied that everything is . . . was . . . in order."

Daett regarded her steadily but his voice trembled. "Were you inappropriate with him, Miriam? Is that why Mr. Bland left you the farm?"

Miriam froze. How could *Mamm* and *Daett* think such a thing? Even the lawyer hadn't asked such a question! Miriam tried to speak, but no words came out.

Mamm stood and reached across the space between them to squeeze Miriam's arm. "I'm sure *Daett* doesn't mean to accuse you by asking so directly, but we have to know if there was any hint of improper behavior between you."

Miriam choked out the words. "He was like a *daett* to me. Was that a sin?"

Daett's face relaxed. "That's *gut* to hear, Miriam. Even though you shouldn't have regarded an *Englisha* man like a *daett*. But it does explain a lot. Mr. Bland must have looked on you like a daughter."

Miriam tried to breathe deeply as *Mamm* said, "We don't hold that against you, do we, *Daett*?" *Mamm* glanced toward *Daett* in his rocker.

Daett nodded. "I should have paid more attention to what was happening with Mr. Bland and you." He hung his head for a moment. "I guess the regular paycheck blinded

100

my eyes, and now we're in this situation."

"Maybe the Lord can bring some *gut* out of this?" *Mamm* asked, looking for the positive.

Daett didn't say anything. He seemed lost in thought.

"I did nothing to ask for this," Miriam said. "But I'll still repent if you believe I did something wrong."

"You did nothing wrong that I can see," *Mamm* said.

They both waited for *Daett*'s verdict.

What he said would be final, Miriam knew. But how could *Daett* hold this against her? She couldn't think of anything untoward that had occurred between Mr. Bland and herself.

"You must give this farm away." *Daett*'s voice was firm. "It's not right for a twenty-year-old girl to have such riches. And how would you care for the place? You can't. And if you could and did, that would be a scandal too great to imagine in our community. A young woman managing a large farm. It wouldn't be seemly."

Miriam swallowed hard. Here was her answer, and it was an option she'd already considered and rejected. Rose and Mr. Rosenberg would consider such an action a great insult to Mr. Bland's final wishes.

How was she to explain this to *Daett,* let alone change his mind?

Mamm's hand had found Miriam's arm again. "Your *Daett* is right, Miriam. And I can see you're struggling to accept his decision. See how much of a hold wealth has on a person? Let this be a warning! Get rid of this farm at once. Surely Rose will know how this can be done."

"She's coming this afternoon," Miriam reminded them. From the look on *Mamm* and *Daett*'s face, this was a relief. The sooner she gave the place away the better. But how could she? And it wasn't because money had a hold on her heart. It was because she wished to honor Mr. Bland's wishes.

A sob rose from her heart. "Mr. Bland's memory shouldn't be offended like this. He loved me like a daughter. Rose even said so. And this was a gift given from his heart."

Daett's lips were set in a firm line. "That is not a good reason, Miriam. Look where this path might lead. There lies nothing ahead but more trouble. And who knows how soon you might be tempted and be led by that temptation completely out of the Lord's will?"

A sudden thought rushed through Miriam's mind. She pondered it for only a moment before she blurted it out. "If I must give the farm away, then I'm giving it to you, *Daett.*"

Daett was speechless.

Mamm spoke up immediately. "We couldn't accept such a thing, Miriam!"

"You don't have a choice." Miriam spoke calmly. "I will tell Rose and the lawyer this afternoon. I will have the lawyer draw up new papers. This is my answer."

Daett still hadn't spoken.

Was *Daett* stunned by her boldness? Miriam wondered. She'd never spoken to him like this. Had the inheritance already corrupted her soul and changed her attitude? Miriam trembled at the thought and hung on to the edge of the couch. What had taken hold of her? Only a few days ago her life had been so calm and secure and sane. They had been poor but happy.

Miriam stood and looked at her *daett.*

He still looked stunned as he sat there silently.

Miriam's body tingled as she fled into the kitchen. If she gave *Daett* the farm, it would change the family's financial situation for the better completely. Why hadn't this course of action occurred to her before? What a perfect solution! *Daett* would no longer be a poor man. Had selfishness blinded her eyes momentarily? *Daett* would just have to accept the farm, Miriam decided. However, she would figure out a way to give it to him so that it would always stay in the family . . . so he couldn't give the farm away or sell it to someone outside the immediate family.

Miriam leaned on the edge of the countertop. How did she dare think such thoughts about controlling what her *daett* could do? How could she even think that she knew what was best? But she *had* thought them. She would speak to Rose about the matter this afternoon. Mr. Rosenberg would know how to write things up so that *Daett* couldn't sell the farm.

Miriam shivered. These were not the proper thoughts for a young Amish woman to have. She knew that. But she hadn't asked for any of this to occur, so she wasn't to blame. Hadn't Rose assured her that her brother knew what was best? She would trust God to guide her, and she would trust Mr. Bland's judgment, even if he was *Englisha.* Hadn't she been there in the moments before he passed and seen the expectation in his heart that he would soon meet his beloved *frau* in heaven? Mr. Bland had been redeemed by the Lord just like she had. And just like her family had.

A soft hand fell on her shoulder, and Miriam jumped and turned around. *Mamm*'s face came into focus. Her concern was written deeply on her countenance. "What's happening to you, Miriam?"

"I don't know." Miriam paused. The words had just slipped out, but they were true. She *didn't* know.

"You should come back in, and we'll pray about this." *Mamm* pulled on her arm.

Miriam stiffened. "*Daett* already said what he said. I've decided to give the farm to him. There's no sense in praying."

Deep hurt and shock spread across *Mamm*'s face. "But we must always pray, Miriam. Have you forgotten that already?"

Miriam's shoulders relaxed. *Mamm* was right, and she should take correction in good faith. Wouldn't that be a sign that she hadn't been corrupted? She nodded and followed *Mamm* back into the living room.

Daett was already on his knees, so *Mamm* and Miriam joined him.

Oh, what a mess, Miriam thought. Where had her peace and *gut* sense fled to?

Daett's prayer rose in a soft whisper:

Dear Lord, look down upon us now and have mercy upon our situation. You know that Miriam didn't ask for this situation to happen, and You know that neither did we. All our lives we have sought to walk before You in humility and brokenness. There has been peace and harmony in our home because of Your grace and presence.

Now this trial of temptation has come. Do not allow it to bring that which displeases You. Break our hearts of the pride that still lies there ready to rise again. Let us not be like Satan, eager to think more highly of himself than You made him. Let us remember that we are dust, that we are made from the ground that our feet walk on.

Teach us to think lowly thoughts. Do not take Your Holy Spirit from us. Help Miriam make the right decision about this matter.

Please forgive me where I may have spoken out of turn and said things that bruised my daughter's heart.

There was a long silence before *Daett* stood. Miriam and *Mamm* followed. Miriam wiped her eyes just as a loud clatter sounded on the stairs behind them. Shirley must have decided that with the end of the prayer, it was safe to return. The smaller children poured down the stairs and out of the stairwell, scattering throughout the house to resume their play.

Shirley soon appeared with a sheepish look on her face. "Problem solved?"

"I wish," Miriam said.

"The Lord will help us," *Mamm* spoke up.

Daett was already headed for the washroom door and his chores.

Shirley could be filled in later on the details, Miriam decided. Right now she had to keep focused on carrying out her plan. Once the farm was safely in *Daett*'s name, the news would be broken to the whole family, whether *Daett* wished it or not. She would then be clear of the matter.

CHAPTER TEN

Rose's car pulled into the driveway soon after lunch, and Miriam quickly made her way across the lawn. There had been grim tension in the house since the morning's conversation about Mr. Bland's farm. Shirley begged for more information, but *Mamm* refused to talk about it. It was best that way, Miriam decided. She pulled open the car door, climbed in, and offered a cheerful-but-strained, "Good afternoon."

Rose wasn't fooled. "How's the family taking it?"

"Not well." Miriam winced. "We just had another round of speaking about it this morning."

Rose pulled out of the driveway. "Did you spill the beans about the money?"

Miriam shook her head. "Things went badly enough with just the farm topic."

"What is your father's advice?"

Miriam's chuckle was forced. "His *orders,*

you mean." She couldn't believe that came out of her mouth and the tone of her voice. How did she dare speak about *Daett* like that?

Rose didn't look surprised though. "So, what were his orders?"

Miriam kept her voice low. "He told me to give the farm away. I told him I would — but I'm giving it to *him.*"

Rose shrugged. "That's fine with me. Was that perhaps what he was after to begin with?"

Miriam gasped before words gushed forth. "Oh, no! *Daett*'s not like that at all. In fact, that's what I need to speak with you about. How can I give the farm to *Daett* and yet make it so he can't give it away to someone else?"

Rose glanced at Miriam. "If you're serious about giving the place away, Mr. Rosenberg can help you. And the paperwork can be drawn up so the farm has to stay within your family. That might be a wise choice anyway. I would have offered to help you manage the place, but even then it might have gotten to be a little much for two women. Unless you have a beau on the line with marriage plans?"

Miriam felt her face redden as she thought of Ivan. "I'm afraid not. There's just little ol' me."

"That might change now, even if the farm is in your father's name." Rose gave Miriam a knowing look.

A leap of hope stirred inside Miriam. She pushed the feeling back at once. This was not something she would entertain. She would never try to steal Ivan just because her family had new wealth — even if the new farm was the nicest in the community. The change of fortune was still so hard to believe!

"It *will* make a difference you know," Rose pressed on. "One wishes sometimes that it wouldn't, but that's just the way things are . . . the way men are."

What if Ivan was told about the two million dollars? The thought burned through Miriam. That would be unethical to use such a low trick. Surely she wouldn't even be tempted. She didn't wish to win anyone's heart with money. What a disgraceful marriage that would make.

"Our people are different," Miriam said.

Rose came to a stop along Main Street and parked. Minutes later the two women were ushered inside by Mr. Rosenberg, who answered the office door himself. "It's a Saturday," he said and chuckled, as if he owed them an explanation. "I'm glad to offer my services whenever it's convenient for you, with or without a secretary present."

He guided them into his office and motioned for them to sit down at a small table with comfortable chairs.

"I can sign what I need to," Rose said. "But with Miriam, it looks like there will be a bit more paperwork involved."

"Oh?" Mr. Rosenberg raised his eyebrows.

"I want to give the farm to my *daett* — and make it so he can't give it away." She was feeling nervous, but that was understandable. She'd never been in a lawyer's office with or without a secretary present.

Mr. Rosenberg thought for a moment. "That's doable. Maybe a trust plan where you control a major interest. I'll look into it. You'll still need to sign papers today. The farm has to be turned over to you before you can transfer the property to anyone."

Mr. Rosenberg grabbed a stack of papers from the desk and sat down at the table. Putting the papers down, he said, "This pile involves the farm. The smaller stack concerns the money. This is your new checkbook and debit card, Miriam. Congratulations!"

"Thank you," Miriam said nervously. Was there really two million dollars in that checking account? She didn't dare look, but maybe it wasn't written down inside it.

The lawyer quickly went over the checkbook and banking instructions with Miriam. "I've also written this down so you can refer to it if you need to," he said. "I need your address and a legal form of identification. I'll send the follow-up paperwork to you. The bank needs an address where you want your monthly statements sent."

Miriam's mind spun. "I didn't bring identification with me. I do have my birth certificate at home. As for the bank, I don't want anything bank-related to come to my home. That would cause all sorts of problems."

Silence settled on the room for a moment. "Well then, use my address for the bank, and I'll keep the statements for you," Rose offered. "You can look at them anytime, of course. And you can bring in your birth certificate the next time we come here. Is that okay, Miriam?"

"Yes, yes, of course. And thank you." Miriam could breathe again. There were more pitfalls along this road than she'd imagined. If the Lord didn't help her, she was sure to fall into one soon. *Help me, please, Lord,* Miriam whispered silently. Guilt rushed through her. Perhaps she had no right to ask help from the Lord with such a large amount of money?

"Let's get started." Mr. Rosenberg interrupted her thoughts. "I'll explain each document as we go along."

Miriam pushed the dark thoughts away. "I'm listening."

With a kind smile, Mr. Rosenberg explained the documents. Miriam signed each one without hesitation when he was finished.

"Now," Mr. Rosenberg said when they'd finished with both stacks, "on to our next project, which I think I can finish within the week. Shall we set up another appointment now?"

"It has to be on a Saturday. I go back to work full-time next week," Miriam said. "I'm sorry if that inconveniences you."

Rose laughed. "Not many young women with two million dollars would worry about missing work."

Mr. Rosenberg laughed in agreement, so Miriam smiled at the joke, although her thoughts were about how little the *Englisha* knew about the community. Money or no money, work was what one did. Was that foreign to the *Englisha?* she wondered.

"How about you let me know when you have the paperwork ready," Rose spoke up, "and I'll pass the word on to Miriam. Then we'll meet the following Saturday at ten o'clock. How does that sound?"

"Okay with me," Mr. Rosenberg said.

"That sounds good to me too. Are we finished?" Miriam stood and moved toward the door. She really wanted to get home.

Rose seemed to sense her urgency and stood quickly.

They said their goodbyes to Mr. Rosenberg. He followed them to the door and was waving when Miriam glanced over her shoulder on the way to Rose's car. He was a kind man, and she trusted him completely. But that was about the only *gut* feeling at the moment. She wanted to get home. The Yoder farm in Possum Valley was her haven from storms. And it would be, Miriam told herself, even when her *daett* realized that he would have to keep the farm according to the terms of the trust. In the end, *Daett* would see the wisdom of what she was planning.

Seemingly lost in her own thoughts, Rose didn't say anything as they drove toward Berlin.

"Do you miss him — your brother?" Miriam finally asked. "I know I do."

Rose nodded. "It's amazing how fast you can forget the little things when there's business to conduct. Amos was such a good man."

"I know." Guilt rushed through Miriam again. Soon she'd be able to forget about the money. But could she? Now she was acting like Shirley — promises and promises when she knew *gut* and well that with two million dollars in a bank account in her name, her whole life had changed. Even if she gave the money away, something inside of her was different now. Life would never be the same.

Rose slowed for the Yoder driveway and pulled to a stop by the barn. "Why don't you call me around Wednesday to see if Mr. Rosenberg has the necessary papers ready. We'll make arrangements then. And don't worry. He'll get everything right."

"That's the least of my worries," Miriam said as she climbed out of the car. "Thanks for your time and patience and assistance."

Rose laughed. "I'm happy to help. Remember, I've benefited from my brother's will too. Helping you is the least I can do."

"You're still kind, and I appreciate it." Miriam stepped back as Rose turned the car and drove down the driveway.

Miriam turned and walked toward the barn. Hopefully *Daett* would be inside. It seemed right that she speak with him alone about the plans for Mr. Bland's farm. The rest of the family would find out soon enough.

The barn door squeaked as she pushed it open. She paused and squinted in the dim light. Chore time was still hours away, so the lanterns hadn't yet been lit. There was no sound as Miriam walked deeper into the shadows. A deep sob rose from near the haymow door. Miriam stopped. Was *Daett* in prayer among the hay bales? Perhaps he was praying for her soul and the danger she was in? Stabs of regret ran through her. She stepped back. She could slip out, and *Daett* would never know she'd been there.

But she couldn't run away like that. And hadn't she looked forward to the peace she would find here at home? No doubt she'd felt the power of *Daett*'s prayers at the lawyer's office in Sugarcreek, and this was where the interceding for that peace had probably come from.

"Daett?" Miriam called out.

The answer came softly. "Come, Miriam. We need to talk."

"Yah, I'm coming." Miriam moved forward and chose a hay bale across from her *daett.* The hay on the floor was disturbed where he'd been kneeling.

Daett cleared his throat. "I've come to a

116

peace about Mr. Bland giving you the farm. The Lord has spoken to my heart. You don't have to give it away if you don't wish to. I spoke too heatedly and without enough prayer."

Miriam stared. *Daett* had never backed down before. Not when he spoke to one of the children. *Daett* was a *gut* man . . . a very *gut* man. A soft sob caught in her own throat. She moved over to *Daett*'s hay bale and slipped her arm around his shoulders. "But I've already decided. I'm giving it to our *family*. That's what my heart is telling me to do."

Daett's face was troubled. "I can't accept something I didn't earn."

"But you have earned it!" Miriam's look was intense. "Consider all the long hours you've put in for your family. Look at how much you accomplish as you work the best you can. What if this is the Lord's doing? He knows I have no use for a farm but you do. Lee and Mark can help you work the place. And we won't be short on money all the time."

Daett attempted a smile. "There's more to life than money, Miriam. I've tried to teach you that. I can't accept the gift."

Miriam took a deep breath. "Then Lee and Mark can work the place because this *is going* to happen, *Daett*. The lawyer, Mr. Rosenberg, is drawing up the papers now. The farm will become a family trust. You'll be in charge of it, but it's arranged in such a way that you can't give the farm away without my permission."

Daett studied her face as he struggled to remain calm. Finally he said, "And does wealth cause my eldest child to disrespect me on top of everything else?"

Miriam clutched one of *Daett*'s hands in both of hers. "I'm sorry. I don't know why I'm speaking so . . . so forcefully like this, but it's not because I don't honor you. I'll never forget that you are my *daett*. I never want to disrespect you. But you have to admit that we've struggled financially for a long time. And it is through no fault of your own. You work hard. Your lameness wasn't your choice."

Pain etched deeply across *Daett*'s face. "I'm shamed before my daughter, I see. And yet this humbling may be what I needed. Apparently pride in my own efforts and a determination to never give up on my principles have displeased the Lord. He has now spoken, and I will bow my head in submission. But this much I still say. Mr. Bland's farm will always be *your* land. Once you and your beloved marry, you will move on to that farm. Until then, the boys and I will tend it for you."

"You must not say such things!" Miriam squeezed *Daett*'s hand even tighter. "I love you, *Daett*."

"I will say them." *Daett* squared his shoulders. "They are the truth. And I did need a humbling. Come, let us tell *Mamm*. This will be a great load off her shoulders. I know the burden of the coming little one has lain heavy on her heart, and she will be pleased that we've settled this problem. And having a bit more wealth won't hurt us, I guess."

Miriam followed *Daett* out of the barn and across the lawn. He gave her a smile as he opened and held the front door for her.

CHAPTER ELEVEN

Shirley sat on the couch with a serious look on her face as she listened to her family discussing Mr. Bland's gift to Miriam. She was glad for Miriam, Shirley told herself. She really was, but what a shocking surprise. And *Daett*'s acceptance of the gift was the biggest surprise. *Yah,* he claimed repeatedly the farm would be Miriam's once she married, but in the meantime he planned to farm Mr. Bland's old place. Well, at least the family wouldn't be so poverty stricken now. She was glad for that.

In the meantime, her fresh resolutions since Monday night not to call Jonas again had drifted ever further away. This news didn't help. If Miriam had a farm she could move on to once she married, where would that leave Shirley and the rest of the family? In the same place they were right now — poor! She didn't need that reminder at this crucial moment of temptation. Yet there it was. Poverty was still staring her in the face.

She shouldn't be bitter, Shirley chided herself. And she didn't want to be. But then she needed to look after her own interest too, which just might include Jonas Beachy. She would call him and see if he would pick her up from home sometime soon. Shirley's heart beat faster at the thought. *Yah,* she felt a lot less guilty about calling him now. *Daett* certainly wouldn't think her logic made any sense at all, but then he wasn't a girl who had to look forward to living life on a shoestring all alone. A better life might lie out there beyond the horizon. Not necessarily with Jonas, of course, but finding more for her life was the thought that counted at the moment.

Shirley got up and slipped into the kitchen. No one noticed as the chatter continued. Lee and Mark could hardly control their excitement as they talked of how they would start work on Mr. Bland's place. Even *Daett* seemed caught up in the joy, although a look of sorrow had crossed his face briefly as she walked past. *Daett* would struggle mightily with this change in the family fortune, Shirley knew.

"This is the will of the Lord as He humbles me," *Daett* had told them as he explained his decision. "I have taken great pride in my ability to make it on my own, so I now must accept what He has given to Miriam through Mr. Bland."

After a few minutes in the kitchen, Shirley continued on to the washroom. She opened the door and stepped outside. If she went past the living room window, her family would see her. They'd wonder what she was up to . . . and notice her going down the road. Then they'd call after her. So, she would go to the barn first and then to the phone shack from there. *Yah,* that was sneaking around, but she couldn't help herself.

Shirley hurried toward the barn. Would Jonas agree to pick her up? She wouldn't dare ask him outright, but perhaps he would offer again. Maybe she could drop a hint. If not, then no one needed to know she'd called him. If she hurried she could be back before her family missed her.

Shirley entered the barn and went out through the barnyard door. From there it was a short jaunt across the pasture to the road. Several minutes later she arrived out of breath at the phone shack. She dialed the number and held the receiver to her ear as she waited. The last thing she needed was for Jonas to think she was overly eager. She quickly cleared her voice before Jonas answered.

Jonas's voice was cheerful enough. "Shirley, I was hoping you'd call."

"How did you know it was me?" Her voice trembled.

Jonas chuckled. "Modern technology. Caller ID. The number shows up on my phone. I figured it had to be you unless your father was calling . . . to chew me out." Jonas's chuckle wasn't quite as hearty this time.

"Oh, no!" Shirley gasped. "I'd never give *Daett* your number. And *Mamm* knows I talked with you on Monday night."

"Then all's aboveboard." His voice brightened. "So what's up?"

What should she say? She had to guide him toward asking her out, but how? "Well, there was also a surprise at our house this week. The old man that Miriam used to work for — Mr. Bland — well, he died and left her his farm."

"That's interesting," he said.

He didn't sound too impressed, Shirley thought. But then a "little" farm probably wasn't much in his world. Shirley went on, "It's complicated and the family is all talking about it. I slipped out to call you."

Jonas didn't hesitate. "I'm glad you did,

but we have to develop a better communication system. In the first place, I'm the one who should be calling you."

Shirley heard the pleasure in his voice and forced herself to breathe. "There's only this phone to call you with. And I can't stay here very long . . . much less wait here. In fact, I should already be going back."

"Maybe we can use carrier pigeons?" he teased.

Shirley laughed. "We don't have carrier pigeons. I'm just an Amish girl, you know. Difficult communication is how we live."

"I was joking," Jonas said. "You know my parents used to be Amish way back when, even before I was born. I wouldn't say I'd want to live like that, but you obviously like it."

Shirley tried to calm the racing of her heart. She didn't know what to say so she settled for "It's okay, I guess — if I can call you once in a while."

Jonas laughed. "I have no problem with that. I enjoy your calls. Probably more than you do!"

On that you're very wrong, Shirley almost said, but that would be inappropriate. She replied instead, "You're very kind. Thank you."

She could almost feel his smile over the phone.

"You don't have to flatter me, Shirley, but you're welcome. So tell me, what are you doing tonight?"

Shirley's mind whirled. At the Yoder house, Saturday night was a time to wind down for the week, clean up, read a book perhaps, and go to bed early. Except when one was on *rumspringa,* as she was. Was this the opening she was hoping for . . . to see if he'd come and get her? Shirley gathered her courage. "Not much, really. What are your plans?"

"I have a movie I should watch." There was a long pause.

Shirley clutched the receiver. "That's nice."

"You should come watch it with me."

Shirley tried to speak but nothing came out.

"Of course, I understand if you won't. Just sayin'." His laugh was nervous. "I know you don't watch movies."

"I . . ." Shirley managed. "I'd love to, but . . ." Here was her chance! Should she accept? Not really — yet, she must! How else would she get to see more of him?

"Maybe some other time?" He sounded hopeful.

"No!" The word came out a shriek, but Shirley rushed on. "If you'll pick me up, I'll come today! I'd love to come."

"Really?" He sounded skeptical.

Had she said too much? Her fingers were numb from clinging to the receiver so hard. If Jonas ran fast in the other direction, she wouldn't blame him in the least. He didn't need Amish girls who clung to his every word.

Her silence didn't seem to bother him. "What if your father chases me off?"

So that's what he was worried about. Shirley almost smiled. She managed to answer in a calm voice. "I'll tell my parents you're coming, and I'll meet you at the end of the lane. There won't be any trouble. I am on *rumspringa,* after all." That wasn't all true, but it was true in part. *Mamm* and *Daett* would have to accept her decision, just like they had to accept Miriam's decision to give them Mr. Bland's farm.

"See you at seven then." His voice sent a thrill through her.

"I have to go now." Shirley hung up the receiver and turned to race down the road and across the field again. By this time someone would have missed her, and they'd be on the lookout. She'd have to break the news of her plans at once. Tonight she

126

would not only ride with Jonas in his fancy convertible, but she would spend significant time with him. It was almost more than her heart could handle. Who would have thought such a thing would ever come to pass? A stab of guilt ran through her. What about her many resolutions and promises? Had they meant nothing? Shirley slowed down to catch her breath. She had to think of some answer because *Daett* would ask the same question.

Shirley pushed open the back barn door to find Lee and Mark just beginning their chores.

They stopped to stare at her. "So that's where you vanished to," Lee said, more statement than question. "Who did you call?"

Shirley plunged into her explanation. "I'm going out with Jonas Beachy tonight." She couldn't keep the chirp out of her voice. "We're watching a movie at his house."

"Now I've heard everything!" Mark made an exaggerated gesture as he pretended to drop his pitchfork on the concrete floor. "This even tops Miriam's exploits. Maybe you and I are falling behind, Lee."

"That's what I'm thinking." Lee glared at Shirley.

"It's what I've wanted to do for a while."

Shirley met their disapproving looks straight on. "Don't worry, I'll behave myself."

"Still making useless promises to yourself, I see," Lee told her.

Shirley lowered her head and fled out the front barn door. Lee spoke the truth. She couldn't keep her promises. But she would somehow keep this one. She and Jonas wouldn't do anything wrong. Jonas was a decent man, after all, despite what her family thought. She took a deep breath as she slipped into the house. At the moment she had no desire for another face-down with anyone. If Lee could handle her so effectively, then how would she survive *Daett*'s rebuke? Shirley's heart pounded as she entered the living room. *Mamm* was still sitting on the couch with Miriam beside her. *Daett* wasn't around, and hope rose inside of Shirley. She could tell *Mamm* without *Daett* here. But just as Shirley opened her mouth to spill the news, *Daett* came out of the bedroom.

He regarded her for a moment. "Where have you been, Shirley?"

There was only one answer she could give. To lie wasn't an option. "I called Jonas Beachy. He's picking me up tonight at seven. We're going to watch a movie."

Mamm let out a little gasp, and *Daett*

seemed to grow a shade paler. He didn't say anything for a long moment. "Has this anything to do with the news earlier in the day?"

What was she to say? She didn't want to blame Miriam or dash cold water on the family's climb out of poverty.

Her silence was answer enough, and *Daett*'s face grew even more serious. He raised his eyes and sighed before praying, "Dear Lord, help us. These are troubled waters that I can never travel alone."

She wanted to throw her arms around *Daett* and promise she'd never see or speak with Jonas again, but she knew that wouldn't help because she wouldn't follow through. She was still going out with Jonas tonight, no matter what. "I'm sorry, *Daett*," she managed.

He didn't say anything. He turned and left the house without a backward glance.

At least the door didn't slam behind him, Shirley comforted herself. Oh, if this wasn't the right thing to do, what sorrow she was bringing on her family. While *Mamm* and Miriam sat in silence, Shirley breathed her own silent prayer. *Help me, dear Lord! Please help me.*

CHAPTER TWELVE

At ten minutes before seven, Shirley slipped out the front door and headed out toward the barn. She would look foolish waiting out by the road, so perhaps the barn was best. She couldn't stay in the house a moment longer. *Mamm*'s sorrowful face was more than she could bear. Promises that she wouldn't be able to keep wanted to bubble up inside of her, but she refused to make them. Her resolve had weakened after supper when *Mamm* asked with hope on her face, "How old is this boy?"

"I don't know," Shirley had answered. She'd wanted to add, *He's old enough to act decently, and we will.*

"He's around eighteen, I think," Miriam offered.

"I wish he was a little older," *Mamm* commented.

Now Shirley reached up to touch her *kapp*. Her hair hung loose in a bun under it, kept there by the application of several extra pins. Thankfully neither *Mamm* nor Miriam had noticed. Shirley had plotted a brave course for tonight, one she wasn't sure she had the courage to pursue. Under the right conditions, she would get rid of her *kapp* and look at least in part like an *Englisha* girl. Wasn't she officially on her *rumspringa* now?

Before Shirley could reach the end of the sidewalk there were footsteps behind her. Had *Mamm* followed her for one last lecture? She whirled around to see Miriam approaching. Shirley relaxed. Miriam might not agree with what she was doing tonight, but there would be no lecture.

"May I speak with you a moment?" Miriam glanced toward the road. "Before Jonas shows up?"

This would be better than waiting out by the road alone, Shirley decided. She nodded.

Miriam appeared worried. "I've been wanting to tell you how sorry I am that this farm thing has so upset our family. If I'm leading you astray, please forgive me. Please don't go with Jonas tonight."

Shirley sighed. "*Yah,* in a way it had something to do with my decision. But in another way it didn't. Look, I'm glad I've taken this step, so don't blame yourself, Miriam. It'll be okay. I'll just have some fun and happy times with Jonas, and there will be plenty of time to join the church later."

"You always make promises." Miriam squinted at her sister.

Shirley glanced away. "Maybe someday I'll be a saint and keep my promises perfectly."

Miriam managed a wry look. "That'll be the day."

"See?" Shirley said. "Even you find a little humor in this situation. It's not as serious as everyone thinks."

Miriam's gaze went to the end of the driveway as Jonas's fancy convertible pulled in and came to a stop. "I'd say it's pretty serious." With that, she retreated toward the house at a rapid pace.

Shirley took a deep breath. She hadn't wanted an argument with anyone moments before Jonas arrived. That was why she'd come outside early, but it had still happened. It mustn't ruin the evening. She turned toward Jonas and smiled as she approached his car.

Jonas jumped out to greet her and open the passenger-side car door. "Good evening!"

He was all smiles and looked so handsome. She managed to hold her composure, return Jonas's greeting, and climb inside the car. It was even more *wunderbah* than she remembered.

"Your sister seemed upset," Jonas said as he climbed into the driver's seat, shut the door, and turned the key. The engine caught with a soft purr.

Shirley waited to answer until they were out of the driveway. "She was trying to persuade me not to go with you tonight."

"Obviously she didn't succeed." Jonas grimaced. "Did your family make more trouble than expected?"

"A little." Shirley took a deep breath.

Jonas seemed to sense her reluctance and moved on. "Have you ever seen a movie?"

Shirley tried to hide her embarrassment at the question. *Nee.*

Again he seemed to understand. "You'll enjoy it!"

On that he was right, Shirley told herself. She'd enjoy anything with him.

"So tell me more about your sister inheriting a farm," he asked.

Shirley took another deep breath. "I guess the whole thing just happened out of the blue on Thursday. Miriam learned of her gift after Mr. Bland's funeral."

"This Mr. Bland must have liked her."

Jonas grinned.

"I do think they'd grown close," Shirley agreed. "Miriam told me he'd become like a *daett* to her."

Jonas appeared pleased. "So it runs in the family then? This openness to non-Amish people?"

"I don't know." Shirley knew puzzlement showed on her face. "How do you mean?"

Jonas motioned with his hand. "You are, after all, riding with me."

Heat rose up Shirley's neck. "Oh, that way. I guess it does."

"Well, I like it," Jonas said. "I think it suits both you and your sister well."

Shirley looked away. If *Daett* ever heard such talk he would grow even more gray hairs long before his time. At the moment she wanted to switch the subject to something more suitable, but what? She could follow through with her plan — if she dared. A quick glance at Jonas showed his concentration fixed on the road ahead of them. With a few quick pulls of the pins, Shirley removed her *kapp* and undid the hair bun. Her long hair flowed in waves over her shoulders. Shirley ran her fingers through them to straighten them out.

Jonas had his mouth open when she glanced at him, but he recovered soon enough. "I wasn't expecting that."

Shirley looked at him with concern. "You don't mind?"

He laughed. "Certainly not! You're . . . well . . . quite something. I'd forgotten how wonderful long hair looks on a woman."

"Your family will think me strange?" Alarm filled her face.

"Not at all." Jonas shook his head as if to clear his mind. "It's . . . it's great. Believe me!" He gave her a quick smile.

This wasn't the emotion she'd expected. Still, this was new territory for her. If Jonas said she looked okay, then she'd take his word for it.

"You can look in the mirror," he offered. "There's one on the windshield clip behind the sun visor."

Shirley reached up, pulled the visor down, and there was the mirror just like Jonas said. She regarded herself for a few seconds. She looked about the same as she did at home. If Jonas liked what he saw, that was all she needed to know.

"Impressive, huh?" he teased.

Shirley shrugged. "It's okay. It's what I'm used to."

"I like your modesty. It's befits you."

His eyes were warm when she looked at him. "Thank you," she said.

Jonas turned into a driveway. Shirley straightened up in her seat. She'd been so caught up in this new adventure that she hadn't noticed they were so close. Now she would get to see this great house and likely meet Jonas's family. It was enough to take her breath away.

"They'll like you." Jonas seemed to read her thoughts.

"I hope so," Shirley murmured as Jonas pulled to a stop in front of huge garage doors. This house was bigger the closer they got, Shirley decided. Jonas motioned for her to stay seated until he walked around and opened the car door for her. Shirley rubbed her face, determined not to look like an eager fool in front of this family.

"Ready?" Jonas didn't wait for an answer as he led the way. He didn't offer to take her hand, which was *gut.* She would only have been embarrassed by the gesture. Jonas was a gentleman and then some. She was right to have come tonight. There was much here she could learn.

Jonas opened the front door, and the silence of the huge house greeted her. His family must be lost somewhere in the vastness, Shirley thought.

Jonas smiled and led her further inside.

In the living room his *mamm* and *daett*

rose to be introduced and shake her hand. They were nice, just like Jonas said they would be. They seemed neutral about her, which was fine. Jonas probably brought girls through here all the time. As Jonas led her upstairs, Shirley was speechless at the grandeur of the house. When they got to a large room at the top of the stairs, Jonas plopped down on the couch as if this was nothing special. It must be so for him, Shirley thought. But her head was spinning.

"Sit here next to me," Jonas said, pointing to the place on the couch beside him.

Fluffy cushions lay everywhere, and Shirley pushed them aside. She ended up closer to Jonas than she'd planned, but she decided not to move. He might think she didn't want to be close to him. How wrong he would be!

"Ready?" He pointed a small black box toward a large television screen. A picture appeared and sound began. "A tour of the Holy Land," Jonas offered, as if that explained everything.

Shirley settled in on the couch. Up on the screen strange lands and sights unfolded before her. Jonas didn't offer any commentary as the movie continued. Obviously he thought it was self-explanatory. She wasn't about to admit that it wasn't. Shirley

137

concentrated until her eyes hurt. The pictures made some sense, but what she really wished for was Jonas's arm slipped over her shoulder. She'd love to snuggle up against him and feel the warmth of his smile turned toward her. But those were highly inappropriate thoughts, Shirley told herself. She was only seventeen and should be thankful Jonas had even invited her into his house. Any further attention was much more than she should expect. And Jonas seemed engrossed in his movie anyway. Still, his form so close to her was more than she could resist. Did she dare slip her hand through his arm? What would Jonas think? She must not, Shirley told herself. But moments later her fingers brushed his arm. A quick glance upward took in his warm smile. He punched the box — the remote, as he called it — and the pictures and sound stopped.

"I'm sorry." He stood up. "I'm forgetting my manners. Would you like something to drink?"

"I'd love that." She gave him her sweetest look. *What I'd like even more is time spent talking with you,* she almost said.

He seemed to understand. His face softened. "That's right. You've never watched a movie before. It must be a little disconcerting. Come, let's step outside on the balcony.

But first a soft drink, perhaps?"

Shirley didn't answer as she followed him downstairs. His *mamm* and *daett* had disappeared. Everything was strange in the kitchen. Ice rattled out of the refrigerator door, and they had soft drinks instead of homemade lemonade. She chose a Diet Coke and waited while he poured it for her. At home she would have served him, but here she was lost in the newness. Maybe in his world the men served more than the men of the community did. If so, Shirley liked the idea.

Soon they made their way back up the stairs with their drinks in hand. Jason pushed open a set of double doors that opened onto a balcony. Shirley drew in a sharp breath at the vista before them. Well-kept Holmes County farms rolled off into the distance, with the immaculately mown lawn in front of them as a starting point.

"Like it?" Jonas stood close to her.

"It's so beautiful," Shirley kept her voice low. "I've never seen anything like it."

He laughed. "I guess I'm used to it."

"I'd never get used to this." The words slipped out. Shirley didn't move for a moment.

Jonas remained relaxed beside her. She slipped her hand in his. The smile didn't leave his face, and his fingers tightened in hers. "I'm glad you came over, Shirley."

The words she wanted to say caught in her throat, but he didn't seem to mind. She decided she was obviously starstruck. She could stay here for the rest of her life and be content. Shirley leaned her head against his shoulder. Her long hair flowed over his arm as she drank the view in. Weren't wonders like this supposed to lie at the ends of the earth? Yet the Yoder family farm in Possum Valley lay only a few minutes away, which didn't seem to distract from the pleasure at all. No matter what else happened in her life, she would always remember this evening at the Beachy home.

"Ready to go inside?" Jonas's voice interrupted her thoughts.

"I'll never be ready to go inside," Shirley whispered as Jonas smiled down at her.

CHAPTER THIRTEEN

In the workshop behind Raymond Beachy's vast display room filled with exotic log-home furnishings, Ivan concentrated on the handcrafted chair in front of him. His mind wouldn't stay on the job, though. With a sigh he straightened his back for a moment. His real ache this morning wasn't his muscles. A stab of regret was running through him. How could he have known things would turn out this way? He couldn't have, Ivan reminded himself. There was no way he could have known Miriam Yoder would inherit a farm free and clear from the old man she'd cared for. Miriam had given the place to her parents for now, but everyone knew what that meant. Miriam's *daett* had made it clear at the last Sunday services that Miriam would have the place back once she married. It seemed a matter of conscience to Eli Yoder, who had always had a hang-up about money. It was a hang-up he, Ivan Mast, didn't share in the least. A farm without debt in Holmes County wasn't a small matter. What a fool he'd been not to wait a few weeks longer before taking Laura Swartz home from the hymn singing.

The mistake had been a natural one to make, Ivan told himself. He could still undo the damage if he acted fast enough. Laura was a fine woman, but Miriam always had the deeper character. He'd known that but had given in to Laura's charms when the family moved back from Oklahoma. There really was no need for recriminations. Ivan would tell Miriam that he'd cared for her all along — which was true. And he'd tell her things hadn't worked out with Laura as he'd expected. Which wasn't a lie, either. He'd lost his head a little. Surely Miriam would understand.

His actions might appear a bit suspicious, now that the news of the inherited farm was known in the community. Miriam wasn't stupid, and she'd always been a woman of strong moral convictions. She might be stubborn. Stubbornness was a trait Miriam got from her *daett*. But Ivan would have to try. He'd never live with himself if he didn't. His work here at the Beachy's furniture business in the past year had strengthened his resolve to make it *gut* money-wise himself. How he'd do that he hadn't been certain. Work by the hour didn't seem to be getting him anywhere fast. But Miriam's inheritance of such a prosperous farm could be his way forward . . . *if* Miriam could be won over. Then he could stand tall among the best in Holmes County and say goodbye to log-home furnishings for *gut.* He'd have to leave Laura's beauty in marrying Miriam, and that wouldn't be easy. Laura's charm and grace had attracted him, and he'd been fortunate no other man had beaten him to the punch. He was a blessed man to have won Laura's affections so easily. But Laura had no money. What a cruel choice he was faced with. Well, maybe Miriam would grow in beauty as she aged, and Laura would go the other way. It was a small comfort, but at least something to hope for.

Raymond's son, Jonas, had breezed through the shop this morning to check on things. He'd taken a moment to chat. "Do you know this Miriam who inherited the Bland farm?" Jonas had asked with a grin.

Ivan figured Jonas knew he knew Miriam and wanted to rub things in.

Ivan had shot back, "Everyone knows her."

Jonas's grin had broadened. "I suppose they do now. I happen to know the family myself. Not too close, of course."

What Jonas meant by that wisecrack, Ivan had no idea at first. And what interest Jonas might have in the Yoder family was beyond him. Eli Yoder was poverty-stricken — and planned to stay so.

When he'd added nothing else, Jonas had continued. "Dad said old Mr. Bland's farm is among the best in Holmes County. There's rich black soil along the river bottom and tourist attractions along the main road — if an Amish man owned the place. Too bad, isn't it?" Then Jonas had moved on, but what he meant was plain enough. The tease burned deep. Jonas and his *daett* should know what they talked about. They were both brilliant businessmen. If they thought he'd messed up by trading Miriam for Laura, then he must have.

So what was he to do now? If he stopped his relationship with Laura and Miriam rejected him, he would have lost both beauty and the prosperous farm. Jonas would think him a total fool after that. *Nee,* Ivan would have to come up with a better plan. There was no question there. How like his luck to have something like this happen. Here he'd the perfect chance to date Miriam and had passed the opportunity up for Laura. Miriam must have been heartbroken when he took up with Laura. He knew her well enough to know that, even though the look on her face the following youth gathering didn't betray her feelings. Would she take him back now?

If he could only be sure. At least there was no question on his part. He would choose Miriam over Laura. One could put up with a lot in a wife — even her lack of outstanding beauty — if there was significant money involved. His work with the Beachys had taught him that much. Money bought a lot of things: prestige, lavish lifestyle, nice homes — all of which he could have even if he stayed with his faith, which he planned to. He certainly didn't have to leave the faith to enjoy the blessings of money.

He'd have to speak with Miriam before he stopped his relationship with Laura. There was a good chance Miriam would overlook his brief time with Laura Swartz and welcome him with open arms. But if Miriam rebuffed him, he would still have Laura to fall back on.

Ivan shook the chair in front of him, letting out his frustration. The truth was, he'd enjoyed his dates with Laura. He realized that more clearly now since he might not have too many more. And there would be tears from Laura. Unlike Miriam, Laura wouldn't take his rejection with classy style. She wouldn't bear her pain inside. It would be out in the open for everyone to see. But what could people say? Dating couples changed their minds all the time. That's what he had to focus on. And he'd warn Laura that if she made a big fuss he'd drop hints in the community about the shallowness of her character. That should limit her crying sessions. If there were tears in public, Laura would know to keep them unaccompanied by nasty accusations.

Now, how would he convince Miriam to forget his time with Laura? That would be the difficult part. And the longer he waited, the harder it would be. For one thing, some other man might make a move on Miriam now that she was well set with a farm when she married. He would have to take the risk that Miriam would accuse him of wanting to marry her because of the inheritance. He'd admit to Miriam that it did add to his attraction, but that in his heart he'd always admired and loved her. He'd tell her that Laura had been a mistake. What other choice did he have?

And he would love Miriam, Ivan told himself. He'd loved her once, so that was proof enough that his feelings were genuine.

And he really wouldn't have been happy with Laura Swartz. Not once things came down to everyday life. He could imagine now that the years spent with such a shallow girl like her simply wouldn't be worth it. Beauty faded, the Scriptures said, once the babies came and middle age crept on.

Ivan moved the hickory chair in front of him and finished the staining. It was a wonder he hadn't ruined the job with the way his mind wandered this morning. That was something the Beachy family wouldn't tolerate. They demanded the highest quality of work. He'd managed so far to retain both the job and his ability to advance up the ladder until he'd been appointed foreman of the department. All well and good. But if could just marry Miriam Yoder and take over her farm, there was no limit to what he could become or accomplish.

He'd get over Laura soon enough. He'd miss her laugh. That much was true. He'd discovered how much he enjoyed it these last few weeks. But then mightn't she eventually lose her laugh once the troubles of life began? Money, on the other hand, wouldn't lose its value. Wasn't that worth the loss of Laura's pretty face? And he'd still see Laura at the Sunday services. It wouldn't be the same though. She'd be someone else's *frau*. Laura wouldn't stay single for long. That much he was sure of. Not as *gut* looking as she was.

It was a shame though, Ivan thought as he picked up another chair, that he'd never had the chance to kiss Laura. He'd figured there would be plenty of time for kissing in their future and he hadn't wished to appear too rushed. That was part of the appeal of a real man, he figured — the lack of need, even though he would gladly have taken Laura's hand on their first date and drawn her face close to his. She would have allowed a kiss that first evening, he was sure. Now he had worried and schemed in vain. Perhaps he could still steal one after he talked with Miriam and knew for sure that she would take him back.

Ivan stood up straight. He couldn't quite do that. Even Laura would figure out what he'd done once he cut off their relationship. He'd better act cool and dispassionate. It wouldn't be easy, but he shouldn't expect things to be easy. Not when a debt-free farm hung in the balance. And Miriam needed a man like him who knew how to manage the place. Truly the Lord was in this situation. The whole plan was clear as day. Now for the next step, and the step after that. He'd take this slow and steady. Soon Miriam's

heart would be his again. He was certain of
that.

CHAPTER FOURTEEN

On Sunday afternoon, more than a week later, Miriam stood listening to the chatter of the crowd in Mose Gingerich's home where the church services had been held that morning. Miriam's thoughts drifted to the past week. Shirley had told her that Jonas planned to pick her up again sometime soon. She'd whispered her plans to Miriam after they'd settled in upstairs for the night. Jonas and she weren't very serious yet, Shirley had assured her. And she didn't plan to become serious. They just liked each other's company. No harm would come of it.

Miriam's job at the Berlin Gospel Bookstore was going well. The paychecks weren't as big as with Mr. Bland, but anything helped. In the meantime, her two million dollars in the bank still seemed unreal. She wondered at times if it really was there. The checkbook in her dresser drawer said the sum existed, and so had Rose.

Perhaps she should use some of the money to solve Shirley's problem. Shirley could be sent on a trip somewhere — maybe to Oklahoma with Aunt Fannie. A little time away might end Shirley's fascination with Jonas. Perhaps Miriam might even go with Shirley. She'd be glad not to have to see Ivan each Sunday and all the warm smiles Laura Swartz sent his way when she thought nobody was looking.

Perhaps Miriam should bring up the idea of a visit at dinner. She'd love to be around her chatty aunt again, and that would be far enough away from Possum Valley to find peace for a while. After she'd found out about the inheritance, she'd even suggested to Rose, half in jest, that she'd flee somewhere. But how could she do that? It seemed as impossible now as it had then. From where could she say the money for the trip had come? Perhaps if she'd mentioned to *Mamm* and *Daett* that she'd received a little extra money from Mr. Bland, she could spend some now. But that would have been a partial lie, to say the least. Besides, what would she do about her job at the bookstore?

Miriam shifted on her feet and glanced around. The services had finished an hour ago, and the second round of people were ready to be served their dinners. Mose waved his arms around to gather the young boys in from the outside. A few of the younger married men had also missed the first round. They made sure Mose didn't miss them by hollering, "We haven't eaten yet!" from the back of the living room.

"*Yah, yah,* I know this." Mose laughed. "But I thought your wives had served you a big enough breakfast you wouldn't be quite so hungry."

This produced hoots of laughter from the older men.

Miriam smiled. Everyone knew that Mose teased, and that no man would miss lunch regardless of how large his breakfast had been.

"Unmarried girls over here!" Mose hollered out.

Miriam moved toward the table with the other girls her age. She'd helped serve the first tables, and now she looked forward to a meal herself. The time was already well after one o'clock, and hunger gnawed at her. The problem hadn't been the breakfast served at home. There had been plenty of food. She'd been unable to eat a full meal out of nervousness. By today everyone would have heard the news about the farm the Yoder family had been given by the *Englisha* man Mr. Bland. And they would have had time to think and talk about the matter. Not that anyone would object, but this would change their status in the community. How that would play out, Miriam wasn't sure, but it certainly would have an impact. *Daett* had stayed true to form and made sure everyone understood that she would have the farm once she married. *Daett* didn't have to add the detail that this made her a more attractive marriage partner. That would just be accepted. This was another reason she hadn't breathed a word about two million dollars. What kind of a stir would that make?

Miriam seated herself at the long table, and Bishop Wagler's call to prayer soon rang through the house. All heads in the vicinity bowed. When Miriam looked up, she caught Ivan Mast's gaze fixed on her. He was seated across the room with the unmarried men. Miriam looked away quickly as blood rushed up her neck. Why did Ivan pay her attention today? His girlfriend, Laura Swartz, sat not three people away from her at the table. What was Ivan up to? When their eyes had met a few weeks ago, he'd glanced away disinterestedly. Today, he was still looking at her — if she didn't miss her guess. Miriam sneaked a peek. Sure enough, Ivan's gaze was still on her.

Well, she would ignore him, Miriam decided. There could be only one explanation for Ivan's sudden interest. She'd once wanted his attentions badly, but she didn't want him because she would own a prosperous farm. What kind of marriage would that be? Ivan had missed his chance. He'd chosen Laura, and his long look in her direction was completely inappropriate. That was all there was to it.

Miriam studied the food in front of her. She'd been hungry moments ago, but now all she wanted to do was get up and leave. Well, she would eat now whether she felt like it or not. Miriam took a bite of her sandwich and accidentally caught Ivan's gaze again. To her horror, she felt a thrill at his attention. Against her will she had to struggle not to smile back at him. There was no sense to this. She wouldn't — couldn't — encourage him! Ivan might even speak with her if she wasn't careful.

Miriam choked on her food, and the girl beside her gave her a concerned glance.

"I'm okay. The food just caught in my throat," Miriam offered.

The girl nodded and went back to her conversation.

She was being immature, Miriam told herself, to even think such things about Ivan. She was still desperate for his attention, and she had to stop it. Both of them would have to live with the choice Ivan had made. It was too late to switch girls now — at least for the reasons Ivan had. She forced herself not to look in his direction as she finished the meal.

His newly found interest in her would pass once the news of the farm wore off and Ivan figured out she was the same girl she'd always been. Decent — at least from a man's point of view — but a little on the homely side. Certainly no beauty like Laura. She didn't need a farm to attract a decent husband. And Miriam wouldn't stoop to that level, either.

Bishop Wagler soon called for a prayer of thanks for the food they'd eaten. Miriam tried not to, but she snuck a quick glance in Ivan's direction after Bishop Wagler's "Amen." Ivan gave her a warm smile, and her heart pounded in her chest. This had to stop! Miriam looked away at once. She couldn't be drawn into this trap! Her heart could never trust this man again. Ivan's attention at this juncture was not a coincidence, no matter how much she might wish otherwise. And what about Laura? She had to notice Ivan's wandering eye. Glances like he'd given her might escape the attention of most of the people around them, but certainly not a girlfriend.

Had Laura perhaps broken up with Ivan? The thought sent such a rush of joy through her that she became light-headed. Miriam pushed the thought and emotion away. She'd have heard that news by now. And it wouldn't change anything anyway. Ivan's interest right now was highly suspicious, and she mustn't forget that. How many times had she longed for this very moment, yet now everything had changed. Now Ivan had an ulterior motive.

Miriam moved toward the kitchen crowded with busy women at work on the dishes. She saw she wasn't needed and returned to the living room to help. Laura had come to the same conclusion and was already there. She didn't want to meet Ivan's girlfriend at the moment, but what should she do? She went to work clearing the table.

Moments later Laura gave her a glare and then returned to the kitchen with her hands full of dirty utensils.

Obviously Ivan and Laura still had a relationship or Laura wouldn't have sent her such a look. Miriam squeezed into the crowded kitchen. She smiled to several women when they nearly collided. All of them returned her smile. Laura's sister, Esther, offered her a dish towel. Miriam set to work with a will, pushing thoughts of Ivan and his antics far from her mind. That's all this was, she assured herself — childishness, which would go away once Laura had time to speak with Ivan and straighten things out.

A bit later Miriam saw Lee go out the front door, no doubt his way to the barn ready to travel home. Lee had his own horse and buggy, and Shirley and she had ridden with him. Mark was forced to drive the girls' horse, Mindy, on Sundays, toting along two of his siblings, which Mark grumbled about. He wanted a horse that belonged exclusively to him, but they could barely afford the three driving horses and buggies they had. For all of them to arrive at the community gatherings crammed into two buggies would have been a shame too heavy to bear. Even now, with three in each of the single buggies, that left four children and *Mamm* and *Daett* for the double surrey. Perhaps Mark would finally get his own horse now that there was income from a debt-free farm in the family. She could put up with the pain Ivan caused in her heart by focusing on the blessings her family would now enjoy.

Miriam slipped back into the living room and tapped Shirley on the shoulder. Shirley was deep in conversation with their cousin Martha, but at Miriam's nod quickly wrapped up the talk and headed outside. Lee didn't like to wait. He would if they hadn't come out of the washroom by the time he pulled up to the end of the sidewalk, but they'd hear about it later.

Miriam led the way to where their shawls and bonnets were stacked. She found hers, and Shirley did the same. Minutes later they were properly attired and outside. Lee was nowhere in sight.

"Wonder what's holding him up?" Shirley muttered. "You sure you saw him head out to the barn, Miriam?"

"I know I did." Miriam couldn't have been mistaken. "Let's go out by the buggies. Maybe he'll come by then."

Lee appeared about the time they arrived near the long line of parked buggies. He wasn't alone. Ivan Mast was sticking close to his elbow. Miriam stiffened.

Shirley giggled. "Didn't I see him make eyes at you today?"

"Shhh!" Miriam commanded with a meaningful glare.

Shirley wasn't finished. "He must be quite impressed now that we are no longer poverty-stricken. Isn't this exactly what you wanted?"

"It's not," Miriam said between her teeth.

The two young women fell silent as the two men approached. Ivan was smiling as he left off his conversation with Lee. He turned his charms on Miriam and Shirley. "You two look cheery this afternoon."

"I expect so," Shirley sang out.

I don't want to be impolite, Miriam told herself. She forced a smile but said nothing.

Ivan's glow didn't dim. "Got to talking with your brother and thought I might as well help him hitch up. Didn't expect to find you girls out here."

Miriam clenched her teeth. Ivan certainly *did* hope to find them with Lee. That's what his plan had been all along, and she wouldn't play his game. "Come," Miriam muttered to Shirley. "We might as well climb in."

Ivan's face fell as the two clambered inside the buggy. He didn't dare come to the buggy door for an intimate chat with Miriam. Instead, he held the buggy shafts as Lee backed his horse in, fastened the tugs on his side, and waved goodbye as Lee drove them down the lane.

Miriam leaned back and let out a relieved sigh. She hadn't seen the last of Ivan's attention, unless she missed her guess.

Shirley's giggle confirmed her suspicions. Lee seemed lost in his own world, but he was a man so he couldn't be blamed. Men often didn't notice the most blatant things when it came to romance.

CHAPTER FIFTEEN

It was Friday evening. Shirley was with Jonas as he raced his convertible down Route 83. The roof was down, and Shirley leaned her head over the doorframe and allowed the wind to meet her full in the face. The sensation was exhilarating. She'd left the house managing to avoid making any foolish last-minute promises to *Mamm*. She had to live in the real world, Shirley told herself. And the real world at the moment was with Jonas. She'd taken off her *kapp* once they were out of sight of the house, and the wind blew her long hair out behind her.

Out of the corner of her eye, Shirley saw Jonas's gaze linger on her before he glanced back to the road. She almost couldn't bear the joy rushing through her. For almost two weeks she'd waited for this moment when she could be with Jonas again. It was as *wunderbah* as she'd imagined. Jonas was exciting and kind, all at the same time.

Jonas laughed and Shirley joined in, their voices mingling with the sound of the wind rushing by and the car tires clinging to the road.

"Thanks for picking me up," Shirley said with a glance in his direction.

Jonas shook his head. "I'm the one to say thanks. I like being with you."

Shirley looked away and didn't answer. She would have to be careful and not say too much about how she felt. They were both young, and this evening her plan was to enjoy the fun of the moment. She did finally admit, "You're too nice to me." She took a deep breath and drank it all in — the exciting car, the daring speed, the beautiful evening, and, of course, the handsome Jonas. How could life be so sweet and full of pleasure when *Mamm* and *Daett* thought this was something awful? What a tragedy such suspicions were. She wouldn't allow their disapproval to dampen her spirits or spoil her *gut* time tonight.

"Family giving you problems?" Jonas seemed to read her thoughts.

Shirley brushed her hair from her face. "Just the usual. At least I didn't get any lectures this time before you came."

"Then they're accepting . . . you and me?"

"I wouldn't say that. But do we have to talk about it? I'd rather not, if you don't mind."

Jonas didn't hesitate. "Sorry. I was concerned, that's all."

Shirley gathered her courage and reached over to touch his arm. "I know . . . and I appreciate that you're concerned. But talking about it makes me think about it. I'd rather just enjoy the time I have with you."

Jonas grinned. "Okay, I understand. So what shall it be tonight?"

"Perhaps a movie? I think I'll do better this time than before," Shirley said.

Jonas laughed. "How about I take you out to eat? Do you have a favorite place?"

"Me?" Shirley laughed. "It's not like our family goes out to eat much. We're Amish and poor. We're not like you or your family."

"Let's not talk about that either," Jonas said. "I'm just a simple man. Money isn't everything, you know."

"Now you sound like *Daett.*" Shirley winced. "I'm sure you're both right. It must be nice to have extra money though."

"Let's not think about it anymore tonight," Jonas said as he slowed down for a stop sign.

"That's suits me just fine. But don't ask

me to choose a restaurant. I don't have any idea what's available or where they are."

He pondered for a moment. "It'll be the City Square Steakhouse, then. I know you'll love it."

With you I love everything, even movies, Shirley almost said.

"Do you like steak?" Jonas asked.

"I love it . . ." Shirley said with some hesitation. "The few times we've had it at home, anyway. I hope I know how to act in a fancy restaurant. I've never been to one." His long look took in all of her.

Shirley felt her heart flutter.

But then Jonas glowed with approval. "Just be yourself, and everything will be just fine."

"Don't give me such compliments." The words came out under her breath.

Obviously he caught the gist. His glow didn't wane. "It's hard not to with a girl like you."

Shirley studied the road for a long moment and imagined how red her face must be glowing. Thankfully, Jonas changed the subject.

"Tell me more about this farm your sister inherited. I hear it's one of the finest in Holmes County."

"Oh, it's nice, I guess," she began. "*Daett* and my two older brothers spent considerable time there the past week. I went with Miriam once to clean the house and put things in order. It seemed like a nice place."

Jonas slowed down as they approached the outskirts of Wooster. He didn't say anything for a moment. "I heard the place is large, acreage wise, and it has lots of business potential."

Shirley sighed. "I don't know how big it is. I do know *Daett* and my brothers will struggle to keep up with both farms on their hands. But they're happy about it. Already a young couple, Lester and Elaine Stoll, who married last fall and have been living in his parents' basement, have asked to rent the house. I heard *Daett* talk with *Mamm* and Miriam about it. I think they've accepted the offer."

"I don't know them." Jonas slowed down even more as they entered the heart of Wooster.

They're poor like us, Shirley almost said, but she bit back the words. There was no reason for her bitterness about poverty to surface. And besides, money seemed to mean about as little to Jonas as it did to *Daett.* Maybe that came because Jonas had never suffered from the lack of it. Or perhaps it was because Jonas was a really nice person. He had, after all, overlooked the fact that she was from a poor family when they first started going out.

"Where do you know this Lester and Elaine from?" Jonas asked.

"They're in our district." Shirley studied the city buildings around her. "They're nice people."

"It's nice that you could find people to live in the house so quickly," Jonas said. "And people you know, at that."

"Yah. And it's nice to have a steady income so soon from the farm. Miriam is happy about that. She's giving everything to *Daett* and *Mamm."*

Jonas didn't comment as he turned into a parking lot. "Well, here we are!"

Jonas jumped out of the car and dashed around to open her door. He took her hand and led the way toward the restaurant.

Shirley felt her hand trembling in his and hoped Jonas wouldn't notice. It was the newness of the place that had her in shivers, Shirley told herself. The truth was that Jonas's hand in hers was the real reason, but that didn't seem decent to think about right now. Perhaps later in the privacy of her bedroom she'd allow her mind to linger on how precious it was.

Jonas opened the restaurant door and held it for her. He quickly walked next to her as they approached the restaurant host.

Shirley was glad her pesky conscience wasn't stirring at the moment, but she feared it would soon exert itself in such a fancy place. And without Jonas, she wouldn't have had a chance to have a meal in a place like this. *Yah,* this was an amazing experience. All the more reason to enjoy it. *Live each moment in what is right.* And this was right! So very right. Thankfully her conscience didn't whisper anything back.

They were soon seated and a smiling lady handed them menus and left. Shirley took a discreet look at their surroundings. Elaborate lights hung from the ceiling. There were long, beautiful art prints on the walls. She noticed the well-dressed clientele had glanced at them while they were being seated. "I know what you said about being myself, but do I look weird or something?" she asked Jonas. "Maybe I should have left my *kapp* on? At least it would go with my Amish dress. Everyone is staring at us."

"You look beautiful. That's why they're looking at us."

Jonas was fudging the truth, no doubt. All these people had seen better-looking girls. For the future, she would have to get an *Englisha* dress for her outings with Jonas — if there were anymore. How would she accomplish that without the money to buy one? She certainly couldn't ask Jonas. Nor could she make an *Englisha*-style dress at home under *Mamm*'s watchful eyes.

Jonas looked up from the menu and stared at Shirley with a smile.

"Don't look at me like that," she whispered. "It embarrasses me."

He grinned but turned his eyes back to the menu. She followed his example, although she was overwhelmed by the myriad choices and the fancy foods listed. When the waitress arrived, Shirley still hadn't decided what to order.

Thankfully, Jonas came to her rescue. "May I order for you, Shirley?"

"Yes! That would be perfect!"

Jonas turned to the waitress. "We'll both have the filet mignon."

Shirley let out a breath of relief. She hadn't even known how to pronounce the words, much less known what "filet mignon" was.

"Potatoes au gratin or baked?" the waitress asked.

"Not baked," Shirley said quickly. She had baked potatoes at home all the time. Why not be adventurous? Whatever au gratin potatoes were, at least it would be something new. Jonas chose au gratin too, so they must be okay.

"This is my favorite steakhouse," Jonas said. "Great food."

"Then I'm glad you brought me here," she said, her eyes still taking it all in.

Jonas reached under the table and gave Shirley's hand a brief squeeze.

Shirley's heart pounded until the waitress returned with salads. After each offered a brief, silent prayer, Jonas began eating so Shirley followed his lead.

Soon the main course arrived. Conversation was light as they enjoyed the delicious steak and side dishes. Shirley watched Jonas carefully and ate slowly to avoid any missteps. She hid her sigh of relief when she took her last bite.

She gently massaged her neck to rub the tension away. Now, perhaps, she could relax.

Jonas finished a moment later and leaned back. The waitress appeared, and he ordered a dessert for both of them that Shirley had never heard of.

When they were finished, Jonas paid the check with a credit card. After the waitress returned the receipt, Jonas asked Shirley, "Are you ready to go?"

"Sure." Shirley rose slowly, careful not to trip over her own feet. She could just see herself flat out on the restaurant floor with

Jonas embarrassed half-to-death. When she was next to Jonas, his hand found hers. She leaned against his shoulder as they made their way out the front door. The faint smell of his cologne filled the air around them.

CHAPTER SIXTEEN

Fifteen minutes later the lights of Wooster were behind them. Shirley relaxed in the comfortable leather seat of Jonas's Porsche. The darkness had settled like a blanket, but the car's headlights pierced through and highlighted the road ahead. Only a few vehicles passed them because Jonas had turned off the main highway not a minute ago. It was a longer way back to Berlin, but Shirley didn't care. The longer the ride home took, the better.

"So," Jonas said as he smiled at her, "good meal?"

"Amazing!" She so wanted to nestle up close to him, but she didn't dare.

The little country road they were on wound itself here and there. A few Amish homes appeared now that they were well out of town. She could tell they were Amish by the gas lanterns burning in the front windows and the occasional buggy dimly visible in the barnyards if lanterns were lit in the barns.

Back to Possum Valley, Shirley thought. Jonas would drop her off, and she wouldn't see him again for who knew how long. She might even have to face a lecture tonight from *Daett* that would tempt her to make promises she wouldn't keep because they'd involve staying away from Jonas.

Jonas slowed down and the car bounced onto a pasture lane and then up a small hill. He pulled the car to a stop and turned off the lights.

Shirley drew in her breath as her eyes adjusted to the view. The sweep of stars reached low to the horizon. This was even better than what Miriam and she could see of the countryside from their upstairs bedroom. Here on this small knoll the country was open for miles, with only a few farms scattered in the distance.

"Like it?" Jonas asked.

"Of course I do. It's beautiful." Shirley gazed across the fields.

This seemed a little early in their relationship for such a romantic spot, but she wouldn't object. Did she dare move closer to Jonas? If not tonight, then when? She had no assurance that Jonas would ask her out again. She scooted closer to him, and his hand found hers. Shirley breathed in the faint smell of the meadow through the open top of the convertible.

Jonas turned toward her. "I'm glad you like the view."

I like being with you even more, she felt like saying. The words felt safer wrapped around her heart than spoken. Never had she felt like this before. And the sad thing was that there might never be a night like this again.

"There are the seven sisters." Jonas's free hand pointed skyward.

She followed the direction he traced and settled her gaze on the star cluster. All she could see though was the outline of his arm visible against the heavens. Jonas was more beautiful, she thought, than the twinkle of a thousand stars. Those she'd seen all her life on the farm. The trace of his arm she'd never seen under the light of the stars. Oh, what if he read her mind? She whispered quickly, "The stars are nice, really nice."

"Do you study the stars?" His voice was tender.

"Not really. I just look at them. They make me feel lonesome most of the time."

"Stars *are* kind of lonesome. They look clustered together, but even the seven sisters are light-years apart."

"Not unlike us." The words slipped out, and she tensed. Why had she said something so foolish? Then she felt him squeeze her hand and figured he was smiling. She relaxed.

His hand let go and slipped around her shoulder. "Yes, you're right. So near and yet so far."

"I know." She tried to breathe evenly as she leaned her head against him.

His free hand swept lower across the horizon now. "Those are all Amish farms. You can tell by the dim lighting."

"*Yah.*" Shirley took a deep breath. "They are my people, the place where I come from."

"Do you like being Amish?" The question came gently.

"I think so." Shirley stared at the star-filled heavens. "It's what I am. How do you be something else . . . something you're not?"

He shrugged. "You leave, I suppose. My parents did."

She said nothing for a moment. "I've always thought I'd stay in the faith. *Daett* and *Mamm* are . . ." She let the thought drift off.

His hand moved on her shoulder. "I'm glad you're with me tonight, Shirley, even if our stars are far apart. It means a lot to me."

174

"Oh, Jonas!" A sigh escaped her lips. "This is precious to me too. You'll never know . . ." He said nothing, so she kept her gaze on the lights across the field. They seemed more appropriate to look at than the stars above. She'd been right the first time. Their worlds were very far apart.

"Do you think we'd find each other as interesting if we lived in the same world?" Jonas asked.

Her voice was faint. "I don't know, Jonas. I don't think either of us can be what we're not. Not me, not you."

"Right. How can we be something we're not?" he echoed. "That's what I like about you, Shirley. You answer deep with deep."

"Oh, I'm not deep at all." Shirley sat straight up on the car seat. "I'm shallow as shallow can be."

He chuckled. "You underestimate yourself."

"No." Her voice was firm. "You think too much of me. Now, the same isn't true the other way around. Don't deny it."

He didn't say anything for a moment. "I like you, Shirley. That much I won't deny. And you seem to trust me."

"Of course I do!"

"That's a good foundation to build on. Don't you agree?"

But what is there to build? Shirley bit back the words. This conversation had become a little *too* deep. They were both young and getting in way over their heads. It was enough that they enjoyed each other's company. Anything more than that would have to take care of itself in its own good time.

Jonas nodded as if he understood. His hand found hers again. "Shall we go for a walk? Work off some of that supper?"

She laughed, but her voice was a bit tense. "Fine with me!"

"Come then." Jonas stepped out of the car and walked around to open her door. He led her across the pasture taking slow steps. The moon peeked over the horizon, and they both paused to admire it.

"You can almost see it inching up." Shirley's tone was hushed. "I've watched it do the same from our upstairs bedroom window."

"So you're a moon-gazer?"

Shirley shrugged. "I suppose most country girls are. It speaks to the soul."

"I like that about you, country girl." His hand pulled on hers.

She hesitated. "You hardly know me. I mean really know me. I'm not that special. I'm so ordinary."

He bent close. "Not to me. Maybe I need to get to know you better?"

Shirley smiled. "That's a pleasant thought. But then maybe it isn't. You might not like what you see."

He gazed at the moon. "I'll like what I see, so don't you worry about that."

Shirley wondered if she should dare say what she really felt right now. She took a quick glance at his face. "You're the best thing that's ever happened to me, Jonas. Other than the Lord, of course. Look at the joy my heart is full of! And I have you to thank."

His chuckle was low. "You do say the sweetest things, Shirley."

She lowered her head.

He reached out and traced her cheek with his finger. "You should let more of your heart show, Shirley. It's beautiful."

She would soon collapse right into his arms if he didn't stop this, Shirley thought. But at the same time she didn't want him to stop. She wanted to hear things like this forever.

His finger moved on her cheek again. "Maybe we should get back. Your parents will be worried."

A protest rose inside her, but Shirley kept silent. What Jonas said was true, and this night had to end, whether she wished it would or not.

He seemed to understand her silence. He led the way back to the car without a word.

She kept his hand in hers. She pulled Jonas to a stop for one last look across the open fields.

"We're right outside of Apple Creek." He spoke as if this were vital information she needed to know. "The lights of town are just over the next hill."

"Have you come here before?" Visions of others girls who had clutched his hand not wishing to go home cluttered Shirley's head.

"Alone. Sometimes. This is my uncle's land."

"It's so beautiful."

"Maybe we can come back again . . . sometime." His fingers tightened in hers.

"Oh, Jonas, I would love that!" Shirley paused. "But you know how it is, and . . . how . . . how we are." Her voice trailed off.

His hands rested lightly on her shoulders. "Yes, I know. And I understand that we may only have this moment." His fingers touched her face again.

Shirley gave in and stepped in closer. She wanted this tonight. His kiss. Never before had a man kissed her, and she wanted kisses from Jonas forever and ever. If Jonas never kissed her again, this one would be all she'd need to get through an entire life-time. She wanted his strong arms wrapped around her. Would he think her too forward?

He pulled her close for a second and then stepped back. He reached up and touched her cheek gently. "We really should get back, Shirley."

Come! she wanted to shout. *Kiss me! I'll never ask for another thing again.* But she didn't. Couldn't he sense the welcome pouring from her heart?

"We shouldn't, Shirley." His fingers lingered near her lips.

Shirley felt no shame in wanting his kiss.

"You are too sweet, Shirley. I shouldn't kiss you." His voice was tender.

"*Yah,* Jonas, kiss me," she whispered. "You know we won't see each other much longer." How she knew that, she had no idea. She just did. Their time together was limited. Tonight she'd seen the truth in the stars. They were worlds apart even though they lived so close.

His face was resolute as starlight played on it. He turned toward the convertible. He paused and then went back.

Shirley saw the struggle on his face. She waited.

He turned even more and his hands

touched both of her shoulders lightly.

She took one last breath before she tasted his lips. They were sweeter than she'd imagined possible, the sensation deeper than the stars in the heavens and much closer than the dim lights of the Amish homesteads. She drank in Jonas's essence until he pulled away.

His voice trembled. "We're way too young for this, Shirley."

"It is right for this moment, Jonas." Her voice was firm. "I will always remember you and this evening . . . this time under the stars. Even when you have long forgotten me, I'll remember this." He didn't answer as she clutched his arm.

Together they turned and walked to the car. Only at the last moment did she let go to enter the car door he'd opened for her. He shut the door and walked to the driver's side. He got in, started the engine, and backed the convertible out of the pasture.

They remained silent all the way back to Possum Valley.

Shirley stayed on her side of the car. She wasn't ashamed of their kiss. But it would be too much to look Jonas in the face or touch him right now.

Jonas pulled into the Yoder driveway and stopped near the barn. He turned the

180

engine off and leaned toward her. "It's been a great night, Shirley. I'll think about us for a long time . . . about you. We have to see each other again soon."

Her voice caught. "I'll never forget you, Jonas. *Never!*"

"Please contact me again if you can. Maybe next week." His smile was hesitant.

"*Yah,* I'd like that, but I'm not sure if I'll be able to." Before he could get out to open her door, Shirley opened it and jumped out. She wanted to kiss him again, but that might spoil the enchantment of what had happened between them tonight. It was best left as it was. She waved to him before turning toward the house.

"Good night, Shirley." His whisper hung in the darkness.

She slipped away. She was on the front porch before the headlights of his convertible arched across the house as he turned and drove down the lane.

CHAPTER SEVENTEEN

Miriam rushed to fill the tub with water for seven-year-old Elizabeth and five-year-old Cheryl's bath. Saturday afternoon was almost gone, and there was still the upstairs to sweep. Her little sisters didn't usually protest their Saturday bath time, and thankfully today was no different. Both little girls were lined up ready to jump in once she finished with the water.

Miriam gave them a warm smile. "No splashing now. I don't want to have to wipe the walls down once you're done."

"We won't!" they chorused as they climbed in together.

"Clean up!" Miriam ordered. "*With* soap. *Mamm* will be in soon to check."

They were giggling as she left.

Yah, Mamm would no doubt find some area that needed more scrubbing, Miriam thought. It surely wouldn't be long before she took on the oversight of the girls' baths.

But as of now *Mamm* wished to remain involved with the household duties where she could. The closer her delivery time came, the more she would need to rest.

A shadow crossed Miriam's face. Now, if the mess in her life could be cleaned up as easily by *Mamm,* how *wunderbah* would that be? But Miriam had more than dirt stuck behind her ears. And so did Shirley, if Miriam was any judge of the matter. That girl had been uncharacteristically quiet since her date with Jonas last night. All day Shirley had worked through her household duties with a dreamy look on her face. *Mamm* had noticed too, judging by the worried look on her face.

"Shirley!" Miriam called out. "I need help with the upstairs."

"Up here already!" a muffled voice answered from above.

So Shirley had begun to clean? That was *gut.* But the thought brought little comfort to Miriam. Shirley probably figured there'd be fewer chances for questions about last night if she wasn't behind on the chores. Miriam sighed and turned her thoughts to Ivan. He'd acted worse at this week's youth gathering than he had on Sunday. Ivan had even managed to corner her in the washroom when none of the other girls were around.

"Hi, Miriam," he'd said. Ivan had appeared innocent enough, like he'd dropped in by coincidence. But Miriam knew this was no casual meeting. After the looks Ivan had sent her way on Sunday, including all evening outside at the volleyball net, she knew he was up to something.

"Hi, Ivan," Miriam had responded. Maybe if she was friendly, he'd go away. Resistance hadn't seemed to work so far.

Ivan's confidence had only seemed to grow. "I'm glad you're happy to see me, Miriam."

Miriam had stifled a sigh. "Ivan, you know I like you well enough. But you have a girlfriend now. Remember?"

"Oh?"

She decided he'd feigned surprise, as if the thought had never occurred to him.

"Who would that be?" he'd asked.

She hadn't fallen for his tease. "Look, Ivan, we really shouldn't be out here alone. Someone might walk through."

His response had been to close the door between the washroom and the kitchen, which didn't help. There was no lock, and a blocked door would arouse suspicion.

"You seemed to care for me not that long

ago — or was I imagining it?" Ivan asked.

Her face had reddened at the comment.

Ivan had fairly glowed with triumph. "Just give me a chance, Miriam. You like me. I know you do."

Miriam had bitten back a retort. Liking Ivan wasn't the problem, and he knew it. His obtuseness was contrived. Did Ivan really think she would be won over so easily? The thought insulted her, but Ivan also knew her well. He knew she'd mourned when he'd started to date Laura Swartz. Even now Miriam's heart beat faster the moment Ivan appeared.

She'd pushed past Ivan, brushing his hand off her shoulder. He had dared touch her with such boldness! The worst of it was that she'd liked it. How many years had she dreamed of the moment when Ivan would show her such tenderness? But not under these circumstances. Still, life gave what it did. Was she being foolish not to grab the chance to wed Ivan — whatever his reasons? But *nee,* she couldn't live her married life with the knowledge that her husband loved a farm more than he loved her. And he didn't even know about the cash inheritance!

"Talk to me, Miriam . . ."

Ivan's voice had lingered in her ears as

she'd rushed into the kitchen.

A few of the girls looked up in surprise at her flustered appearance, but thankfully Ivan hadn't followed her. "People will think what they wish," Miriam told herself. That they didn't know Ivan had spoken with her was *gut* enough for now. But sooner or later someone would put two and two together — probably Laura Swartz. Now, if there was a repeat performance by Ivan tomorrow after church there would be trouble for sure.

Miriam sighed. Now was not the time to be distracted by Ivan Mast. Shirley was upstairs hard at work. It was time to get upstairs if she didn't want awkward questions asked of her. Miriam took the steps quickly and found Shirley in Lee and Mark's bedroom.

Shirley had the dusting brush in her hand. She looked up when Miriam entered. "You don't have to rush about. I'll finish up here, Miriam."

Stopping in front of her sister, Miriam felt compelled to ask the question on her mind. "Shirley, what happened between you and Jonas? Tell me the truth about last night."

Shirley looked away and didn't say anything.

"I want to know," Miriam persisted.

Shirley turned her head and regarded her

sister with a steady gaze. "You make it sound as if I did something wrong. It was the most *wunderbah* night of my life!"

"I was afraid of that." Miriam sat on the bed and groaned.

Shirley's voice took on a dreamy tone. "We walked under the stars, Miriam. I thought I would die from joy. And, oh, Miriam! Then it happened. We kissed! I've never kissed a man before and never want to again — unless it's Jonas, of course. It was perfect!"

Miriam knew something like this had happened. Her voice caught as she said, "You know this can't go on. You can't marry a Mennonite, much less someone who goes to a far different church like Jonas Beachy does. You *have* to stay Amish!"

Shirley's face darkened. "I know that, Miriam. Jonas and I both know we're from different worlds. *Yah,* any relationship between us will eventually end, but until it does I'm going to enjoy Jonas while I can."

Miriam stood up and busied herself with the broom. Should she trust Shirley? Giving Shirley a sharp glance, Miriam said, "This sounds like another one of your empty promises to me."

Shirley shook her head. "I saw this one written in the stars, Miriam. We were talking out in that open meadow, and Jonas pointed out how far apart the stars were . . . and yet how close they looked."

"I think you're trying to cover your guilt." Miriam tried a glare to see if it would rattle Shirley's obstinacy.

Shirley didn't back down. "I know I'm right, even if I can't fully explain why."

Miriam sighed. "Then we'd better pray that we find a solution to our problems."

Shirley lifted her eyebrows. "What problem have you got?"

Miriam swept with greater vigor. "Believe me, I have plenty of my own — with Ivan."

"Ivan?" Shirley said. "What about Ivan? I thought he was going with Laura Swartz. Is he coming back to you now?"

"Trying to," Miriam said. "But it's not going to happen."

The sisters worked quietly for a few minutes, each lost in her own thoughts. Then Shirley glanced out the window.

"We have a visitor," she said with a sly smile.

Miriam clutched the broom handle. "Surely not Jonas!"

Shirley laughed. "*Nee*. He's driving a buggy, not a Porsche. And besides, Jonas wouldn't be so bold as to come without my knowing beforehand." She stared out the window. "I believe it's Ivan, which would be your concern, not mine."

Miriam crept over for a peek past the dark-blue drapes. *Yah,* it was Ivan. He was sitting in his buggy while deep in conversation with Lee. Had Lee heard him drive in and come out of the barn to meet him? Or had Lee known Ivan was coming? Either way, what business did Ivan have here? Hopefully not her! She glanced at Shirley. Was she putting two and two together? If so, soon her whole family would know Ivan was interested in her, and they too would assume it was because of Mr. Bland's farm.

Shirley whispered in her ear. "What's going on? Is this the trouble you referred to?"

"Probably," Miriam whispered back. The truth was she didn't know why Ivan was here. Maybe he really had come to see Lee. *Nee,* whatever reason Ivan would give for the visit, he'd really come to see her.

The two young women headed downstairs and found *Mamm* with Elizabeth and Cheryl. The little girls had their hair freshly washed and combed. Both girls chimed at the same time, "There's someone here!"

Are visitors so scarce at our house that it's such a major event? Miriam thought with irritation. But her anger was better directed at Ivan and not at her family.

189

"He's coming in!" Elizabeth and Cheryl both glowed as Lee and Ivan appeared on the front porch.

Miriam almost fled back upstairs, but that wasn't practical. *Mamm* would call her back if Ivan wished to speak with her, and that would add embarrassment on top of embarrassment.

Shirley opened the door before Lee could. "What a surprise!" she sang out. "Ivan Mast in person."

A deep chuckle from Ivan greeted her welcome.

Mamm whispered, "I don't know why Ivan's here, but you'd better go greet him."

Spurred into action, Miriam pasted on a smile and crossed the living room floor as the two men came inside.

Ivan's face brightened even more at the sight of her. "Good afternoon, Miriam."

Lee took Shirley's arm. "I guess we'll make ourselves scarce then." Lee pulled Shirley along as he headed for the kitchen.

That left Miriam and Ivan face-to-face by the front door with *Mamm* and the younger girls looking on. Miriam didn't want another word with Ivan when the others could hear, so she brushed past Ivan and went onto the porch. He followed. She took the first rocker she came to and waited for him to sit in the other. Then she burst out, "You do have your nerve, Ivan! Coming here uninvited. How am I going to explain this to my family?"

His smile was broad. "I think it's the most natural thing. You can tell them that Ivan Mast has come to his senses. Now tell me the truth. Haven't you wished for this moment many times?"

Her face burned. How did Ivan know her heart so well? Yet he had still spurned her for Laura Swartz.

"If my dating Laura bothered you, well, I'm sorry about that." His tone softened. "That'll be over soon, Miriam. I came to tell you that and ask if you could forgive me for my misjudgment in that matter."

She stared at him. No words would come out of her mouth.

"*Yah.*" He nodded as if she'd asked a question. "You have a right to ask. I will be speaking with Laura at length on Sunday night, and we will part ways."

"Then why are you speaking with me now?" Miriam asked.

Ivan had a pleased expression on his face. "I can see that you care, and that's *gut*. I'm here to tell you what my plans are because you wouldn't let me speak to you earlier this week when you so abruptly cut me off.

That's why I've come over now — when we would have more time without the fear of anyone walking in on us."

Miriam wanted to roll her eyes. It was too much. She couldn't imagine that Laura would give up so easily. Ivan was a catch, and any young woman would jump at the chance to date him and, perhaps, marry him. And what made Ivan think she'd take him back if he did break it off with Laura? Didn't he realize she would never accept a date that depended on the farm as bait? That Ivan thought so made anger run all the way through her.

Ivan watched her carefully. He must have read her thoughts because he hastened to add, "I hope you don't think that in my heart this has anything to do with the farm you inherited from Mr. Bland. I heard about it, of course, and it does make you a more attractive prospect, but that's simply not the real reason I'm here. I still care about you, Miriam. I should never have dated Laura in the first place. You're a decent woman and will make a real jewel of a *frau*. I hope you will give me a chance to prove myself."

Before she could think of a proper answer, Ivan was on his feet. "I don't want to bother you long, Miriam. But I did wish to say that. I'm willing to wait a few weeks until you think things over, and then I will officially ask you home for a Sunday evening together. After I've spoken with Laura, of course."

Miriam really didn't want to agree to such a thing now . . . or later, but Ivan was already on his way down the steps. She couldn't find her voice to call after him.

Ivan briefly turned toward her. "Thanks for the time, Miriam." He lifted his hand in a quick wave. "The best to you and to us."

She watched him until he climbed into his buggy and drove down the lane. He had a big smile on his face when he drove past her.

CHAPTER EIGHTEEN

Supper was over that Saturday evening, and the younger children had been sent to bed. Lee and Mark were in their rooms for the night when Miriam took a seat on the couch. She hadn't discussed Ivan's visit this forenoon with anyone, and her family had respected her silence. But now was the time to speak in private with *Mamm* and *Daett*. And this conversation might well lead to Shirley's involvement. She was upstairs but could be called down at a moment's notice. Shirley might not be happy, but if necessary she'd be included.

Miriam glanced at *Mamm* sitting in her rocker beside *Daett*. "I need to speak with the two of you."

Silence hung heavy as they looked her way and waited.

A lump caught in Miriam's throat.

Mamm seemed to understand and spoke first. "Is this about Ivan?"

"Yah," Miriam managed.

"Ivan is a member in *gut* standing with the church," *Daett* said with a pleased expression on his face.

Miriam decided to get right to the point. *"Mamm, Daett . . .* I need to get away for a while. I need to be somewhere else."

Daett's look turned to surprise. "Because of Ivan?"

"I suspect that's only part of the problem," *Mamm* offered. "Maybe you'd better explain, Miriam."

Miriam gathered her thoughts. How much should she say? She couldn't go and accuse Ivan, and yet . . . Her words came slowly. "Ivan says he's going to end his relationship with Laura Swartz. He wants to bring me home from the Sunday-night hymn singings. But I think he's only paying me attention because . . . well, because Mr. Bland gave me the farm."

Daett's pleased expression returned. "Maybe Ivan's finding out that Laura makes a poor substitute for my daughter."

Miriam forced a smile. "That's nice of you to think, *Daett.* But Ivan's not coming back because he's tired of Laura. He's after the farm. I'm sure of it." There! The words were out.

Mamm didn't appear too shocked, but

Daett lost his pleased look. "You don't really think Ivan would do such a thing?"

"*Yah,* I do," Miriam said, now on the verge of tears.

Mamm didn't show too much incredulity, but *Daett*'s opinion of Ivan was too innocent.

"I'd take some time to think about this, Miriam," *Daett* said. "Surely Ivan is offering you some space if you have doubts."

Miriam nodded.

Daett's pleased look returned.

"I'd like to leave for a while to ensure that space. And I'd like to take Shirley with me." There! That had also been said even if she had no idea how such a thing was possible. She didn't mean to hurt *Daett* by the implication that she didn't trust his advice. Her instinct to flee was strong, and she trusted that more. What she didn't trust was her heart if she stayed here. What if she gave in to Ivan's pleas? The years when she'd longed for his attention might simply overwhelm her. She needed a place away from him . . . and even away from Mr. Bland's farm. A place where she could think everything through.

Mamm reached over to touch Miriam's arm. "Don't you think you're overreacting? I know things have been stressful the last while, but running away never does any *gut*. And where would you go? Plus there's not the money for travel, Miriam."

Miriam took a deep breath. All this was true except the last part, but Ivan had pushed her over the edge this morning. She wouldn't turn back now. Plus there was Shirley to think about. Maybe that was the point she should make. She looked at *Mamm* and *Daett* again. "Do you know that Shirley's pretty serious about Jonas Beachy? And it's more than just a little *rumspringa* fun, if you ask me. They're kissing already."

The look on *Daett*'s face showed that he wasn't pleased in the least with this information.

Miriam realized she probably shouldn't have revealed what Shirley had told her, but her sister hadn't asked that her actions be kept secret. And *Daett* would find out soon enough.

Right now his words came quickly enough. "And you would take Shirley with you?"

"*Yah,* of course." Miriam didn't hesitate.

"And Shirley would go to this place too?" *Mamm* sounded skeptical.

Daett gave *Mamm* a sharp glance. "I'm still in charge around here, although one begins to wonder with all that's been going on," he said with a frown.

Miriam twisted her fingers together. If *Daett* knew about the money she'd inherited, he would really be concerned. She had never kept something like this from him, but that was apparently what money did to a person. Money began to dictate actions, and there didn't seem much she was willing to do about it. The checkbook upstairs in the closet drawer was a secret that had sealed her lips tighter than a lid on a cooking jar after it came out of the pressure canner.

Daett continued. "But what's the use of sending Shirley away? With the modern ways people like the Beachy family embrace, Jonas can follow Shirley anywhere." He glanced at *Mamm* with a sorrowful expression. "We must have failed somewhere in our training."

Mamm was quick to give *Daett* a smile because she was that way. She always knew what *Daett* needed. And encouragement was just the ticket right now.

Daett took a deep breath. "But maybe we should try it. Anything is worth the effort to save one of my daughters."

"But where and how?" *Mamm* didn't sound too happy with the idea.

Daett didn't have to think too long. "Your sister Fannie is having a baby soon, isn't

198

she? That's in Oklahoma. Maybe young Jonas would leave Shirley alone if she went out there. And it might give Miriam time to think about . . . well, about her situation."

And come to her senses, Miriam added silently. She pushed the bitter thought away.

"And where would the money come from for this trip?" *Mamm*'s voice cut through Miriam's thoughts. "And how long would they be gone?"

Daett didn't hesitate. "We have the rental income from Mr. Bland's house now, and soon there will be farm income. Surely we can do this for our daughters' sakes. As for the time, you know more about the kind of help Fannie will need, but what about two weeks? Although I don't suppose Jonas will forget Shirley in just two weeks."

Miriam's mind spun. This sounded like a good idea.

"Well, maybe the girls could stay a little longer," *Mamm* said. "Like a few months instead of weeks. I'm sure Fanny and William would appreciate having more family around."

Daett frowned. "Then Miriam would need to quit her job at the bookstore, and her income . . ." He let the thought hang without adding the embarrassing fact of saying they needed her money.

That's true, Miriam thought. Her family hadn't survived without her income the past few years when she worked for Mr. Bland. But couldn't they now? Hadn't she done her share with the farm she'd landed in *Daett*'s lap?

Daett must have thought the same thing because he said, "I'm sorry. I forget that I needn't think like that any longer. If Miriam gets married, we'll have to live without her help, so why not practice now? And she has done plenty already. There is the Bland farm income. We'll get by."

Mamm stared at *Daett*. "I guess I did suggest this, but both of my oldest daughters going? How will I make it without them? And for a few months — with the baby on the way?"

Daett didn't answer at once. Finally he said, "Perhaps it's time Naomi helps out more. It'll be *gut* for her. We must do what's best for all the girls."

Mamm spoke up. "We'd better ask Shirley about her feelings. Or maybe we should think about this for a while before we decide."

Daett set his lips in a straight line. "Call Shirley. I've had enough of this. Shirley will do what I tell her."

Mamm hesitated but then got up and

called up the stairs for Shirley.

Seconds later soft footsteps padded down the stairs.

Mamm took her seat again.

Shirley came in and sat on the couch next to Miriam without a word. Her chin was set, though, so Shirley was ready for a fight of some kind.

"We've been talking," *Daett* began, "and we've come up with a solution to some of our problems that are . . ."

"Problems like me?" Shirley interrupted.

Daett shook his head. "You know we love you, Shirley. We probably don't do that perfectly, but we try the best we can with the faults we have." *Daett* cleared his throat. "I know you intend no harm by going with young Jonas. Still, you also know how hard it is for you to keep your resolutions. We've been talking, and we think it would be best if you went away for a while. We want you to accompany Miriam to see your aunt Fannie in Oklahoma and help her with her new baby."

Shirley considered this for a moment. "I'm not going to forget Jonas, *Daett*." Her voice was resolute. "We both know we'll have to go our separate ways eventually."

Daett's face was full of compassion. "You say that now, Shirley, but we all know how you are about promises. You may feel like you'll stop seeing Jonas by mutual agreement, but the more you're together, the less likely that will happen. This trip with Miriam will help you keep your commitment to not get involved with him."

Shirley was silent for a moment before she stood. "It doesn't look like I have much choice. I will need to tell Jonas."

"You're not to tell Jonas where you're going," *Mamm* said.

Shirley's chin was up again. "It's not like he's going to follow me to Oklahoma, *Mamm*. But, *yah*, I will tell him where I'm going. That is only right."

Mamm's voice was strained. "Then we'll accomplish little with this sacrifice."

"We must trust the Lord." *Daett* spoke up. "This trip is the right thing to do, and we must not doubt even with obstacles in the way. Both Shirley and Miriam will be better off in Oklahoma for a while."

Shirley stared at Miriam.

Miriam couldn't read her expression. Was Shirley mad? Did she blame her for all this? Well, at least the future was decided. She could deal with Shirley's feelings later. All that mattered now was that she'd be able to escape the Ivan Mast problem. And that would be happiness enough.

CHAPTER NINETEEN

Sunday evening Ivan's buggy crept down the road toward the Swartz home. Laura had lingered at the hymn singing, deep in conversation with one of her many girl-friends. Ivan had been impatient to leave, but now he was in no hurry either to arrive at Laura's home or for this evening to end. The time had come to tell Laura goodbye, and the agony in his heart was worse than he'd expected. Why Laura hadn't noticed the attention he'd paid Miriam today was beyond him. A temper tantrum or a barrage of questions from her would make this much easier. Instead Laura nestled against him with her head on his shoulder. She took great liberties for the length of time they'd dated, but Ivan couldn't blame her. So far he'd done nothing but encourage the woman's feelings for him. How he would change that suddenly, he still didn't know.

"It's a sweet night, isn't it?" Laura whispered. "The full moon will be up soon."

The last thing we need is a full moon, Ivan almost said. He answered instead, "I didn't know that."

"Oh . . ." Laura cooed. "I thought you were the romantic type. Don't you know that lovers who meet under a full moon have their hearts sealed together? Like forever?"

He'd never heard of such a thing, but it sounded like something Laura would come up with. Practical Miriam wouldn't talk about full moons or hearts sealed together forever. And practicality was what he needed right now.

"Let's pull over and wait for the rise of the moon." Laura's head rose from his shoulder to peer outside the buggy. "Right over there in that clearing. That's perfect."

What could he do but respond positively? So Ivan pulled off the road and brought the buggy to a bumpy stop in the field. What he *should* do, Ivan told himself, was slap the reins and race toward the Swartz place and drop Laura off without a word. Laura didn't seem bothered by his silence. She likely thought it romantic.

"It'll be up all the way soon." Laura's head was on Ivan's shoulder again as her gaze fixed on a distant tree line. "We have all

204

evening, you know. And it's much nicer out here than just sitting on the couch at my house."

This wasn't how he'd planned to spend his last evening with Laura. Ivan had tried to send hints her way all week but to no avail. This was not *gut* at all. Even so, this was going to be the end for them, so why shouldn't he enjoy their last hours together? Her fingers found his, and he took them gently.

She sighed and moved closer. "You're such a dream, Ivan. I never thought I'd do this well with a handsome man."

"I'm not much, you know. Just a laborer at a furniture shop."

Her fingers tightened on his. "Don't be so modest, though that's what I love about you, I guess. You know *gut* and well that not everyone could have gotten that job. I may not be too intelligent, but I know that. The Beachys have high standards, and they pay well. And you're a foreman now, aren't you?"

"I see you've been checking." He liked the feeling that ran through him at her words. These were not things that Miriam would have mentioned or likely even knew about. Because the truth was that he did get paid well. He just wanted more. But he wasn't about to admit that to Laura. Especially tonight. He glanced down at her uplifted face. Her beauty stabbed his heart.

"You can do even more, Ivan." Her voice was gentle. "I like a man with ambition."

He was a fool, Ivan told himself. Laura fit him perfectly. He ought to settle down now and ask the woman to marry him tonight instead of what he'd planned to say.

"See? Here it comes." Her finger traced the dark horizon where a soft glow of light was bubbling up.

"Is that saying true?" Sudden fear raced through him. What if there was something that happened between a man and a woman who sat under a full moon? He'd never get away from Laura. He'd never get his chance for a farm that was free for the taking . . . well, almost free anyway.

Laura's laugh was soft. "You wouldn't object, would you?"

"Of course not." His reply was quick. It isn't a lie, Ivan told himself. He didn't really object. It was just that other matters were interfering.

"Then let it happen." Her voice was hushed as the moon rose higher, half of its round globe visible now.

Did the woman actually believe in this? She seemed to, but Laura wasn't given to such superstitions. This was just her way to show her affection for him. She might also wish to give him a glimpse of the depth of possibility and where she wished their relationship would head. *Marriage!* Ivan stiffened at the thought.

Laura glanced up at him. "You're not afraid of the moon?"

He laughed with effort. "No. I like it here with you. It's a nice moon."

She leaned tightly against him. "You know, Ivan, I was afraid I was losing you. I don't know why. Please don't be angry with me for doubting. You're the first serious boyfriend I've had. And . . ." Her voice broke as her hand clung to his. "There's not something wrong is there, Ivan?"

Now was the moment to speak! Ivan tried but the only sound to come out was a croak.

She sighed. "I know how you feel. It must be the jitters of first love. I am your first love, right Ivan?"

"Yah," he managed to squeak out. "I've never really dated before."

"Not even someone from another community?" Her eyes searched his face in the moonlight.

"You were my first hymn-singing date, Laura. Honest!" He tried to keep the strain out of his voice.

She settled against his shoulder again. "I can't say that I've never dated, but none were like you, Ivan. We'll make a great couple by the time all is said and done. I know I have a lot to learn, and I can be immature at times. But I'm trying. I want to be everything that any *gut* husband would want in a *frau.* I feel so unworthy at times."

"Someone as beautiful as you will have no problem finding a husband!" The words burst out of Ivan's mouth.

Laura laughed with joy. "Ivan, when you speak like that, you make me feel so *gut.*"

"But you know you're *gut* looking. Surely you do!" He looked down at her in the gentle light.

A smile played on her face. "But I need to hear it, Ivan. And sometimes outward beauty isn't enough, you know. Not for a decent man like you."

Ivan glanced away. He would never get said what needed saying tonight. Not after words like that. And yet he had to. How could he take Miriam home from the next hymn singing if he didn't terminate his relationship with Laura first?

"You *do* love me, don't you, Ivan?" Her fingers traced his chin and paused near his mouth. He'd shaved this morning, but the stubble had grown enough to reveal where a lengthy beard would one day grow — once he had said the marriage vows and no longer used a razor on his chin.

Ivan forced a chuckle as he said, "I love you a lot!" What else could he say? That he could find no love in his heart for this woman? She would see through that. And he would soon kiss her if they didn't move on. Ivan took up the reins. "We'd best be going, Laura."

Her laugh was tender. "You don't have to fear, Ivan. I'm just little ole me."

She was much more than that, and she knew it, Ivan decided. She also knew about Miriam. He was certain of that now. His gumption was frozen in place. Apparently he'd met his match. Laura wouldn't let go easily, that much was plain to see. She'd probably planned this moon thing. Maybe that was why she'd been so slow to leave after the hymn singing tonight.

"I know we haven't known each other for long, Ivan." Her fingers stroked his face again. "But it feels like we have. Like years, in fact. Like we've always known each other."

It did indeed, he thought, but he kept his thoughts silent. He'd already said way too much.

"When was the first time you thought of

me as . . . as . . . you know what I mean, Ivan. When?" The moonbeams bathed her face now as she looked up at him. "When, Ivan? I'd like to know."

Her beauty almost choked him, and the charm of her voice pulled his heart in. The ache from earlier had ceased. Ivan let the reins slip from his hands. Why had he even thought to leave this woman for Miriam? Compared to this, Miriam's suspicious nature packed cold ice around his heart. And Miriam had never spoken to him in this tone of voice.

"Your beauty has charmed me plenty." He kept his voice low to match hers. "Since the beginning of time, I think."

She laughed. "I knew you had romance in you, Ivan. All you needed was the moon to bring it out."

"We can't live under the moon though."

Her face filled with concern. "We'll have each other, Ivan. That will be enough. You know it will."

"Living on love." He couldn't keep the sudden bitterness out of his tone.

Her voice was pleading now. "Ivan, it is possible. And it's true, you know. I will *always* love you. Kiss me, Ivan. Kiss me now and see if it isn't true!"

He shouldn't do this, Ivan told himself.

Never! And yet his resolution had flown away. What did owning a farm free and clear mean anyway? And what if he was mistaken and Miriam didn't give in? He shouldn't have made that promise yesterday to Miriam. His confidence had carried him away.

"Ivan . . ." Laura's voice was a husky whisper. "Ivan, you love me. I know you do. Don't do this to us. Whatever you're thinking, don't do it. You'll never love anyone like you love me."

How could she know this? he wondered. His silence confirmed that she was right. She held his heart in her hand. Resistance seemed out of the question — even if he wished to. He moved one hand at a time and placed them on each side of her face.

She didn't hesitate, her gaze uplifted to his eyes.

He touched her lips with his fingertips before he kissed her. The softness of her lips melted something deep inside of him. Still she was keeping her distance, he noticed. She was chaste even while she was kissing him. And it had the effect she probably knew it would. He drank deeply of her essence and only drew back after a long moment.

Her face beamed up at him. "You love me, don't you?"

"I do." He bent his head again, and she didn't resist him.

"That's enough." She finally pulled away from him but stayed close enough to lay her head on his shoulder again. He followed her gaze out over the shadowed landscape to where the woods lay in darkness under the round moon. Maybe there was something to this moon thing, after all. Even though she would have had this effect on him seated on her living room couch with a storm outside. Still, Laura hadn't taken any chances, and she also hadn't failed. There would be no words from him tonight about terminating their relationship. Not after that. He was a fool, but even he wasn't that big a fool.

"We should get back," she said. "*Mamm* and *Daett* will wonder what's become of us."

She held his arm while he drove. The buggy bounced across the ditch edge and back onto the blacktop. Ivan had noticed there had been no *Englisha* cars on the street while they'd been parked. Usually there was traffic this time of the evening, even on a Sunday night. Had Laura prayed for and received uninterrupted time alone with him? That wouldn't surprise him. As if to confirm his suspicions, the headlights of a car behind them bounced on the road ahead of the buggy. The vehicle soon passed them.

Ivan watched the red taillights fade into the distance. This was just as well. Perhaps his pursuit of money was foolishness, and he'd been saved from it — at least for the time being. Miriam wouldn't be disappointed if he never showed up again to speak with her. She would soon hear that his relationship with Laura was continuing. That would doom any chance of getting Miriam's farm, but at the moment he didn't care. Laura's kisses had made him reconsider the whole matter. He'd never kissed a woman before, and if this joy continued, he might never kiss anyone other than Laura.

They soon pulled into the Swartz driveway. Laura stayed beside the buggy while he tied his horse, Billy, to the hitching post. Her smile glowed in the full moon when Ivan approached her. He stepped closer.

Her finger came up to trace his cheek. "No more tonight, Ivan, but I do have pie inside. Your favorite — cherry."

"Gut," he said, although what he really wanted was to kiss her again. He would always want to. He was certain of that.

CHAPTER TWENTY

On Wednesday evening Shirley paced the floor of her upstairs bedroom. She'd changed clothes an hour ago, and Jonas was due at any moment. She wanted as perfect a "last time together" as possible now that the trip to Oklahoma was all planned. A call had been made from the phone shack to Aunt Fannie in Oklahoma. No one had answered, so *Mamm* had left a message stating the time when she'd be back at the phone on Monday evening. Aunt Fannie returned the call as planned, and *Mamm* came back from the phone shack sober-faced but with the plans lined up.

"Fannie was thrilled," *Mamm* had announced. Clearly *Mamm* wasn't, but that was to be expected.

As for tonight, Shirley was determined that there would be no tears. *Yah,* her heart had grown close to Jonas, yet there had been an inevitability about the eventual outcome of their relationship from the first and, certainly, since the evening they'd spent together under the stars. That special night their hearts had met and parted ways. Jonas was a *wunderbah* man, but they were worlds apart in ways Shirley couldn't even figure, beginning with their faith, their parents, and their financial statuses. For once she felt practical about it. She glanced out the bedroom window. There was no sign of Jonas yet, but she knew she'd hear his Porsche pull in soon. Since her younger siblings now knew about Jonas, she could go out and wait for him on the front porch — but tonight she didn't feel like it. Perhaps she wanted to act like a true girlfriend who had a real future with her boyfriend. Such a girl could afford to stay inside — and perhaps even cause him to have a short wait before she went down the stairs.

Both *Mamm* and Miriam had been worried when she told them she planned to spend her last evening in Possum Valley with Jonas. They probably thought he would persuade her to stay, but then they didn't really know Jonas. He understood her as she understood him. Hadn't the stars spoken to both of them? But neither *Mamm* nor Miriam would understand that either. She was too young, they'd say. Stars spoke what young people imagined them to speak. Well, she knew what they'd said, and that was that.

There was only one thing Shirley disapproved of about this trip to Oklahoma: Miriam's intention to leave Ivan. Miriam shouldn't do such a thing. She should trust Ivan even if he might have been influenced by the farm in his desire to renew their relationship. What was wrong with that reasoning? Hadn't Shirley first been attracted to Jonas because of his fancy convertible and the knowledge of how rich his family was?

The truth was that *Mamm* and Miriam still hadn't gotten over their shock that she'd so easily agreed to go on the trip to Oklahoma. No doubt they expected she had something up her sleeve — like an elopement. Shirley laughed at the thought. Jonas hadn't asked to marry her, and he wouldn't. Nor would she agree to it if he did. *Yah,* they did love each other, but didn't she have some sense? And what about her desire to live a decent life among the people of the faith? That hadn't changed. Didn't her intentions count for something?

At least *Daett* still trusted her. "Let Shirley go out with the boy," he'd said. As if *Daett* could have prevented her from going anyway. But it was *gut* to feel trusted by *Daett* and not to have a fuss with her family the last night before she left Possum Valley for a long time. She was happy tonight, and that was what mattered. Later there might be sorrow, but not tonight.

Shirley peeked out of the bedroom window as the sound of a car pulling into the driveway reached her. Shirley gave out a little squeal and dashed down the stairs. Now that he was here, she wanted to see him. So what if he would notice her eagerness and be pleased with his power of attraction. Right now she didn't care.

"Please be careful and act decent," *Mamm* told her from the kitchen doorway.

"*Yah,* I will," Shirley promised as she dashed out the door.

"Hi," Jonas greeted her as he got out and walked around to open the car door for her.

"Hi, yourself!" Shirley said as she climbed in.

Jonas got back into the driver's seat and shut his door.

Even as they pulled away from the house, Shirley began to remove her *kapp.*

Jonas drove out of the lane and sped off, his face beaming.

The joy of the moment was strong even though they both knew this was their last night together for a long time. How alike they were, and yet so far apart.

"Isn't this trip of yours kind of sudden?" Jonas asked, glancing at Shirley.

"*Yah.*" She hesitated, and he seemed to understand.

"Is it because of me?"

Before she could answer, he said, "Never mind. I don't think I really want to know the answer."

How like Jonas, Shirley thought. He didn't want her to feel uncomfortable answering that question. Maybe later in the evening she would broach the tender subject. But if further words on the matter were left unsaid, she would be just as happy.

Jonas glanced at her again, his gaze a tease now.

Shirley laughed and raced her fingers through her hair, knowing it would be a long time before she'd take her hair down in front of a man again. She'd not do it again until she said her marriage vows with a good Amish man. With Jonas the rules seemed different. And this was as it should be, Shirley decided.

Jonas watched as she continued combing her fingers through her hair. "Beautiful," he said as he reached for her hand and squeezed her fingers before he let go to make a tight curve on the road. "Where to?" he asked once he could take his eyes off the road.

"Anywhere is fine with me." She gave him a warm smile.

"Come on now," he teased. "Surely you have some preference?"

"I really don't, Jonas. Remember, I don't know much about your world."

"Well, then, how about dinner someplace close? Like the Good House?"

"Sounds good to me." Anything sounded good to her right now as long as Jonas was with her.

Jonas looked Shirley's way as he took another curve in the road. "So you're really going to leave Possum Valley? Just like that?"

She nodded. Somehow talk about stars sounded foolish right now, what with his presence so close to her.

"Will I get to see you once in a while?"

Shirley sat up straight. Should she say what she wanted to say? *If you come visit me in Oklahoma.* But, *nee,* that wouldn't be right. She didn't want Jonas out in Oklahoma. She let her silence speak for her and eventually said, "Let's not spoil our last night together. I've really enjoyed being with you, Jonas. I wish this would never end, but it has to. And there's nothing either of us can do about it."

"Agreed." Jonas was smiling a bit ruefully. He took his convertible around a few more curves before pulling into a full parking lot. "Looks like we have plenty of company tonight."

"But I have you," she said. "You're all the company I care about."

Jonas grinned as he got out, walked around, and opened her car door. He took her hand and helped her out. They held hands and walked into the restaurant.

After a brief glance at Jonas, a smartly dressed man ushered them to an open table. "Your server will be right with you."

"Does he know you?" Shirley asked when the man left.

"Maybe." Jonas shrugged. "I come here often. They have the best crab cakes in the area."

It must be nice to have people know you, Shirley thought. But that was what happened when one's *daett* had lots of money. Not wanting to follow that line of thought, she changed the subject. "So, what have you been doing with yourself?"

Jonas shrugged. "The usual. Working at Dad's place. I help him out where I can. I grew up around the business, so it's not really that hard. Dad has me doing different jobs to learn the business."

Shirley smiled. "I've done mostly house-work. I've never done outside work like Miriam did taking care of Mr. Bland. That job seemed boring at first, but it turned out more exciting at the end when Mr. Bland left Miriam his farm."

Jonas's eyes twinkled. "Are you sure that's all Mr. Bland left your sister?"

Shirley glanced at him. "You're teasing, of course."

He shrugged. "Maybe. I'm not sure. Dad has heard rumors, that's all."

"Rumors about what?" Now Shirley stared at him.

Jonas looked away. "This could be wrong, of course, but Dad sits on the board of the bank Mr. Bland used, and rumor has it that a fairly large sum of money was also left to your sister."

Shirley laughed. "Miriam's not said a word about anything but the farm, and she'd be the last person to have secrets. Miriam's like 'Miss Upright' herself. She would have said something. And believe me, the farm is more than anything we'd ever dream of hoping for. The Yoder family is poor, Jonas. Like really, really poor. And *Daett* seemed to like it that way."

"Sorry." He reached over to touch her

hand. "I didn't mean to stir up anything, Shirley."

"Oh, I'm okay." Shirley took a deep breath.

Their waitress appeared. "Good evening, Mr. Beachy. Glad to see you again."

Jonas smiled up at her and gave her his order.

Shirley noticed he hadn't even opened the menu, so she wouldn't either. Besides, she didn't know one thing from another in these fancy places. "I'll have the same," she said. "I like what he likes."

The waitress left.

Silence fell between Shirley and Jonas until he finally said, "Thinking mighty deep thoughts there?"

"Not deep, no," Shirley said. "Deep thoughts would be Miriam, not me."

His hand reached across the table and touched hers briefly. "I wasn't trying to put you on the spot. I like to hear what you think, that's all."

"Probably not this time. I think I'm getting just a little bit sad."

"You know I'll miss you, Shirley," he said, squeezing her hand. "I wish things could have turned out differently. But I understand . . . I guess."

"I think we both understand that we

couldn't ever be . . ." Shirley took a deep breath and forced the words out. "I'd love it if we could be a couple forever, Jonas. If only we weren't from such different worlds. If only it wasn't so . . . so . . ." Shirley sighed. "I think this trip to Oklahoma is for the best, even if it wasn't my idea."

His eyes met hers as he teased, "You never know. I might go to Oklahoma on business sometime."

A smile played on her face. "I will be back, you know. My plans for the future aren't definite, but I won't be gone forever."

He squeezed her hand again. "Tomorrow isn't definite. Nothing is but God. You have been a joy, Shirley. I'll never forget you."

She felt tears forming. "You know I feel the same way, Jonas."

The waitress interrupted them by bringing their salads, but Jonas's hand lingered for another moment on Shirley's.

Shirley smiled at the certainty of a good-bye kiss when Jonas took her home. They would have to stop along the road before they arrived home because a long pause sitting in Jonas's convertible in the driveway would more than likely bring *Daett* out to investigate. Stopping before they arrived at her house, she'd linger within his arms. The memory of their short time together would be all the more precious as they said farewell. It could neither be added to nor taken away from forever. One thing was for sure — she would never forget Jonas.

CHAPTER TWENTY-ONE

Miriam took in the open stretch of grassland outside the bus window. The driver had called out the name of the small town moments before. "Antlers," he'd said. A very western name, Miriam thought. And appropriate to the area. They had now left the last of the town's houses behind. She glanced over at Shirley, who was shifting on the seat beside her trying to doze off again. She clearly wasn't interested in the passing landscape.

It wouldn't be long now until the driver announced their destination: Coalgate, Oklahoma. Aunt Fannie and Uncle William's home was just outside the small town of Clarita, but the bus didn't stop there. Miriam glanced through the window again and wondered if much would change for them. Shirley would be happy whatever the countryside looked like. She likely had other things on her mind — like Jonas Beachy and their last evening together.

Shirley had been beaming when Jonas dropped her off at home on that last evening. Up in their bedroom, Shirley and Miriam had talked. Shirley had let out a long sigh and looked rapturously at the ceiling. "What a *wunderbah* man — but one I can't have. But his kisses, Miriam. Oh, it's like heaven has come down to the earth!"

"All I can say to that is I think it's a good thing we're leaving tomorrow," Miriam had muttered. "It's high time we got you out of here."

Shirley had laughed but then turned serious. "Jonas said you might have been given some money by Mr. Bland. He's heard some rumors. His *daett* sits on the bank board."

Miriam deflected the question. "The farm alone was plenty generous of Mr. Bland, don't you think?"

Shirley had shrugged and said, "*Yah,* that's what I thought."

Miriam had breathed a sigh of relief. She hadn't lied, nor had she been forced to admit the truth. Obviously Jonas was only repeating rumors and didn't have anything to substantiate it. The very thought though had turned her face pale. How had Jonas's *daett* come across even a rumor of the inheritance? The lawyer and Rose had assured her that any money in a bank account was a closely kept secret. If Jonas's father had heard about the money and shared the knowledge with his family, how long before someone else would find out? What if Ivan heard about it? He worked at the Beachy's business. Then his eagerness to pursue her hand in marriage would really skyrocket. It was *gut* of the Lord to provide a way of escape for her. She and Shirley might have to work hard for a while as they adjusted to the Clarita community, but they would succeed.

Miriam leaned back. Would Ivan follow her out to Oklahoma? She couldn't imagine that he would. She'd given him no encouragement that she would welcome further attention from him. Shouldn't her sudden departure be enough of an answer to his overtures? Surely the man would get the message! And she could look forward to a fresh start out here on these grassy plains without any hassles or temptations from Ivan. Miriam sighed. Why was her heart so weak when it came to that man? She should have been able to distance herself from his charms without the drastic measure of a long-distance trip to Oklahoma. Well, no matter. The Lord must understand. Hadn't

He helped out with these plans?

And this was for the best, Miriam told herself. For Shirley and for herself. Aunt Fannie had written about how much they enjoyed the community, so no doubt she would also enjoy Clarita. She already liked the change in landscape. The wind here could blow for miles across the grass with nothing to slow it down. Aunt Fannie had also written about how friendly the people were. There weren't that many Amish who lived here compared to Possum Valley. That made for closeness, Aunt Fannie had written. "We have few secrets among the community people."

Miriam stared out of the window. How then would her secret be safe here? She sat up straighter. The inheritance money *had* to remain a secret. She would need to keep her mouth shut that was for sure. Not one word to anyone. Not even to Aunt Fannie, especially because she hadn't told *Mamm* and *Daett* back home. Another thought raced through Miriam's mind. What if there was a man in the community who showed an interest in her? Would she be able to trust him? She was wary after Ivan's deception. The communities at Clarita and Possum Valley were closely connected, so news usually traveled freely between the two. How would a man act if he found out about the two million dollars? It was bad enough when people just knew about the farm. *Nee,* she must say nothing about the money. Nor could she trust herself to a man until she knew for sure he would love her for herself and not for what came with her. There wouldn't be another Ivan Mast in her life. Not again. But, of course, first there had to be a man who would show interest in her, and that might not even happen. Miriam glanced over at Shirley. If there were any available men in the Clarita community, they would certainly go for Shirley's *gut* looks instead of Miriam's plainness. Hadn't Ivan proven that point? Laura Swartz was *gut* looking like Shirley, and Laura had been Ivan's first choice, regardless of what he said.

The whine of the bus engine lowered as it slowed down. The driver's voice came over the intercom, interrupting Miriam's thoughts. "Our next stop is Atoka," he announced. "There will be a thirty-minute lunch break."

"Good! I'm starving!" Shirley said.

Miriam too was hungry. She thought some food might help calm her wandering mind too.

Moments later they were off the bus and

had purchased sandwiches and orange juice from a small deli. A courtyard lay off to the side complete with picnic tables. Shirley led the way over, and they sat down.

Miriam unwrapped her sandwich. "Do you think we'll be able to settle out here okay?"

Shirley thought for a moment. "I think so. Although I'll miss Jonas. And *you should* miss Ivan."

"Ha! I want to get away from Ivan, and *you should* want to get away from Jonas. Besides, there will probably be plenty of unmarried men here. You can take your pick." Miriam took a bit of her sandwich. She didn't add, "Unlike me." Bitterness was never right. Besides, she'd been the one who wanted to come to Oklahoma as a means of escape.

A mournful look crossed Shirley's face. "I've been thinking about Jonas. Seems like he's close to my heart even as we travel further away."

Miriam allowed sympathy for Shirley's plight to flood her heart. "You do miss Jonas, I know. But a relationship with him could never be. You also know that."

Shirley nodded. "I agree. It wasn't for the best."

Miriam held her sandwich with both

hands. "You do surprise me, you know —
how easy you were to persuade about coming. I thought you'd put up a fight."

"Maybe I'm trying to be practical." Shirley
gazed down the street.

Miriam reached over to touch Shirley's
arm. "I'm sorry I haven't been more sympathetic about Jonas. I suppose what shouldn't
be is still hard to get over."

Shirley gave her a quick glance. "Thank
you."

Miriam hastened to add, "I'm not supporting your affection for Jonas, believe me.
But I have my own heartache. Maybe that
helps one to understand more." *I have
secrets too,* she almost added.

"I still think you should have given Ivan a
chance," Shirley chided.

Miriam winced. "You know the answer to
that. He only wanted me because of the
farm."

Shirley appeared pensive. Just as she was
ready to speak, the bus driver announced,
"Time to go, folks. We're loading up."

Both young women stood. Shirley whispered, "I think you should plan to go home
when *Mamm*'s time comes. You might reconsider Ivan then."

They paused to throw away their food
wrappers and napkins. Miriam gave a short

laugh as they went up the bus steps. Shirley was grasping at straws. Naomi would take care of *Mamm* at home, and there would be no money for a return trip so soon. She certainly couldn't use her own money without offering some kind of explanation.

Shirley whispered, "I'm afraid you're going to meet someone out here and fall for him." Shirley took her seat beside Miriam and added, "Just because he's not Ivan."

Miriam frowned. "*Nee,* Shirley, you're the one who will find a new beau in Clarita."

Shirley shrugged. "I don't think so."

Miriam raised her eyebrows. "You sure stick up for Ivan, considering how he acts — chasing me to get my farm."

"Well, what's wrong with that?" Shirley shifted on her seat. "I think Ivan's nice, and you did like him a lot not that long ago. What's wrong if the farm brings you together? You'd still be married to him, and he'd have to love you."

"Not in the right way, he wouldn't!" The words slipped bitterly, and Miriam turned away.

Shirley appeared dreamy eyed. "I was attracted to Jonas because of his family's wealth. I freely admit it. So what's wrong with that? And yet in the end it was true love, Miriam. I've kissed him, remember?

And sweeter moments I've not had with a man before. And I know I'll never love someone like that again."

"Let's change the subject." Miriam looked through the bus window at the passing landscape. "Anything other than money and love."

Shirley ignored her. "Money can lead to love, Miriam. Really, it can."

"Nee," Miriam insisted. "Money and love are a dangerous mix. Little *gut* can come out of the two together. *Daett* would say little *gut* comes out of money when it's mixed with *anything.*"

"Only the heart proves anything," Shirley muttered. "And mine's still back in Holmes County with a man I can never marry."

The bus was slowing down for the next town. The sign that flashed by the bus window read "Coalgate," the place where Aunt Fannie and Uncle William would pick them up. Shirley's glance had followed hers, and she sat up straight on the seat, her mournful thoughts about Jonas apparently forgotten. At least for the moment.

The bus ground to a stop at a small filling station. The driver spoke over the bus speaker: "Coalgate."

Miriam gathered her bag from the over-head compartment and followed Shirley off

233

the bus. She strained for a glimpse of Aunt Fannie and Uncle William, but she couldn't see anyone she recognized. In their Amish attire, they should stick out, but by the time the driver retrieved their suitcases, there was still no sign of them.

"Is this the right place?" Shirley's voice revealed her worry as the bus disappeared up the street.

"I'm certain," Miriam's kept her voice steady. "We'll wait on the sidewalk. Aunt Fannie and Uncle William can't be long in coming." This was not the time to let fear take over.

"Maybe the bus was early?" Shirley's voice trembled, but it changed a moment later. "There they are!" She waved vigorously.

Miriam waved too as a car with Uncle William in the front passenger seat pulled up to the curb. Aunt Fannie had the back door open before the vehicle even came to a full stop.

"Oh, you poor dears! You've been waiting for us." Aunt Fannie rushed over to give both girls a big hug — well, the best she could in her condition. Aunt Fannie laughed. "I'd squeeze you tight for an hour, but you see how far my stomach protrudes."

"And it's a very *gut* condition to be in." Uncle William chuckled. "May I at least shake hands with my nieces?"

"Oh, I'm so glad to see both of you!" Aunt Fannie gushed before she let them go. "And I'm so sorry we didn't get here early."

Miriam offered her hand to Uncle William with a shy smile. She hadn't seen him in a while, but he was still a handsome man. Aunt Fannie, as the youngest in *Mamm*'s family, had done well in her choice of husband.

Shirley offered her hand to Uncle William. Her chirp had returned. "You know, it's awfully nice of you two to have us."

Aunt Fannie dismissed the praise with a wave of her hand. "What's *wunderbah* is you two coming all the way out here. And to help with my baby, at that. I never thought I'd see the day."

Aunt Fannie didn't know their real reasons, and for that Miriam was glad. She focused on more cheerful thoughts as Uncle William loaded their suitcases, and Aunt Fannie introduced them to the driver of the vehicle, Mr. Whitehorse.

The *Englisha* man nodded and said, "Welcome to Oklahoma. Are we all ready to go?"

"Yep!" Uncle William proclaimed as he climbed into the front passenger seat again.

The two girls joined Aunt Fannie in the back.

"Now, tell me all about your trip," Aunt Fannie said as Mr. Whitehorse drove them down the street toward Clarita.

Shirley chattered away about the hours on the bus and the people they'd seen. Aunt Fannie likely wouldn't rest until it was all told, Miriam thought as she looked out at her new surroundings. She'd let Shirley tell most of the story. Sudden weariness rushed over Miriam, and she tried to relax as they drove into the countryside. She'd arrived in a "new country" for a new start. From what Miriam had seen so far, this was a land that held much promise for both Shirley and herself. For that she was thankful.

CHAPTER TWENTY-TWO

Miriam watched with interest as Mr. White-horse pulled into the driveway of an obviously Amish homestead. She didn't know exactly how the Byler place would look from Aunt Fannie's brief descriptions in her letters, but there were buggies parked in the yard and there was a large greenhouse. *Yah,* this had to be Aunt Fannie and Uncle William's home. Plus Aunt Fannie's chatter had stopped. They had arrived! Aunt Fannie certainly wasn't the quiet one of the family, but that was one of the things Miriam had always liked about her aunt.

"Here we are!" Uncle William announced as they all got out of the car.

Aunt Fannie waved her hand about. "This is it. Our western spread. Well, a nursery really. But you already knew that."

"It's beautiful," Shirley gushed. "I'll love it here."

Aunt Fannie laughed. "I'm glad you like

it. Make yourselves right at home."

Mr. Whitehorse opened the trunk and set their suitcases on the ground. "There you are." He added, "And again, welcome to Oklahoma."

"Thank you," Miriam said. She turned to face her aunt. "You'll be getting off your feet now that we're here. I'm taking over until the baby comes."

"I . . . I have to do *something,*" Aunt Fannie sputtered in protest, but she appeared relieved.

"I certainly agree with Miriam," Shirley added. "No more work for Aunt Fannie now that the Yoder sisters have arrived!"

Uncle William glowed. "Now that's what I call the Lord's *gut* timing. But don't spend all your time at work. The community will have plenty of youth activities. You won't want to miss any of those. And we do have a shortage of unmarried girls, I believe."

"William!" Aunt Fannie scolded, even as a young man came out of the greenhouse door. He shielded the sun from his eyes as he looked in their direction.

Shirley drew in her breath and whispered, "I told you, Miriam. There he is!"

Aunt Fannie and Uncle William must have heard, Miriam was sure. She felt blood rush up her neck. What kind of impression did

238

this create with Uncle William? He would think they had discussed being on the lookout for suitable boyfriends. In her case, it was exactly the opposite. She'd fled one potential suitor, and she didn't want another one.

"That's my nephew Wayne." Uncle William grinned from ear to ear. "He helps out at the greenhouse once in a while." Uncle William lowered his voice. "And he's available."

Miriam tried to think of an adequate response, but the words stuck in her throat.

Shirley had no such inhibitions. She smiled her sweetest as the man approached.

"Introduce them," Aunt Fannie whispered to Uncle William, as if she were in on the conspiracy.

Which maybe she was, Miriam thought. From all appearances, her aunt and uncle had been the ones who had discussed this matter at length. But no matter. Miriam simply didn't want a boyfriend. And this handsome man would go for Shirley anyway. They always did.

"This is Miriam and Shirley Yoder, my nieces." Uncle William was obviously happy in his role as potential matchmaker. "And this is my nephew Wayne Yutzy."

Miriam was just sure her face would burn

up with embarrassment. But there was nothing she could do except follow Shirley, who had already stepped forward to shake the young man's hand.

"Hi, Wayne," Shirley said with a sweet smile.

"Hi." Miriam offered her hand. "Glad to meet you." She smiled even as the blood continued to heat her face. She'd never been *gut* with words at moments like this. Shirley was the one who said exactly the right thing with just the right touch.

Wayne grinned. "I heard you two were coming. I hope you'll enjoy your time in Oklahoma." He glanced at Aunt Fannie. "You have some super-nice relatives."

"There now!" Aunt Fannie scolded. "Your silver tongue will get you nowhere. And these young women will be told all about your tricky ways."

Wayne and Uncle William both laughed, so Aunt Fannie must be teasing, Miriam decided. It was just as well. All she needed was to meet a man full of tricky ways, though she had to admit Wayne looked way too honest to have many tricks. But what did she know about men? Besides, Shirley doubtless had Wayne's full attention by now, which Miriam should be thankful for. This could be another sign of the Lord's blessings on this trip — Shirley falling for a young Amish man so soon after their arrival in Oklahoma.

"We'd better get unpacked," Miriam commented, which probably sounded stupid, but that's what came out of her mouth.

Thankfully Shirley covered for her. "I'm sure we'll see you later, Wayne."

Aunt Fannie didn't waste a beat. "Wayne's staying for supper, so you'll both be seeing him then."

"I'm sure neither of them can wait," Uncle William offered.

Hopefully he's still teasing, Miriam thought. She definitely *could* wait. She said nothing, anxious now to get inside and settle in.

"He's fallen hard for you, Miriam," Shirley whispered on the way to the house.

"Shirley, he was looking at you the whole time!" Miriam whispered back.

Aunt Fannie obviously overheard because she whispered at the door, "He'd be such a decent catch. You couldn't go wrong, Miriam."

Why do you think I could catch him? Miriam almost asked.

Aunt Fannie raised her eyebrows. "Don't tell me there's a boyfriend back home? One I haven't heard of?"

"There is." Shirley didn't waste any time exposing the truth.

"There is not!" Miriam protested.

"It can't be both ways." Aunt Fannie was perplexed. "Surely you're not attached to a man, Miriam? Your *mamm* would have told me."

"I'm not." Miriam set her face in decisive lines that seemed to convince Aunt Fannie.

Even Shirley backed down a little. "Well, let's just say she *could* be."

A happy smile spread over Aunt Fannie's face. "That's different. At least our men are still in the running then."

"Ivan's a very decent man in Possum Valley, and he likes Miriam very much." Shirley wasn't finished. "He's asked Miriam most emphatically to date him, and she might still agree."

Aunt Fannie stared at both of them. "Is that so, Miriam?"

"No, it is *not* so!" Miriam picked up her suitcase and waited for directions.

Aunt Fannie shrugged and waved her hand toward the upstairs. "Your rooms are up there, girls. Take your pick. It's not like there are any young folk in the house."

Miriam made a beeline for the stair door. Shirley was right behind her. The sound of Aunt Fannie's voice followed them up the stairs. "I'd come up and help unpack, but I'm in no condition for stairs right now."

"You stay right where you are!" Shirley's voice was firm. "We're okay."

"She's absolutely right," Miriam spoke over her shoulder. "We'll be right down when we're unpacked."

At the top of stairs Miriam waited until Shirley caught up. "What are you up to anyway?"

Shirley didn't appear bothered in the least. "I'm not up to anything. You know I think you shouldn't fall for someone else. Ivan's the man for you."

Miriam groaned. "Don't worry, I'm not going to fall for someone else. But I'm not going to be with Ivan either."

Shirley studied her. "Then you aren't interested in this . . . this Wayne fellow?"

"Of course not!" Miriam snorted with her response.

Shirley smiled. "Then it's settled."

Miriam's thoughts went another direction as she looked around the upstairs. The house must have been built not that long ago according to how fresh and cheery everything appeared.

"Not like our old farmhouse back home," Shirley observed. "It reminds one of freshness and money."

"Don't say that," Miriam corrected. "I don't want to think about money. Now which room is yours? It looks like we have four choices."

Shirley pointed. "That one."

"Then I'll take the one next to you." Miriam dragged her suitcase into the room.

Shirley stood at the door for a moment. "Aunt Fannie and Uncle William must plan on lots of children. Or they did!"

Miriam smiled. "The Lord doesn't always lead the way we think He will. I mean, look at us."

Shirley nodded and went into her new room, presumably to begin unpacking.

Miriam flung her suitcase on the bed and rushed about hanging her few dresses in the closet. The rest of her things fit easily into the dresser drawers. Her two pairs of shoes went on the closet floor. The suitcase went under the bed. Out in the hall she peeked into Shirley's room. "I'm going down."

Shirley glanced up. "Be there soon."

Miriam knew it would be a while though. Time enough for her to tell Aunt Fannie about Ivan without Shirley's interruptions or positive comments about his attention and how Miriam should take Ivan back.

Going downstairs, she found Aunt Fannie on her rocker with a broad smile on her face. "Done already?"

Miriam nodded and took a seat on the couch. "I don't know how much *Mamm* told you about our reasons for coming here. Perhaps you should know that it's about more than just helping you with the new baby."

Aunt Fannie's attention perked up, but she didn't comment.

Miriam continued. "Shirley was seeing a . . . well, a man the family considered worse than *Englisha* because his family was formerly of our faith, and they are now very wealthy and of the world. The lure of his money was strong, and it was best that Shirley remove herself from temptation before things went too far."

"I see," Aunt Fannie said. "And what about you, Miriam? What were your reasons for coming?"

Miriam hesitated and then said, "For several years I was a caregiver for an *Englisha* man. He was like a second *daett* to me in some ways. Anyway, when Mr. Bland passed on a little while ago, he left me his farm. It's one of the nicest farms in our area. When Ivan Mast — a young man I used to like — found out, he wanted to break up with the girl he'd been seeing and come back to me. He claimed his renewed interest in me wasn't just because of the farm, but I didn't believe him. Shirley, however, doesn't think it matters why he's interested in me. She thinks I should encourage his attention toward me."

"Life gets so tangled sometimes, doesn't it, dear? Your *mamm* explained some of this to me. This will be a good time for you not to worry about things back home. Just enjoy your time here, and let us take care of you while you take care of us," laughed Aunt Fannie. "And if it's a fresh start you both need, then the Lord must have willed this trip."

"I agree. And thanks for being so understanding." Relief flooded through Miriam. *Yah,* she would gather her strength here in this new country so full of promise. Sure, someday she would return to Possum Valley, but for now she'd forget all about the troubles she'd left there.

"So tell me about the family back home," Aunt Fannie invited, changing the subject.

Miriam waited for a moment and then began speaking after the stair door opened and Shirley came into the living room and sat down.

CHAPTER TWENTY-THREE

Later that evening the supper table was laden with mashed potatoes, gravy, a pot roast, and fresh salad from Aunt Fannie's greenhouse. Shirley sat at the table with her hands folded. She sent a brief smile toward Wayne across the table from her.

He smiled back, but his attention was clearly fixed on Miriam — and had been ever since he'd come in at Aunt Fannie's call for supper.

Now *that* was a change, Shirley thought. She still hadn't made up her mind whether she should be interested in Wayne, if only to distract him from Miriam, but here was her answer. Wayne apparently wasn't distractible. Still, she hadn't really tried yet — other than a smile or two, which could be interpreted as friendliness. Maybe Wayne needed a more overt message. No, she would stay out of this, Shirley decided, though it would have made her feel better if Miriam had given in to Ivan's attention. That man was obviously motivated by money, yet just as love had grown in her heart for Jonas, so love would have grown in Miriam's heart for Ivan. But, *nee,* Miriam had rejected Ivan as unworthy of her love, and now another Prince Charming was apparently riding to the rescue.

"You're awfully quiet." Aunt Fannie sent Shirley a questioning look. "I remember you as the talkative one of the family."

"I figure young Mahlon Troyer will get her talking soon enough," Wayne teased, mentioning someone from the youth group they'd been talking about.

Shirley almost gasped. Wayne sure was oblivious to her interest in him. Thankfully Miriam came to her rescue.

"Wayne, Shirley left her heart in Holmes County. For now, anyway."

Wayne leaped right in. "Oklahoma is perfect for love and marriage. There's much less competition out here."

Aunt Fannie cleared her throat.

Wayne's face reddened a little. "Of course, that can work the other way too." He studied his plate of food.

Thankfully Aunt Fannie filled the awkward space with quick chatter. "Well, I'm sure everyone will be glad to see you two girls. We don't have that large a community, so all of us are close — in heart, at least, even if we are spread out a bit." Aunt Fannie laughed. "Don't worry, we drive horse and buggy to see each other. At times the distance seems farther with all the open spaces, but you'll get used to that. The *Englisha* people here are all of the solid, down-to-earth type. Our neighbors are willing and ready to drive us to Coalgate or even further for our shopping or to pick up our visitors, like Mr. Whitehorse did this afternoon. I'm already coming to think of you two as residents, not visitors. You're like part of the community already. In fact, we haven't told anyone how long you're staying. Your *mamm* just said it might be for more than a week or two or three. And by the time the baby comes, I'm sure you'll be settled right in — permanently, if that's your desire, of course. We have plenty of room."

"I'd like that, as would the others, I'm sure," Wayne said, having recovered from his embarrassment.

Uncle William pushed away his plate. "Isn't there pie or something?" He looked around. "There ought to be for our celebration of two *gut*-looking young women arriving in Oklahoma."

"Of course there are!" Aunt Fannie gave

Uncle William a fake glare. "Blackberry and rhubarb. You surely can't eat both."

"I can try." Uncle William's laugh filled the kitchen.

"Spoken like a true man." Aunt Fannie began to get up.

Miriam reached over and pulled on her aunt's arm. "I'll get the pies. You're to rest now, remember?"

Aunt Fannie sat down with a grateful look.

Miriam got up to bring over both pies and slide them onto the table.

Shirley noticed that Wayne's gaze followed her sister's every move. She was torn between being a bit jealous that he seemed to prefer Miriam and yet happy that he might cheer her up.

Shirley took a piece of rhubarb pie and passed it to Wayne while Uncle William cut the first piece out of the blackberry.

"Wayne, you're also eating both, aren't you?" Shirley teased. The words came easily now that she didn't have an ulterior motive.

Wayne didn't respond to her tease other than to give her a quick smile. That hurt more than she wanted it to.

Wayne leaned across the table. "Miriam, did you bake these since you arrived?"

Uncle William laughed, obviously pleased with this evaluation. "Amish wonder woman

Miriam. That's a little much to expect there, Wayne."

Miriam was blushing furiously. Uncle William knew Aunt Fannie had made the pies before they arrived, and the same went for the rest of supper. Miriam and Shirley had done little but put on the final touches and prepare the table. Wayne must know this, but he was wasting no time to show his interest.

Wayne joined in the laughter. "I know she could have if she'd tried!"

Aunt Fannie jumped in. "Well, we Amish women do know how to cook delicious meals and desserts."

Shirley could see her sister was enjoying being in this new place and having a handsome man shower her with praises and smiles. Miriam wasn't used to receiving it so quickly. Shirley offered a pleased smile toward her sister.

Uncle William said, "Well, that was an excellent meal!"

"I agree," Wayne added.

"Wayne and I still have work to do in the greenhouse tonight. I'll come back in for evening devotions when we're done. But right now let's pray and give thanks." Uncle William bowed his head.

They all followed his example, but not

before Shirley saw Wayne take the opportunity for another glance at Miriam. He'd be back in before he left tonight, Shirley was sure. She pushed the thought aside as Uncle William spoke the prayer. It was time to support Miriam in her new venture, not oppose her.

"Amen," Uncle William said.

The two men rose and headed toward the washroom.

After hearing the sound of water running, Shirley heard the outside door open and shut quietly.

"Shirley, is something wrong?" Aunt Fannie asked. "You haven't been the girl I know all evening."

"I've just been thinking," Shirley said distractedly. *Yah,* she had to admit being so silent was unlike her. She didn't spend a lot of time in introspection. But perhaps that was going to change with their arrival here. Maybe this move was changing her already. She didn't know whether to smile or shudder at the thought.

Aunt Fannie smiled. "Oklahoma can set you to thinking. There's something about the open skies and the land. It deepens the soul."

Catching Miriam's pleased expression,

Shirley replied, "Maybe that's just what I need."

"The Lord has His reasons for your arrival here. Never doubt that." Aunt Fannie rose and picked up several plates.

Shirley didn't respond verbally. She touched Aunt Fannie's arm. "You go sit in the living room, Aunt Fannie. Miriam and I will clean up the kitchen. Then we'll come in and chat afterward."

"You're both such angels!" Aunt Fannie gushed. "This is so *wunderbah*. I thought I'd have to make do the best I could until the baby came . . . and afterward because, well, Lester Weaver's eldest daughter, Mary, hasn't taken care of a mother and newborn baby before. So . . ." Aunt Fannie's words faded away.

Miriam placed her hand on Aunt Fannie's shoulder. "Just go. We're all thankful for the Lord's leading in this."

"Well, okay." Aunt Fannie set the plates on the counter and then vanished into the living room.

"Miriam, Wayne clearly likes you," Shirley whispered, even though their aunt had gone. "And I have to admit that I'm glad of it."

"Really?" Miriam glanced toward her. "That's a change. What brought that up?"

"I've been thinking." Shirley lowered her

head. "That's all."

"Are you glad we've come then?" Miriam started filling the sink with water.

Shirley hesitated. "I don't know. It's too early to tell. There's a lot going on inside of me. And watching Wayne watch you . . . it just affected me a bit."

Miriam smiled. "Don't write too much into his attention. He doesn't know me that well. I still think he'll go for you."

Shirley picked up more plates from the table and brought them to the sink. "You underestimate your charms, you know."

"Like my farm?" A pained look crossed Miriam's face. "Do you think Wayne knows? Why else would he choose me over you?"

"He might know . . . or he might not," Shirley said. "But even if he does, don't make the same mistake you did with Ivan. If Wayne persists in his attention to you, why not accept it and be happy?"

"*Nee*, Shirley. It's right what I did with Ivan." Miriam poured a small stream of dishwashing detergent in the sink. "And if Wayne has the same notion as Ivan, he'll get the same treatment."

"There's a simple way to find out," Shirley said. "I'm going to ask Aunt Fannie about Wayne." With that she went into the living room and approached her aunt.

Aunt Fannie looked up from her knitting. "Is something wrong?"

"No, I just have a question." Shirley twisted her hands together. She felt uneasy asking, but she felt they needed to know. "Does Wayne know about the farm Miriam inherited? Was he paying attention to her tonight just because he knows about it?"

Aunt Fannie shrugged. "I don't think so, although I'm quite sure William mentioned the inheritance to him at some point. Still, it's not that big a deal out here. Things aren't like they are back in Holmes County where money is such a focus and land is hard to come by. We trust in the Lord and each other here."

"*Gut.* That's what I thought." Shirley took a step backward. "I'll tell Miriam." But she didn't have to. She turned around to see Miriam in the doorway, a troubled expression on her face.

"So Wayne knew?" Miriam said to no one in particular.

Aunt Fannie rose and wrapped Miriam in a quick hug. "*Yah,* but it's nothing to be concerned about. Wayne's not like that. Trust in the Lord to watch over you and guide you."

Miriam didn't appear convinced as she

turned and headed slowly back to the kitchen sink.

CHAPTER TWENTY-FOUR

Miriam awoke with a start. A quick glance at the alarm clock on the dresser showed the time was a little after two o'clock. What could have awakened her? Aunt Fannie's house was still new to her, but it wasn't known for creaks and groans like her home in Possum Valley was. And she usually enjoyed such eccentricities anyway. Something else had disturbed her. It was Sunday morning. Had the thought that she would see Wayne soon awakened her?

Miriam frowned. She didn't look forward to the questions Wayne's attentions were raising. Were his overtures genuine or influenced by his knowledge that she would come to marriage with a debt-free farm? Was she being overly suspicious because of Ivan? Whatever the answer, it didn't seem like enough to awaken her in the middle of the night. Had Shirley perhaps been disturbed by nightmares and cried out?

Miriam pushed back the covers and tip-toed out into the hallway. Her nightgown swayed around her legs. She quietly opened Shirley's bedroom door across the hall. She was asleep, so that couldn't have been the cause of the disturbance. Miriam paused at the top of the stairs. At first there was no sound, but soon she heard faint noises coming from the living room. Someone was up.

Was Aunt Fannie in labor? Miriam clutched the handrail. That must be it! Perhaps Uncle William had gone for the midwife, and buggy wheels in the driveway had awakened her. Miriam hurried back to her room and pulled on her housecoat before rushing downstairs. She'd awaken Shirley later if necessary. The birth wouldn't happen right away, so they didn't both need to get up so early. She came through the stair doorway to find the kitchen lit by a kerosene lamp. Aunt Fannie was pacing the living room floor in her bare feet. Pain was etched on her face.

Looking at Miriam, Aunt Fannie asked, "Did I disturb you?"

"You're *supposed* to disturb me," Miriam said. "Did Uncle William leave for the midwife yet?"

"*Yah,* but I told him to be quiet." Aunt Fannie moaned quietly.

258

Miriam rushed to her aunt's side. "We're here to help no matter the hour. You should have awakened me. Now, is there anything I can do? Anything you need or want?"

Aunt Fannie tried to smile. "*Nee,* I just need to walk the floor a while. You should go back to bed."

"But surely there's something." Miriam tugged on Aunt Fannie's arm. "A water bottle for your back? Warm milk?"

Aunt Fannie's voice was firm. "You go back to bed. I'll call you when I need you."

"You can't climb stairs." Miriam stated the obvious. "Besides, there's no way I can sleep now."

"Then rest on the couch," Aunt Fannie relented. She began to pace again.

"I'll dress first." Miriam didn't wait for an answer before she retreated up the stairs. She changed in her room and paused in the hallway. Should she let Shirley know? But that would mean the two of them would be downstairs, which wasn't necessary. Better just let Shirley sleep for now. It would be good to have someone rested to help later.

When Miriam came back downstairs, Aunt Fannie was still pacing in the kitchen. Miriam peeked in, but her aunt waved her away. "Get some sleep."

Miriam lay down on the couch in the living room and pulled a light quilt over her. She dozed off and on until the sound of buggy wheels awakened her. Miriam jumped up and ran to meet the midwife at the door. She was middle-aged and introduced herself as Susie.

"Now, you must be either Miriam or Shirley, from what William told me," she said.

"I'm Miriam. Shirley's upstairs asleep."

Aunt Fannie appeared, and Susie's attention shifted to her. The two women disappeared into the downstairs bedroom.

Miriam paced the living room floor like her aunt had done in the kitchen earlier. She should be busy with something other than her own problems, but what? Maybe she should make tea for Aunt Fannie? Wasn't tea *gut* for pain? Oh, how little she knew about the birth of babies! Rather than tea she decided coffee was the answer. Although coffee wasn't *gut* for mothers-to-be, or so she'd heard, Susie might want some. And *she* certainly did. The same might go for Uncle William, who must still be outside. They'd also need breakfast soon, so she should plan that. She could prepare bacon, eggs, and toast. That should hit the spot for everyone. Miriam entered the kitchen and had the coffeepot on the stove when Uncle William came in from the barn. He grinned sleepily. "Coffee, I assume. I could use some of that."

"It'll be ready soon," Miriam promised. "There won't be much sleep for any of us now until the baby comes."

Uncle William sat down at the kitchen table. His hands fidgeted.

"Aunt Fannie will be okay, I'm sure." Miriam poured the hot water over the coffee in a filter. Moments later she set a coffee cup in front of her uncle.

Uncle William sipped as he mused in the quiet kitchen, "It'll be our first, you know. A boy, I'm thinkin'."

Miriam gave him a quick glance. "Maybe. But I'm sure you'll be happy with a girl too."

"*Yah,* I'll be perfectly happy. If Fannie's okay, the rest doesn't matter." A concerned look flitted over Uncle William's face.

Miriam turned away to fill her own cup. Would someone one day love her as Uncle William loved Aunt Fannie? Would she find a man who cared for her above all else? Others had found such love, so why couldn't she? Miriam pulled a chair out from the table to sit down and consider breakfast preparations. Uncle William would need his food, as they all would.

"I'll have breakfast going soon," Miriam offered.

He nodded but didn't reply, a distracted look on his face. Footsteps behind them brought Uncle William to his feet in a quick bound. His chair clattered against the wall.

Susie greeted him with, "Fannie's fine, William. Relax! This has happened many times."

"But not to us!" The words burst out of Uncle William's mouth.

Susie didn't appear fazed. "It'll be okay." She patted Uncle William's arm. "Just stay out from underfoot. Miriam will help me when the time comes."

Uncle William grabbed his cup and vanished into the washroom. Moments later the outer door slammed. No doubt he'd keep himself busy with some chores, Miriam thought with a smile. Even imaginary ones, if necessary.

Miriam began to pull together the things she'd need for breakfast. Susie looked up from her coffee and said with a wink, "You can call me when you have breakfast ready, if you don't mind."

Miriam didn't hesitate. "I certainly will. Are bacon, eggs, and toast *gut* enough?"

Susie laughed. "As starved as I am, anything is enough." With that, she returned to

262

the bedroom and Fannie.

Miriam busied herself with breakfast, and nearly thirty minutes later she called Susie into the kitchen.

Susie came in and helped herself without any encouragement.

Miriam left for the barn. When she called Uncle William's name, he came at a run in the lantern light. Miriam stifled a smile. "No baby yet!" she called. "But breakfast is ready. Are you hungry?"

"That I am." Uncle William rubbed his beard as if breakfast was a foreign thought to him, but he followed her back into the house.

Susie had already finished and put her empty plate on the counter.

Uncle William sat down, and Miriam put the hot food on the table. He motioned for her to sit, and they bowed their heads in prayer.

"Help Fannie, dear Lord," Uncle William whispered at the end, just before saying "amen."

They ate in silence, and moments later Miriam remembered Shirley was still asleep upstairs. She wouldn't be happy about all of this missed activity. But there would be plenty to come later in the day. With Shirley's newfound determination to help out, she could even assist in the birth. It would be a *gut* experience for both of them.

"You'll miss your first Sunday service," Uncle William said with concern. "And seeing Wayne again, of course."

Miriam chuckled. "That can wait. We came out to help you and Aunt Fannie, remember?"

Uncle William gave a wink and said, "But perhaps that's not all. No telling what the Lord has in mind for your stay in Oklahoma." Then he jumped to his feet and left for the barn again.

Uncle William wasn't gone for more than a few minutes before Susie appeared from the bedroom. "It's time, Miriam. Do you want to call your sister?"

Without a word Miriam raced up the stairs and woke Shirley. "Aunt Fannie's time has come! There's breakfast in the kitchen if you want to eat first."

Shirley bounded out of bed. "I'll be right down. I'm not going to miss this."

Miriam left Shirley to dress and hurried back downstairs. She entered the bedroom. Susie was by Aunt Fannie's side.

"Come," Susie told Miriam. "Stand by her and hold her hand. If I need help, I'll let you know."

"I'll take that job," Shirley said from the

doorway, so Miriam stayed where she was.

Aunt Fannie's face was red and sweaty.

"Fan her," Susie ordered. "And there's cold washcloths on the tray over there."

Miriam brought them to Shirley, and her sister gently swabbed Aunt Fannie's face.

Susie whispered, "Pace yourself, Fannie, but when the contraction comes give it your best."

Low moans escaped Aunt Fannie as the minutes ticked slowly past.

"Some more towels," Susie instructed. "And push the tray closer. We're close now."

Miriam noticed the focus on Susie's face. She admired the woman's steady and unhesitating movements, but it was a job she never wished to have. There was too much pressure involved, and a child's life and that of the mother was at stake. Yet Susie made the process appear perfectly safe and normal.

"Here we come!" Susie said. "You're looking good, Fannie!"

With a final push and a fierce gasp, Aunt Fannie gave her all.

A moment later Susie received the wiggling form, gave it a gentle tap, and a cry filled the room. A smile crept across her face. "A healthy man-child is born!"

Miriam held out a towel without being asked.

Susie shook her head. "He goes on the towel on the tray. We have to snip his umbilical cord first. Wiping comes afterward."

"Did I hear you say it's a boy?" Aunt Fannie's voice was weak.

"*Yah,* that he is!" Susie acknowledged.

"He will be Jonathon," Aunt Fannie whispered. "William picked the name himself. It's that of his favorite uncle."

Susie's smile grew broader. "We'll have little Jonathon to you in a minute."

Aunt Fannie's face had already begun to glow, and Shirley had tears in her eyes. Now Miriam was glad they'd come all the way from Possum Valley. This moment alone was worth the effort, no matter what else might happen in the future.

The bedroom door burst open behind them, and Uncle William rushed in. He came to a stop beside the bed and reached for Fannie's hand. Together they gazed transfixed as Susie lifted baby Jonathon. She smiled as she placed the babe in Fannie's arms.

CHAPTER TWENTY-FIVE

Miriam winced as the sound of the washing machine motor filled the basement. With the birth of baby Jonathon yesterday, Aunt Fannie ought to have peace and quiet on this Monday morning. But Uncle William had told them differently at the breakfast table.

"Don't be tiptoeing around the house now. Fannie wants everything to continue as normal."

Which meant the morning wash should be done on time. Miriam had peeked in on Aunt Fannie after Uncle William left for the greenhouse. Both baby Jonathon in his crib and Aunt Fannie on the big bed were sound asleep.

"I'll keep an ear open so I'll know if they awaken," Shirley had whispered over her shoulder.

Miriam had glanced at Shirley. "If she can't take the noise, you'll let me know?"

"*Yah,* I will," Shirley had said, barely containing her excitement.

Miriam ran the first load of wash through the wringer. Soon there would be diapers too, and washday would be more frequent than once a week. The thought of diapers caused the joy of little baby Jonathon to sweep over her again. How much greater must Aunt Fannie's joy be? Miriam wondered. Baby Jonathon was her first child. Was this how her own *mamm* had felt when Miriam had been born? With the freshness, the newness, the hope of the future held in her arms?

Miriam slipped the wash apron with its pockets full of clothespins over her head, and headed out the basement door with a load of wet wash. Somehow she couldn't imagine that her own birth had evoked such emotions. She was just a common girl and couldn't have made much of a splash. And yet wouldn't she be overjoyed with the birth of her first child? Well, once she'd found love and trust with a man. She would hold her first baby in her arms and weep for joy no matter if it was a boy or a girl.

Goosebumps rose on Miriam's arms as she walked up the outside stairwell. Such joy, the coming of a child. And yet at this time in her life, these were indecent thoughts to have. She wasn't even dating anyone! Still, such thoughts came unbidden with the memory of baby Jonathon's birth yesterday still fresh in her mind. And she shouldn't be blamed for such thoughts. Didn't all young Amish women think of these things? *Yah,* they did. And even as she had witnessed what Aunt Fannie went through in labor, she knew the birth had been worth the pain. Afterward, when baby Jonathon's cries filled the room, the biggest smile had crept over everyone's face. Clearly the birth of a child was always worth the effort.

The same must hold true for her if and when she gave birth, Miriam told herself. Right now she didn't know which way was up or down, but once love settled in her heart, then she would know. A man would stand by her side someday, someone like Uncle William. And he would promise to love and hold her dear all the days of their lives no matter if she brought a farm into the marriage or not.

Miriam approached the wash line and set the hamper on the ground. She reached for the clothespins. *Yah,* somehow she must trust again even though Ivan had shattered her heart when he'd chosen Laura Swartz over her. And to make matters worse, he'd

269

planned to cut off his relationship with Laura once there was land involved. How could Ivan have been so cruel and shallow? How could she have loved a man like that in the first place? Maybe she had best seek advice from someone else when it came to choosing a boyfriend instead of following her own instinct.

Miriam sighed. This was an academic question anyway. She hadn't been to the church service yesterday, and already Wayne seemed like a distant memory. He did work for Uncle William, so maybe she'd see him before the next Sunday service. She decided she didn't want to wrestle with that thought of him right now. Nor did she want to think about the farm or the money in her secret bank account. The memory of them brought up conflicting and bitter thoughts. A lot of *gut* money did anyone. *Yah,* one could buy things with money — except for the things that really mattered: home, love, trust, and a baby like Jonathon. Money couldn't even buy fresh wash on the line put there by willing hands moved by a desire to help. Money destroyed all of that. Miriam shook her head. So why did she still have the checkbook upstairs? There were lots of people who would willingly take the money off her hands in a heartbeat.

Miriam pondered the question. Maybe she didn't want to pass this trouble on to someone else. But that was much too sanctified an answer. More than likely she just couldn't let it go. Her attraction to the money was too strong. *Daett* had been right. Money was dangerous. It took a grip on the human heart and never let go. Wasn't she an example of that very thing? Who else had such a secret they didn't share with anyone? She hadn't kept secrets before the money came. She wanted the life she used to know *and* the money. It was an awful thought, but true.

Miriam pinned one of Uncle William's shirts on the line with two clothespins as she held a third in her mouth. She would have to work through this money stuff sometime, but not this morning. It was a little too much considering how tired she was after yesterday. And thoughts about the money and farm were stealing the joy of baby Jonathon's birth right out of her heart. Miriam shoved the two problems away and continued until she had the last piece of this load of wash up. With the hamper in one hand, she headed back to the stairwell. At the corner of the house she glanced toward the front steps and stopped short. Wayne Yutzy was standing there ready to knock on the front door. She gasped.

He turned, and his face lit up at the sight of her. His hand paused in midair. "There you are."

"What are you doing here?" The words cut through the air, and Miriam winced. She hadn't meant to be so abrupt. She didn't want to let her bitterness show around Wayne. Her problems weren't his fault.

Wayne didn't seem to mind. He laughed. "I work here part-time, remember? I wanted to stop by and give my congratulations on baby Jonathon's birth."

Wayne knew he wouldn't talk with Aunt Fannie or see baby Jonathon so soon after the delivery, and he already knew the baby's name, so obviously he'd spoken with Uncle William. Wayne was here for reasons other than congratulations, Miriam decided. Wayne had come to see her.

"He's a healthy baby boy," Miriam announced. Hopefully nothing gave away her thoughts or how she felt right now. What an embarrassment that would be.

"I missed you at church." Wayne was all smiles. "Though it's understandable with the birth and all . . ."

Miriam shifted the hamper to her other hand. "Aunt Fannie needed us. We're not going home anytime soon, so there will be other opportunities." Now why had she said something so stupid? It sounded eager and hopeful, when she meant to convey neither sentiment.

Wayne grinned. "That's what William said this morning, which I'm very glad to hear. I hope you decide to make Oklahoma your home. I suppose it's a little early for that decision. But maybe your Aunt Fannie's healthy baby boy will help. Show you how great an effect you have on the community."

"I'm afraid we had nothing to do with that," Miriam countered.

Wayne's smile didn't dim. "Well, I'm still glad you're here. There's a youth gathering this Thursday evening at Roy Troyer's place. Everyone is looking forward to meeting you and Shirley. I hope you'll come."

"Of course!" The words leaped out of Miriam's mouth.

Wayne replied just as quickly. "I'll pick you up then, since I have to drive right by here."

"Oh, we can't impose on you like that." Miriam's hand flew to her mouth. "I'm sure you have sisters to take along."

Wayne appeared sheepish. "*Yah,* I do. But they're old enough to drive themselves."

Miriam kept her voice firm, although it

was an internal struggle. "We'll come by ourselves. No need to pick us up. You need to drive your sisters."

"But you will be there?" Wayne raised his eyebrows. "Surely you don't have to stay home and take care of the baby." Wayne rushed on before Miriam could answer. "One of my sisters can stay with Fannie if necessary. They'd love to help out, and they get to attend the youth gatherings all the time."

"We'll be there," Miriam told him. "Uncle William can tend to Aunt Fannie if there's a need. But likely she'll be on her feet by that time. At least if she's like *Mamm* always is after giving birth."

Wayne's face brightened. "Great! I'll introduce you around, okay? There aren't that many of us. We're all nice people. You'll feel right at home."

"Thank you," Miriam told him. She wasn't sure she liked this. Yet, it wouldn't be mannerly to deny Wayne's request.

"Maybe I'll see you before that. If not, until then." Wayne gave a wave of his hand and disappeared around the corner of the house.

Wayne at least knew when to leave, Miriam thought. So he wasn't without manners like Ivan. She couldn't begin to sort out the flood of emotions swirling inside her. There was delight with Wayne's visit mixed in with her determination to proceed with caution and even outright distrust of the man. How foolish she'd been to think that a move across the country would take her away from her troubles.

Miriam took the stairwell steps one at a time. Back at the washing machine she paused as Shirley appeared from the direction of the kitchen. "I see Wayne was here."

"Yah," Miriam muttered a bit more sharply than she meant. She didn't mean to snap at Shirley, but at the moment she wanted to be left alone with her thoughts.

Shirley pressed on. "Aunt Fannie is sleeping right through your washing machine racket, as is baby Jonathon. Looks like they're both happy campers."

"Gut." Miriam ran the second batch of wet wash through the wringer. Shirley hadn't come down to inform her of Aunt Fannie's sleeping status, though that was a comfort to know.

Shirley sat down on a wooden stair. "Miriam, we're due a fresh start out here in Oklahoma, don't you think?"

Miriam forced cheerfulness into her voice. "*Yah,* I think you're right. This trip is the best thing that's happened to us in a long time."

"Oh, Miriam!" Shirley hugged herself. "I'm so glad to hear you say that. There are times out here when I feel like a completely different person. I don't know why, but that's just how it is. Back home in Possum Valley I tried so hard to be the person everyone wanted me to be. You know, making promises and more promises. Could that all change out here?" Shirley gazed at the basement ceiling. "Oh, I want it so badly."

"So you don't love Jonas Beachy any longer?" The words slipped out before Miriam could stop them.

A sorrowful look passed over Shirley's face. "I'll always love him, Miriam. You know that. That part of my heart will never change, but we weren't meant for each other. It simply couldn't be. I'm going to grow a new love that will fill my heart completely and overshadow what I felt for Jonas."

"That's *gut* to hear." Miriam turned back to the wringer. Shirley might be wrong, but Miriam wouldn't sow the seed of doubt in her sister. That much she owed Shirley.

Shirley hugged herself again and went back up the stairs.

CHAPTER TWENTY-SIX

Thursday evening of the youth gathering, Shirley and Miriam hitched up Sally, one of Aunt Fannie and Uncle William's driving horses, and followed the directions they'd been given to the site of the gathering. Both girls sat quietly as they headed down the driveway and out onto the two-lane road, with Shirley at the reins. As the horse settled into a rhythmic pace, Shirley's thoughts drifted to the letter they'd received from *Mamm*. She'd reported that several girls had asked about her at the last Sunday service and said they really missed her. Otherwise there had been just the usual happenings in Possum Valley. *Daett* and Lee had repaired a leak on the barn roof at Mr. Bland's place. Beyond that, *Mamm* had wished them the Lord's blessings and hoped everything was going well.

Seated beside her in the buggy, Miriam repeated the instructions Aunt Fannie had given them before they left the house. "Two miles south on 48, then turn left and go just over the little bridge. There will be no sign or road name, but the Troyer place is the third on the left. There will be plenty of buggies parked in the lawn. You can't miss it."

Shirley held the reins tight. "I wish you'd allowed Wayne to bring us . . . or at least we could have followed him. Driving a strange horse to an unfamiliar place makes me nervous."

Miriam didn't appear too sympathetic. "Sally's a good horse, and we need to maintain some decency and self-reliance. We don't want to rely on Wayne — or anyone else for that matter."

Shirley gazed across the open fields. "Well, unlike you, I want to fit in. And I think we can — if you'd have the *gut* sense to relax and let people help you instead of pushing them away."

"You're not consistent." Miriam gave Shirley a withering glance. "First you want to keep me away from Wayne, and now you want to push me right into his arms."

Shirley winced. She'd admitted that to herself just this morning, but it still hurt when Miriam said it aloud. "It's not that, Miriam. I'm not pushing you. But you were so stung by what you think were Ivan's wrong motives that you just won't trust any man now. Even if Ivan *was* after your farm, you don't need to be so distrustful of Wayne. He's not Ivan. And, *yah,* I'll say it. I was wrong about the money thing. I should never have chased after Jonas just because of his fancy convertible and family money."

Miriam reached over to touch Shirley's arm. "I'm not after a confession. I'm glad you see your mistakes. And I can admit mine too. Maybe I *am* wrong about Wayne."

Shirley allowed her relief to show. "Then you'll relax around him? And around any others? I'm sure they'll try to make us feel welcome."

A slight smile stole across Miriam's face. "For your sake I'll try. And Wayne did tell me he wants to introduce us to everyone else. So if he's there, that's what will happen."

Shirley pushed thoughts of Jonas out of her mind. She gushed. "This is so *wunderbah*! And all the men are so handsome out here. It must come from the wide-open country that expands the soul."

Miriam chuckled as she shifted on the buggy seat. "Now you're a philosopher."

Shirley giggled. "I know. I hope this is going to be the home of my dreams and promises."

"Well, just don't over-expect," Miriam warned. "Don't set yourself up for a disappointment. That's really what happened with Jonas. You always knew it would have to end, and yet you kept pursuing it. Don't let that happen here."

Shirley kept her voice resolute. "I'll be careful. I promise."

Miriam forced a smile. "*Gut!* Now, there's our road."

Shirley pulled on the lines, and Sally made a tight left-hand turn. Shirley could tell Miriam didn't trust her promise. And who could blame her? Her record hadn't been *gut* so far. But all that was about to change. She might not have a new start like this again, so she'd make her best effort. Here no one, other than Miriam and, perhaps, Aunt Fannie, knew about Jonas. And if they found out, they'd give her high marks because she was preferring to find an Amish man over an outsider. Shirley shut the thoughts of Jonas out of her mind as they approached the third driveway on the left. She pulled on the lines again, and Sally turned in. Several buggies were already parked along the driveway, and there was a homemade softball field laid out beside the barn. The youth present turned and watched as Shirley pulled Sally to a stop. One of them stepped away from the others and came their way.

"There's Wayne!" Shirley whispered.

"Good evening, girls." Wayne smiled at both of them, but his gaze lingered in Miriam's direction.

"Hi," Shirley greeted as she got down from the buggy.

Miriam muttered something unintelligible as she too climbed out.

Shirley undid the tug on her side of the buggy while Wayne worked on the other. He was speaking to Miriam in a low voice, so Shirley wasn't sure how the conversation was progressing.

Miriam had a smile on her face when she turned toward Shirley. Shirley smiled too and relaxed.

"You girls wait here," Wayne called out, "while I take the horse into the barn."

"*Nee,* we can't do that," Miriam protested. Shirley agreed. They couldn't stand around in awkwardness until Wayne returned. Nor could they follow him into the barn. Girls didn't go in there unless they had a horse to drop off, and usually the boys took care of that. Their only option was to go by themselves to meet the others.

Wayne's hopeful smile had fallen, but he

accepted the inevitable. "I'll see you when I come back then," he said, mostly in Miriam's direction.

"Come." Shirley pulled on Miriam's arm while Wayne led Sally toward the barn. The small group of young people was coming forward to meet them. First the girls came and offered warm smiles and friendly *gut* evenings.

As the boys introduced themselves, Shirley listened for the name Mahlon Troyer, which Wayne had mentioned the other night at dinner. Mahlon was the second of the unmarried men to greet her. He had a kind face, she thought. And he was handsome, just as she'd suspected he would be. Probably just a year or so older than she was, if she guessed right. Shirley dropped her gaze after a brief moment. She mustn't appear too forward. This was, after all, a community much more restrained than the Possum Valley community. Aunt Fannie had told them they didn't even practice *rumspringa* here. Perhaps this came from their smaller numbers or maybe they did have a deeper devotion to the Lord as Aunt Fannie claimed. Either way, Shirley liked it so far. A girl who had given her name as Betty Troyer came up to stand beside her. She wondered if this was Mahlon's sister.

"So, it's Miriam and Shirley Yoder from Holmes County. We've all looked forward to seeing the two of you ever since we heard you'd arrived."

"We're happy to be here," Miriam said.

"How's the new baby?" Betty asked.

Shirley was surprised at this abrupt change in the conversation, but she replied, "He's doing great! Aunt Fannie's up and about even though the midwife told her to stay in bed a week."

Betty laughed. "Can't stay in bed for long around here. Not even with two of your nieces in the house to take care of you."

"Fannie claims her muscles will freeze in place," Shirley said and then joined in the laughter.

"It's a nice evening," Miriam offered.

"*Yah,*" Betty agreed. "This is pretty typical. Oklahoma evenings are usually pretty nice this time of year."

A few seconds of awkward silence passed before Betty said, "The baseball game will start soon. We'll have enough players tonight with the two of you. A few of the girls only last for an inning or so."

A few moments later Wayne appeared from the barn and headed toward Miriam, who was speaking with two girls she decided could be twins. They'd introduced themselves as Naomi and Miriam Kuntz.

Mahlon walked up, and Shirley turned on her sweetest smile. He gave her only the briefest of nods and turned to Betty. "I can't find my glove. Did you get it out after we arrived?"

Betty motioned toward the side of the barn. "Over there. I set it out with mine."

Mahlon appeared relieved. He turned to go but paused and looked at Shirley. "I'm glad you're here, and your sister Miriam too. Betty will keep you entertained, I'm sure."

Shirley hid her disappointment.

"Brothers," Betty muttered. "They're so helpless sometimes."

"*Yah,*" Shirley said, feeling an unexpected desire for her own brothers. They were anything but helpless, she thought with a smile.

CHAPTER TWENTY-SEVEN

Later that evening Shirley held the reins in the soft darkness of the prairie night as Sally's hooves beat a steady rhythm on the road home. Usually Shirley would have enjoyed the sound, but tonight it — along with everything else — grated on her nerves. How could her first evening with the Clarita community's young people have been such a total flop? Nothing really happened. There had been no rudeness or unkindness shown to her. Perhaps the total ordinariness of the evening had been what disappointed her. She'd been shown no special attention by any of the boys, even Mahlon Troyer. Did they think she was unworthy of attention? Had they even noticed her?

She tightened her grip on the lines. This was a new experience to say the least, and she hadn't taken well to it. Never before had Miriam been the center of attention at a youth gathering. This was definitely not what Shirley was used to. But it's *gut* for me, Shirley chided herself with a quick glance at Miriam seated beside her. Miriam seemed lost in a cloud of happiness. Why shouldn't she be thrilled? Wayne Yutzy had hovered over her all night to the point that Miriam seemed to have lost her resistance to him. And after those first moments when they'd arrived, even Betty had spent most of her time in conversation with Miriam.

Shirley pushed her bitter thoughts away. This was the right kind of experience for her. She needed a little humility in her life. Besides, Miriam needed this moment of glory without her sister tainting her joy. With that thought, Shirley brightened as best she could and forced herself to chirp, "What a *wunderbah* evening, don't you think?"

"That it was." Miriam's face beamed. "All the folks were so friendly."

"I know." Shirley let the silence fill the buggy again.

For a few minutes Miriam gazed across the darkened prairie. "It's almost too much to believe — that we really are in a place where everything is so different. No one cares about money around here. I'm sure they've all heard about the farm, but it wasn't mentioned once. I think Aunt Fannie might be right about Wayne. He doesn't seem to care either."

"They *are wunderbah* people." Shirley kept her voice steady.

"I'm so glad you enjoyed yourself." Miriam glanced toward her.

Shirley forced a quick smile. "Betty Troyer talked with me right away."

Miriam sighed. "Betty . . . I know. She's Mahlon's sister. They're both so nice. He'll warm up to you before long."

So Miriam had noticed his lack of attention. Shirley said quickly, "It's a relief really. No boys hanging around me. It was . . . different."

Miriam laughed. "Come to think of it, that was true for you tonight. My, how our roles have switched."

"It's *gut* for me." That wasn't a lie, Shirley told herself. She really did think it was okay . . . or she *should* at least tolerate it with good grace. Which was about the same, wasn't it?

Miriam's mood darkened. "Do you still think Wayne's sincere? I doubted him, but you believed in him. I'm slowly changing my mind. Have you changed yours at all?"

Shirley reached over to squeeze Miriam's arm. "*Nee,* and don't you doubt that man for a moment. You deserve the good that's happening to you."

"I don't know about that." Miriam settled back into the buggy seat. "It's so new . . . and kind of scary . . . and unbelievable."

"Believe it because it's true!" Shirley said as they turned into the driveway. *You believe it too, Shirley,* she told herself as they climbed down from the buggy. *This is your new life.* But pain twisted inside her despite her best efforts.

"I'll put Sally away," Shirley offered once they had the horse unhitched and out of the shafts.

Miriam nodded and disappeared into the darkness as she walked toward the house.

Shirley found a flashlight under the buggy seat before she turned off the buggy lights. She steadied the beam on the barn door and led Sally forward. She followed willingly enough. Shirley had the harness off the horse moments later and put a scoop of oats in Sally's stall bin. Grabbing a currycomb, Shirley gave the horse a fast brushing. "That'll tide you over for the night." She gave the horse a pat on the neck.

Sally nickered as if saying thanks.

Shirley laughed. "You're welcome!"

Shirley left the barn, closed the door, and then turned off the flashlight. Above her a great splash of stars twinkled. They were brighter than the stars at home, she thought. But then everything seemed brighter around here. With a sigh, she paused beside the buggy for a long look upward. This was the underside of heaven, someone had once said. Maybe it was Miriam, but she wasn't sure. It could have been almost anyone. It sometimes seemed that all the women around her in Possum Valley were more mature spiritually than she was. Shirley had always known that, but she'd made up for it by depending on her beauty and good nature for advantages. After tonight that obviously wasn't going to be enough here.

Thoughts of Jonas raced through her head. She ought to call him. He would give her the attention she craved. His voice would fill with joy at the sound of hers. He'd ask, "How are things going, Shirley? Having a good time?"

She would probably spill her heart to him. What would that gain? "Then surely you're coming back soon," he'd say. And she would weaken. Her heart would leap in agreement, and soon she'd be on the bus back to Ohio. Everyone would understand. Miriam could stay and have her little heaven on earth. So what was the problem?

She put the flashlight back under the buggy seat and took one last look toward the heavens as she walked to the house. She'd have to make a practice of this — spending more time alone under the stars. That would be a pleasant practice on the prairie — once she'd developed the necessary discipline to do it regularly.

The front door squeaked when she entered. The soft glow from a kerosene lamp came from the kitchen doorway. Who would still be up? Certainly not Aunt Fannie. She'd be in bed with baby Jonathon in a crib next to her. Miriam should be upstairs by now. Uncle William was an early riser, so he would be long asleep by now.

With a soft step, Shirley peered through the kitchen doorway. Miriam was sitting at the table with a letter in front of her. Her face was lined with worry when she glanced up.

"What is it?" Shirley approached and stood beside her sister.

"A letter from Ivan." Miriam held up the paper. "Aunt Fannie didn't want me to see it before the youth gathering."

From the look on Miriam's face, Aunt Fannie had decided correctly. Shirley pulled up a chair. "What does he say?"

"Read it for yourself." Miriam pushed the paper across the table.

Shirley squinted at the smeared handwriting. The man wasn't the best or neatest scribe. She focused and read silently.

My dearest Miriam,

I know you think I have no right to such an address, but please hear me out. The news of your departure was quite a shock to me. It was so sudden and so soon. I had thought we would speak again about the matter between us. I can't believe you considered me so lightly that you left without even one word of goodbye. Surely you can understand how I feel.

I admire and respect you greatly. So if you would, please give this letter serious consideration. I had hoped to talk with you in person here in Possum Valley, but you have left us with only the option of letters. I'm not much of a letter writer.

I'm so sorry about any hard feelings I may have caused between us, Miriam. I'm trying to understand how my actions might appear to you. I dated Laura instead of you after our *rumspringa* time, but let's not cut off the friendship and possibilities that remain between you and me. How awful that would be. Can't you see that?

I value your friendship greatly. I hope

you will at least write back. This silence that now hangs between us isn't for the best. I know I haven't always acted as I should have, I willingly confess that. But I assure you that the affection we used to share was real. My heart was genuine.

You are a jewel, Miriam. You're precious, and you will make a great *frau* someday. I know it may seem like a lot to ask right now, but will you at least answer this letter and tell me your thoughts? That would be a great comfort to me. I'm sure it would ease the uncertainty that grips my heart.

Your great admirer,
Ivan Mast

"What do you think?" Miriam asked before Shirley had time to gather her thoughts.

Shirley wanted to say, *You should write back at once, and maybe we can both go back to Possum Valley.* But that wasn't the right choice, she was sure. And Ivan hadn't really expressed love for Miriam. "I don't know, Miriam. He hasn't broken off his relationship with Laura. There's nothing in there about that."

"Maybe he wants to be sure about me first? If I accept his affections, then he'll break if off with Laura. Could that be it?"

Shirley nodded. "There you have it. He's putting you last. If you don't respond, at least he has Laura as his backup."

"That confirms what I've thought all along. It's the farm Ivan is interested in. If he has to settle for me over Laura in order to get the land, that's what he'll do."

"I see how it can look that way," Shirley forced herself to say. Perhaps Miriam had been right about Ivan. He was trying to play both sides.

"Well, thanks for your help." Miriam rose. "Maybe we ought to get to bed. Morning will be here soon enough."

Miriam slipped the letter into her dress pocket.

The storm might be over for tonight, but Shirley knew Miriam wouldn't let this go so easily. "You should burn that letter," Shirley said at the stair door.

Miriam shook her head. That was a radical move and wouldn't solve anything. "I'll have to write him back," she said softly. "But I don't know what I'll say."

"You'll think of the right thing. You always do."

"Thanks, Shirley," Miriam whispered at the top of the stairs where they parted ways.

"Good night." Shirley closed her bedroom

door. Moments later she slipped under the quilt on the bed and, between the window drapes, watched the stars twinkle until she fell asleep.

CHAPTER TWENTY-EIGHT

On that same Thursday evening in Possum Valley, Ivan shifted on his buggy seat. He'd parked in the Swartz driveway moments ago, and Laura should have climbed out by now. Instead she was sitting beside him still chattering away.

"We raked the lawn this afternoon — *Mamm* and I did, along with my younger sisters. And the garden too, although that was weeded by hand, not raked. *Mamm* said something must be done about how things look around the place. We bring in *Englisha* people to buy things from the garden all the time, and things have to appear decent. Not that this would make the produce any better, of course, but for appearance's sake. *Englisha* people are that way, *Mamm* says. They place a lot of stock in how things look. Which isn't right, but that's how things are." She reached over to take Ivan's hand in hers. "But all is right in our world, Ivan, isn't it?" Laura didn't wait for an answer. "I'm so thankful the Lord has given us all these *gut* things to enjoy. Sure we don't always have the nice things the *Englisha* enjoy, but we have made the better choice. That's what I tell myself often."

Laura leaned her head against Ivan's shoulder. "Even today I thought about what might lie ahead of us . . . you and me. We too can have the Lord's blessing, Ivan. I just know it. In our future there's a little farm somewhere . . . someday! I know I haven't been seeing you for very long, so forgive my forward thoughts, but I can't help myself. There's so much about you that's better than any other man I've ever dated. You're decent. You're hardworking. You have that excellent job at Beachy's. And you're handsome!" Laura laughed. "Anyone would have to be blind not to see it. And I'm certainly not blind. I have my faults, yes, but when it comes to men, I know what I see. And I'm so thankful that you've chosen me, Ivan. So very thankful. I'm going to be the dream of your life and a blessing to you for all your days."

She wants something from me tonight, Ivan thought. And he didn't have to guess to know what it was. Laura didn't know about the letter he'd written to Miriam, but she must sense his uneasiness despite his efforts all evening to hide his feelings. Whenever he looked at her, Laura's smile had pierced his confidence in the rightness of his actions. Confound the woman! Ivan told himself. Why is this so difficult?

"What's wrong, Ivan? You haven't heard a word I said." Laura's fingers traced his face in the dimness of the buggy lights. "Don't you like being with me anymore?"

"Of course I do!" he protested. "But shouldn't you go in now? This isn't a Sunday night when we have our regular date time. And I'll see you then, you know."

She moved closer. "You're with me right now, and I'm not in a hurry to leave."

Laura would kiss him tonight again, Ivan thought. And Amish girls didn't give away kisses without a reason. Ivan let go of the reins. Laura lifted her face toward him. He took his time, and her hands held him close. He finally pulled back to gaze into her eyes. "You are the sweetest thing, Laura."

A happy sigh escaped her. "I'm so glad you like me. Can you come inside for a moment now? We still have food in the pantry, I'm sure."

He laughed. "Your kisses are all I need, Laura."

"I know that's not true, Ivan." Her fingers

traced his face again. "You still haven't told me what's wrong."

His laugh died in his throat. He choked out, "It's nothing you can help with."

"Tell me, please," she insisted.

"Just money problems." He took a stab at an answer. Perhaps that would throw her off track. And it was, in part, true. Miriam's farm was like money in the bank.

She appeared skeptical. "You shouldn't have any money problems. You have a *gut* job at Beachy's. You're not wasting your money, are you?"

A wild thought raced through his head. Maybe if he played it right, Laura wouldn't want to marry him. What Amish girl wanted a man who couldn't manage money? If Laura cut off their relationship, he'd have the issue decided without being the bad guy. But then she'd be gone forever. And if Miriam didn't return to him, he'd have lost Laura. Ivan gripped the reins in both hands. *Nee,* he didn't want to lose Laura unless he was certain about Miriam.

Laura cleared her throat. "You're probably just worried about what will happen after marriage. How you'll support a family. Or maybe you think I'll spend all your money. Is that it, Ivan?"

He chuckled. "No, Laura, it's not you. I

know you're *wunderbah.* What woman could kiss like you can and not be a *gut frau* for any man? I just can't give you what you deserve, that's what's wrong." There, he had said something close enough to the truth to get by.

"Ivan, are you still thinking about Miriam?"

Laura's voice broke through his thoughts with a jolt. Thankfully it was dark, and she couldn't see his face very well. With quick effort Ivan pasted on a grin. "How could I think of her with you around?"

Laura stared off into the darkness. "You know she's not right for you, Ivan. I wish you'd forget about Miriam Yoder."

"Who says I haven't?" Ivan worked to keep his voice steady.

Laura didn't move on the seat beside him for a long time. "Okay. Let's just leave Miriam out of it then. I don't want to think about her either. You did choose me over her . . . didn't you? Why would you want to go back now? Is it because you used to love her before you loved me? Or is it because she now owns a farm in the free and clear?"

"Laura, please." His voice trembled.

Her fingers found his hand again. "I can't help it, Ivan. I think these things, especially when your heart drifts away from me. I can tell, you know. Women can."

"Why would I kiss you if I didn't love you?" Ivan didn't wait before he added. "You're the sweetest thing, Laura. I wasn't lying about that."

"Did you ever kiss her?"

He looked down, and her face was lifted toward his. "Of course not!" The words burst out of him. "We never even dated."

"There are such things as stealing kisses behind buggies and barns." She still looked up at him.

Ivan snorted. "Miriam Yoder stealing kisses? I don't think so!"

"Maybe that's it." Laura's fingers tightened on his. "Miriam is more proper, and decent, and all that. She doesn't have to kiss you to gain your affections."

"Laura, don't go there." Ivan's voice rose a notch. "Forget Miriam. Are you not the one I asked home from the hymn singing?"

"Yah." Laura didn't sound convinced. "And I'm glad you did. So let's forget about Miriam and money and stolen kisses. Let's go inside. I'll find some pie, I'm sure."

He shook his head. "We shouldn't on a week night. Your parents will think I can't wait to marry you."

Her face fell. "Well, can you?"

"Please." He tried again. "That's not what

I meant at all, Laura. I want your parents to think well of me — as a future son-in-law. They'd already wonder if they knew I kissed you so often."

A smile crept across her face. "I can tell them I'm to blame for that."

He squeezed her hand. "Don't tell them, Laura. Let's keep it our secret."

"You're a decent man, and they know that." Her smile had broadened. "I'm glad you kissed me. I love you, Ivan."

"And I love you." He held her hand until she climbed out of the buggy.

"At least walk me to the door," she pleaded.

"I'd like that." He climbed down from the buggy and gave the reins a quick twist around the hitching post.

Laura took his hand. Together they walked up to the front porch. She paused to look up at him. "Good night, Ivan. I've enjoyed being with you tonight. I always do."

He didn't answer but pulled her close.

She clung to him until he let go again.

"That's a proper good night," he whispered in her ear.

Laura giggled and disappeared inside.

He'd handled things well tonight, Ivan thought. He strode back to the buggy at a brisk pace, undid the reins from the hitching post, and climbed back into the buggy. He glanced up at Laura's bedroom window. *Yah,* she was watching him leave, just as he knew she would. The thought sent warm circles around his heart. That woman was certainly sweet and pretty. He was a fool not to ask her to be his *frau.* His letter to Miriam was a foolish move on his part. Ivan stared off into the darkness. What if Miriam wrote him back? What if she accepted his attention? But Miriam wouldn't, Ivan comforted himself. Neither would she reveal his letter to anyone or expose him. She wasn't like that. And if she did, there was a logical explanation. He could say he'd been heartbroken over her sudden departure.

What a fool he was, Ivan told himself. Somehow he had to straighten out this matter. But how? Well, he could pray, he supposed, like his people usually did about such matters. But that seemed wrong because the love of money had crept into his heart. He might as well be honest, he reminded himself. And the Lord had already said lots of things about the love of money. The preachers mentioned this sin often in their Sunday sermons. They spoke of sorrows that pierced the heart and left only ashes in one's hand. He should have known better than to base his pursuit of Miriam on her farm, and yet he hadn't seemed able to help himself. "And what man could?" Ivan spoke aloud into the darkness.

His horse pricked up his ears as if he'd heard. He whinnied long and hard. Ivan shivered in the buggy. There was no way horses could understand words, but he'd better not say such thoughts aloud again — even if only Billy was around to hear. Somehow he'd find his way through this. The resolution might come when Miriam refused to answer his letter. She was much too decent a girl to fall for his words anyway. He was confident of that. He relaxed as he drove into the night. He had nothing to worry about. He'd soon forget about Miriam's farm, like he should have earlier. He could look forward to Laura's kisses on Sunday evening. There would be plenty of those, he was sure.

CHAPTER TWENTY-NINE

Saturday morning Miriam was rocking baby Jonathon in the Byler living room. He'd been colicky all night, and from the look on her face, Aunt Fannie was exhausted

"Why didn't you call me?" Miriam scolded. "I'd have walked the floor with him."

Aunt Fannie glowed in spite of her weariness. "He needed his *mamm,* but thanks for the offer. I'm sure there will be other times when I'll be only too happy to have you or Shirley take over. You both are really *gut* with him."

"That's nice of you to say." Miriam allowed the praise to sink in. She was glad they could help.

Aunt Fannie stood. "I do believe I'll try to catch a nap. You seem to have things under control. Oh, and by the way, later this morning there will be a surprise."

Shirley appeared in the kitchen doorway.

"A surprise? Oh, do tell us now! You know how I am with surprises."

Aunt Fannie chuckled and disappeared into the bedroom without another word.

Shirley shrugged and returned to the breakfast dishes. Miriam settled into the rocker with baby Jonathon. Uncle William had gone out to open the greenhouse right after breakfast, and Wayne's buggy had driven in an hour ago. Perhaps there would be a chance to speak to him later, Miriam hoped. The glow of the youth gathering on Thursday night still hung over her and explained her new openness to Wayne. She would be cautious, though. After all, this initial happiness would no doubt wear off before long, maybe even tomorrow when she would see everyone at the community service. Then her emotions might plunge like a rock. Besides, she'd probably imagined half the stuff at the youth gathering anyway — so many cheerful conversations and the kind acceptance from everyone.

Then there was Shirley's reaction to the evening. If Miriam had imagined all those *gut* things, why had Shirley seemed so down all evening? Only on the way home had she seemed the least bit cheerful. Miriam stopped the rocker as baby Jonathon squiggled in her arms. She transferred the babe to a blanket on the floor in a corner of the room and slipped another blanket over him. He soon settled into sleep, and Miriam walked to the window to gaze out across the lawn. She needed space to think. Had Shirley's sudden cheerfulness on the way home been put on for her benefit? This was a startling thought and seemed unlikely, but what other explanation was there?

She glanced at Wayne's buggy parked off to the side of the driveway. Cars were already pulling into the small parking lot. This would be a busy day, and perhaps she should be out in the greenhouse helping. It would be nice to chat with Wayne between customers. Was it really possible that his attention was genuine and unaffected by the farm Mr. Bland had given her? How unlike Ivan!

The letter from Ivan still lay in the bottom of her dresser drawer. Miriam flinched at the thought. How did the man dare think she would even respond to such a letter? The nerve of him! Did he believe her so needy that she would cave in to such a strange relationship? Or was Ivan consumed with his own self-importance? Either answer wasn't a *gut* one. She shook her head. She shouldn't think ill of the man. The Lord judged hearts, and she should leave such things to Him. She would choose to believe the Lord gave *gut* things much more than He gave bad ones. And so why couldn't He be blessing her life here in this new community? Hadn't she prayed and longed for a place of peace, a place that contained bright promises for tomorrow? Why was she astonished when the Lord supplied her needs?

Miriam drew in a long breath and stepped away from the window. She must talk with Shirley. If Shirley was troubled, Miriam could understand why. The poor girl had never had something like that happen to her. In Possum Valley, Shirley had always been the center of attention at any youth gathering.

Miriam tiptoed over to baby Jonathon. He hadn't stirred yet, so perhaps his colic had calmed down. Making sure she kept Jonathon in sight, she made her way to the kitchen to see what Shirley was doing.

Shirley glanced up with a weak smile when Miriam walked in. "Is Jonathon asleep?"

"*Yah,* finally." Miriam picked up a towel and began to work on the just-washed dishes. She glanced at baby Jonathon after drying each one.

"It's your touch." Shirley smiled a bit

brighter this time. "You have a way with babies."

Miriam shook her head. "Don't say such things. I have enough problems with pride already."

Shirley laughed. "You? Problems with pride? What does that say about me then?"

"I guess it says we're both needing the Lord's mercy, I suppose." Miriam reached over and give Shirley a quick hug. "I'm sorry I haven't said more about the youth gathering. I don't think you enjoyed it much, but I was too wrapped up in myself to really notice."

"I must say it was a new experience," Shirley admitted with a hint of bitterness.

Miriam frowned. "I'm so sorry, Shirley."

"It wasn't your fault." Shirley gave a little shrug. "There's something different about this community. I'm not used to it yet."

"I know. I've sensed it too." Miriam touched Shirley's arm. "Will you be okay?"

Shirley pasted on a sweet smile. "*Yah,* I'm okay. I really am. I'm trying to lessen some of my faults, and this may be just the motivation I need. But that's me. As for you, you should be happy."

Miriam gave Shirley a quick glance. "It's so new to me — getting so much attention. I'm not sure what to think. But I don't want to reject the goodness of the Lord."

"There you go!" Shirley washed the pan in her hands with vigor.

"Enough about me," Miriam said. "Are you sure you're okay? I mean *really* okay?"

"As *gut* as can be expected." Shirley motioned with her hand. "Now, stop paying me attention. I'll soon burst out crying, and that's what I *don't* need."

Miriam reached over to give Shirley's shoulders another fast squeeze. "We'll make it through together, Shirley."

"*Yah.* Whatever the Lord has for us, let's accept it. And that goes especially for you, Miriam."

"I'll try. I've been wondering what I should do about Ivan's letter. The nerve that man has!"

"I guess just trust that the Lord is working the best out for him too," Shirley offered.

Miriam glanced at her sister. How fast did things change here? Shirley had never talked like this at home.

At her look, Shirley nodded. "I know that doesn't sound like me. But enjoy it because tomorrow I may be back to the same person I was before."

A soft step at the kitchen doorway interrupted the conversation. Both girls turned around.

"He's sleeping." Aunt Fannie had a pleased smile on her face.

"You're up?" Miriam scolded gently. "That wasn't much of a nap."

"I can't sleep," Aunt Fannie said. "I just toss and turn. Maybe I'll sleep better tonight . . . if Jonathon cooperates."

"Are you going to tell us about the surprise now?" Shirley teased. "I can't wait until this afternoon."

"You're too excitable, Shirley," Aunt Fannie said good-naturedly. "Oh, all right. I thought we would run into town — just the three of us — for a little shopping. That would give both of you time to look around the big town of Coalgate."

"But what about helping Uncle William in the greenhouse?" Miriam spoke up.

"You can do that this afternoon," Aunt Fannie said. "Uncle William and Wayne can handle it this morning. And Coalgate isn't that far anyway. I phoned Mr. Whitehorse yesterday and scheduled everything. His wife, Leola, is coming along too."

"Then it's settled." Shirley glowed.

Miriam smiled at her sister. Even back at home a trip to town never failed to cheer Shirley. "When is Mr. Whitehorse coming for us?" she asked.

Aunt Fannie glanced at the clock. "At ten. That should give us plenty of time to get ready."

Shirley rushed to finish the last of the dishes. "Oh, I'm so excited!"

A short while later Aunt Fannie stayed with the baby while Miriam and Shirley went upstairs to their rooms.

With the door closed behind her, Miriam pulled the checkbook from the dresser drawer. "Why do I even want to see you?" Miriam murmured under her breath. "It can't be because you've become my friend because you haven't." Even so, Miriam studied the checkbook and debit card, along with the instructions the lawyer had given her. She then reached back into the drawer and took out Ivan's letter. She slipped all three into her large dress pocket.

She opened her bedroom door to find the hall empty. Stepping out she closed the door behind her and hesitated at Shirley's door. Should she call? Shirley was probably trying on her best Sunday dress for the venture into town. Miriam nodded her head and smiled as she moved on. She was glad some things hadn't changed, even if it was only Shirley's excitement about a town trip.

Miriam took the stairs down and walked

into the living room. Aunt Fannie must have taken baby Jonathon with her into the bedroom while she changed clothes.

The bedroom door opened, and Aunt Fannie came out cradling Jonathon.

"May I hold him?" Miriam asked.

Aunt Fannie nodded and carefully passed the boy to Miriam.

Miriam took him into her arms and cooed into this face, "Are you ready for a town trip, little one? You're so adorable, you sweet thing." Miriam kissed him on the cheek. "We're all going on a trip in an *Englisha* car, and you're going along! Won't you just love that?" Through the living room window, she saw Mr. Whitehorse's car pull up next to the house.

CHAPTER THIRTY

Early that afternoon Miriam stepped out of the Coalgate library and crossed the street at a brisk pace heading toward the bank's ATM. They had all eaten at a Subway restaurant after visiting a thrift store. Then they'd parted ways from there. Shirley was still at the dollar store searching for inexpensive treasures. Aunt Fannie was picking up a few things in the grocery store. Miriam would have time enough for this short side adventure to see if there really was money in her new bank account. She wasn't sure she knew how to do it. The instructions from the lawyer were in her pocket, but they hadn't made much sense. How was it possible to access an account when her bank was in Sugarcreek more than a thousand miles away?

Miriam gathered her courage and approached the ATM. A man had just finished pocketing his cash. He gave her a quick glance as he walked by, and Miriam almost said out loud, *I don't know what I'm doing. Please help me.* Embarrassment stopped her. What if Shirley or Aunt Fannie unexpectedly came out and saw her at an ATM? she thought. Word would get out fast, and her deception would become known. Bishop Wagler back home might even excommunicate her. But surely that was an irrational thought brought on by her guilty conscience. The bishop would do no such thing, she was sure.

After one last, quick glance up and down the street, Miriam slipped the card into the slot with an arrow. The machine pulled it in and beeped. Miriam jumped. Then she planted both feet on the ground and read the instructions the lawyer had given her and the ones that appeared on the screen. Soon the machine gave her a list of options.

"Withdraw cash," Miriam said aloud. "Why not try that?" She'd planned to only check to see if the money was really there. But wouldn't a little money in her pocket feel *gut*? And if the money wasn't there, she wouldn't be able to get cash. A thrill ran through her. Her heart was betraying her, Miriam acknowledged. Did that make her a friend of money?

Miriam pushed the thought away and

punched the button with twenty dollars beside it. Immediately the machine responded. A twenty-dollar bill spit out of a slot. Miriam took a deep breath and retrieved the money. So far so good. How much money was really in her account? There was only one way to find out. "Check balance," Miriam read. She punched that button. She gasped when machine spit out a slip of paper with the number $2,008,234.00. There was no question about it. She had over two million dollars in the bank! The money had grown. Now she couldn't stop herself. *Daett* had been right. Money did strange things to one's heart. Miriam held her breath and pressed the withdraw button again — the $500 one this time. The bills came out of the slot. Miriam stuffed them into her handbag without looking at them. Surely her face must be burning red by now. She gasped at how easy it had been. She pocketed the debit card and cash slip before hurrying away. What was she going to do with all this money? There was no place to spend it without being obvious. They already had enough funds for incidentals. *Mamm* had given it to them the day they left for Oklahoma.

When she saw Shirley walking toward her, Miriam almost rushed the other way, but she forced herself to move forward calmly.

"Where have you been?" Shirley asked.

When Miriam didn't answer, Shirley's look turned to concern. "That's right. You went to the library. Were you reading novels you shouldn't be?" She giggled at the thought of Miriam doing such a thing.

Miriam gave a strangled laugh. "Of course not! I'm just out of breath from hurrying to find you." *But I have five hundred dollars in my pocket,* she almost said out loud. *And more than two million dollars in the bank!* Shirley probably wouldn't believe her! Only a trip back to the ATM machine would accomplish that. Not a good idea. Better to let Shirley think what she would about a trip to the library.

Shirley shrugged. "Well, okay. Look what I found!" Shirley drew a small, leather-bound tablet from her pocket. "And for only a dollar! Isn't that just perfect for a little diary? I would have bought two of them, but this was the only one left. And no wonder since it's such a *gut* price."

Miriam took the offered tablet and turned it over in her hand. "It is *wunderbah.* You've always been a smart shopper."

Shirley smirked. "That comes from necessity — not having much money. But let's not speak of that now. Maybe I'll meet a rich Amish man out here who will make me forget Jonas."

"Don't say that!" Miriam scolded.

"I was only teasing." Shirley gave Miriam a bright smile. "Come, we'd better find Aunt Fannie."

Miriam agreed and followed Shirley across the street. "I want to help in the greenhouse this afternoon."

"And say hi to Wayne?" Shirley glanced over her shoulder with a grin.

"Sounds *gut* to me!" Miriam shot back, although she could feel her neck get warm. How bold she'd become! It's the money, she told herself. It's given me confidence. But then again, maybe it was the community in Clarita — being in a new place and all. That was the happier thought of the two, and certainly a lot more acceptable than depending on money for strength. In fact, she wanted to forget about the money . . . even if she had five hundred and twenty dollars in her pocket.

"You're falling hard for Wayne, aren't you?" Shirley teased.

Miriam ignored Shirley's comment by remarking cheerfully, "Let's head back to the car. It's almost time to go."

Moments later the two stopped beside Mr. Whitehorse's car. Baby Jonathon was nestled in Leola Whitehorse's arms. She was gently cooing to him. Mr. Whitehorse and Leola greeted them with pleased looks. Leola was obviously happy.

"She's always been excellent with our children as well as our grandchildren," Mr. Whitehorse commented.

"How many grandchildren do you have?" Miriam asked.

He held up five fingers and appeared a bit disappointed. "Children don't have large families nowadays. We had eight ourselves."

"There will be more," Leola said as she continued to coo at Jonathon. "At least I keep hoping so."

"I'll check on Aunt Fannie," Shirley said. "You can wait here, Miriam."

Before Miriam could respond, the nearby grocery store doors were pushed open and Aunt Fannie appeared with a cart filled to the brim. Both girls rushed forward to help unload. Mr. Whitehorse got out of the car to open the trunk.

"Why didn't you ask us to help you?" Miriam exclaimed. "I didn't know you had this much shopping to do."

"Now, now," Aunt Fannie chided. "I'm just fine. I wanted you girls to spend some time in town doing what you wanted to do without worrying about me."

"You should have let us help anyway," Shirley said. "I did find this treasure." She held up the leather tablet.

Aunt Fannie placed a bag of groceries in the trunk and then took Shirley's find. She examined it carefully and glowed. "Now that is worth a trip to town, isn't it? I'm sure you got it at a bargain."

"For a dollar!" Shirley beamed. "I went to the dollar store and shopped carefully like any decent Amish woman would."

Aunt Fannie handed back the tablet. "You'll be a complement to a fine young man someday. Speaking of young men, I never did hear how Thursday night went. I guess I was too taken up with baby Jonathon."

Mr. Whitehorse was listening with an attentive ear as he loaded the rest of the groceries into the trunk.

Miriam noticed, so she didn't say anything. Shirley bit her lip before she finally replied, "Well, Miriam is off to a running start with the youth group."

"That's *gut* to hear. I can't say I'm surprised. But what about you, Shirley? Did you enjoy yourself?"

Shirley frowned a bit and wrinkled her brow. "I'd say so. It didn't go quite how I'd hoped, but I'm okay with it."

319

"That doesn't sound *gut,*" Aunt Fannie said. "Were the youth nice to you?"

"Yes, Aunt Fannie. Everyone was very welcoming. I'm just spoiled and used to a lot of attention, that's all."

"She's having a difficult time adjusting," Miriam said as she stepped back so Mr. Whitehorse could close the trunk lid. She wasn't about to say any more with *Englisha* around. There wasn't that much for her to say anyway.

"Well, it'll go better next time," Aunt Fannie consoled.

Shirley nodded as if she agreed, but Miriam knew it was because her sister didn't want to discuss the matter further.

They climbed into the car, and Leola handed Jonathon to Aunt Fannie with a smile. "He's such a little darling. Sweet as my own pumpkins were. I'm glad we kept one of the child safety seats our kinner used for their children."

"That's kind of you to say." Aunt Fannie kissed Jonathon on his cheek. "We sure love him. And I'm glad too." She strapped baby Jonathon in, and then fastened her own seat belt. She leaned over and gazed at her precious son. "Lord, bless him and all the other little ones You see fit to give us."

"May there be plenty!" Mr. Whitehorse

seconded as he started the car, pulled out of the parking spot, and headed out of town.

Peaceful silence reigned inside the car as the miles rolled away. Miriam watched the landscape pass to take her mind off the ATM machine and the money in her pocket. The difference in this country from Holmes County was pronounced. It seemed quite like another world. She liked that. The uncrowded feeling and the sense that great vastness lay just beyond. Perhaps that explained why people loved each other deeply on the prairie. At least the community in Clarita did. And even though they were *Englisha,* Mr. Whitehorse and his wife seemed no exception. Even the *Englisha* were affected.

She settled back in the car seat with a sigh. There was peace here and promise. She could feel it even with the turmoil brought by the sight of all those twenty-dollar bills spit out by the ATM. She shouldn't have taken five hundred dollars out. She'd have to spend the money unobtrusively, but how and where? There wasn't anything she needed. Spending frivolously was a fault she didn't wish to add to her character. Perhaps she could give the money away. There ought to be opportunities to do that in the community. Maybe she could leave the money stuck in Mr. Whitehouse's car? Would he be surprised that an Amish woman had that large sum of cash? But then Mr. Whitehorse would ask Aunt Fannie about mislaid money, and soon it would come down to the two sisters. Miriam knew she wouldn't lie about it.

No, it was best to wait. The Lord would help her. In the meantime, she'd think about something else. Sunday lay ahead, and she would see the youth group again. She could imagine it already, and happiness surged inside her. Maybe Shirley would even enjoy herself this time. Wouldn't that be an added blessing? Miriam decided she'd pray for that. And there was Wayne, of course. She might have a chance to speak with him this afternoon after the groceries had been unloaded and Aunt Fannie and baby Jonathon were settled in the house. Shirley could put the groceries in the cupboards while she went out to help Uncle William.

The car bounced as Mr. Whitehorse turned in at the Byler driveway. Wayne's buggy was still in its place, so he was here. Miriam smiled even as she reminded herself not to appear overeager to see him. Yet her heart had softened even further toward Wayne. She wouldn't continue to see wealth as an obstacle between them unless he did something to suggest it. Wayne wasn't like Ivan, who had dated someone else and then wanted to come back when he learned of the inheritance. From all appearances, Wayne and the community accepted her for her own sake. Someday she might even tell Wayne about the money, although the very thought struck fear in her heart. But now it seemed at least remotely possible to be forthcoming about it.

"What are you thinking about?" Shirley asked as the car came to a stop.

"I'm not saying," Miriam replied as she opened the door and climbed out of the car. And that was the truth, Miriam told herself. Shirley wouldn't want to know what she'd discovered in her heart.

Shirley glared at Miriam, but thankfully she didn't ask more questions.

CHAPTER THIRTY-ONE

Later that afternoon Miriam slipped through the back door of the greenhouse to see if Uncle William and Wayne needed help. With the parking lot still full, it seemed likely she could do something to help out. She peeked around a tall bunch of bushes.

Uncle William caught sight of her. He rushed over with a big grin on his face. "Glad to see you, Miriam! I thought I'd never get more help this afternoon."

"I'm sorry about that." Miriam smiled. "I guess we got carried away with our shopping, and the library, and . . ." Miriam caught herself before she mentioned the ATM.

"Reading novels while Wayne and I are rushing about here working up a sweat?" Uncle William scolded, but his smile belied his words.

"Well, I'm here now. Put me to work!"

Uncle William waved his hand toward the

cash register. "If you could help check out the items and, when necessary, carry them out to a customer's car that would be great."

Miriam didn't hesitate. "Sure, wherever I'm needed."

Her heart pounded when she saw Wayne was running the cash register at the moment. She moved forward and told herself to "act normal." She liked the man, yes, and he obviously liked her. She would allow herself to be open to whatever God brought about.

"Hi, Miriam!" Wayne called as she approached. "Good to see you. I've been waiting all day for the privilege." He smiled.

The customer standing at the register with three flowerpots in her hands gave Miriam a kind look. "Help has arrived, I see," she commented to Wayne.

"And the best kind of help!" Wayne said with enthusiasm. "Let me carry those pots out for you now that we have help. Miriam can run the register."

Miriam moved around the counter. "You'll have to show me how. I've never operated this brand of cash register. Maybe I should just help carry out purchases." She didn't wait for a response from Wayne. She grabbed the woman's flowerpots and waited as she finished paying the bill. Miriam followed the woman out to her car and watched as she opened the trunk.

The customer turned to Miriam with a smile. "This is the best place for them — if they don't tip over."

Miriam nodded and set the pots among the grocery bags. She guessed, "Shopping down the road at the Amish store?"

The woman's face glowed. "Yes. Exactly. I love the place and come by here every week, if I can. Wholesome people, you are."

"We try to be." Miriam lowered her head. She didn't want to think about the secret money in her pocket, but the thought flashed unbidden through her mind.

"That's such a sweet and humble spirit to have." The woman closed the trunk lid. "Is that young man your boyfriend?"

As her face got red, Miriam sputtered, "*Ach, nee,* not really. See, I'm rather new here and . . ."

The woman was still smiling. "Well, perhaps when I come by next time, you'll have a different answer." She winked at Miriam and then climbed into her car and drove away.

Miriam watched the car disappear down the road. What had the woman seen that made her think Wayne was her boyfriend? She pulled her thoughts away from the woman's words and hurried back inside.

"I thought she'd kidnapped you," Wayne teased.

She looked down. Under no condition would she tell Wayne what the customer had said. Miriam glanced up apologetically. "We got to talking a little and I dawdled. I'm sorry."

"I was only kidding," Wayne protested, giving Miriam a genuine and encouraging smile.

The line at the register had grown longer. Miriam grabbed the two hanging baskets the next customer purchased and bolted out the door. She had to pause and wait for the customer to catch up. "Get it together," Miriam told herself silently. Wayne had her all flustered. Ivan had never affected her this way. Why was Wayne getting to her in the short time she'd been here? She couldn't seem to stop smiling.

When the elderly customer caught up to her, he muttered, "You young people are sure spry. What's the big rush? Don't you Amish have all the time in the world?"

Miriam was instantly contrite. "I'm sorry."

The man clucked with his tongue. "No apologies necessary. I was just teasing, young lady."

Miriam held up the baskets and regarded

them for a moment. "Who are these for?"

"My wife, of course." The man laughed. "Did you think I had a girlfriend at my age?"

Miriam winced. "I'm sorry. I was just trying to . . ."

The man patted her on the arm as he opened his car door. "Don't be so serious. No offense taken. I was teasing again."

Miriam nodded. "Thanks for the reminder. I'll be more cheerful next time you come."

The man glanced back at the greenhouse. "I know it gets busy in there. Hang in there."

"It's not just that." Miriam set his last basket inside the car. "I have some things I'm working through." Why had she said such a thing to a man she didn't even know?

He seemed to take it in stride. "Don't we all!" He got into his car. "Now you take care. Take time to enjoy what the Lord gives you in life. Take that from someone who knows." He nodded and looked very wise as he started his vehicle and shut the door.

Miriam quickly headed back to the register. Already two customers had come out with their purchases. At this rate she'd prove herself next to useless. Wayne would want to know why she'd stayed out so long each time. She wouldn't defend herself even though it seemed as if the *Englisha* insisted on small talk.

Miriam's heart was pounding when she entered the greenhouse.

Wayne glanced up. "I declare! You vanish forever every time you go out that door."

Miriam forced herself to relax and shot back, "You would too if you'd been through what I've been through today."

"Baby cries getting to you?" Wayne grinned.

The next customer was ready to leave. Miriam didn't respond to Wayne as she followed the young lady and her small child. They could have carried their purchase by themselves, but she wanted to get away from Wayne. The elderly customer's words were still ringing in her ears: "Enjoy what the Lord gives you in life." Was she to enjoy Wayne's attention? The prospect delighted and overwhelmed her at the same time.

"Thanks so much!" the young woman gushed as Miriam set her flowering plants in the backseat of the car. "Joshua, get in the car, please."

"He's cute and obedient," Miriam commented as the child climbed into his seat and buckled up.

"My husband and I are trying to raise him right, but it's hard," the woman said. "You

Amish are such good examples for the rest of us. We're so honored to have a small Amish community near where we live."

"Thank you." Miriam's voice caught. "That's kind of you to say."

The woman smiled. "I guess we all do the best we can with the Lord's help."

"That's true," Miriam agreed.

The woman waved as she pulled out of the parking lot. Little Joshua sitting in the back did the same.

Miriam didn't watch long. She returned to the greenhouse.

"Getting better at this, I see." Wayne teased at the sight of her.

Miriam gave him a sweet smile. "I'll get even better, you'll see."

Wayne chuckled. "That's not hard to believe."

Eventually the line of customers thinned out, and Miriam could relax a bit. "Is it always this busy on Saturdays?" she asked.

Wayne nodded and leaned against the counter. He motioned with his hand. "Come closer and I'll teach you how to run this thing. It's not right that you carry the customers' purchases out while I stand around."

"You're working just as hard as I am," Miriam protested.

Wayne didn't answer as he punched some buttons on the register. "There's nothing to it. You enter the numbers, hit this button, and when you're finished, press this one. There — just like this."

"It can't be that simple," Miriam said. She was distracted by standing so close to Wayne. She backed away a couple of steps.

Wayne laughed. "It's not going to eat you, you know."

But you might, she wanted to tease back, but the words stuck in her throat. She didn't want to be ruffled by his presence and yet she was. Could she really open her heart again? The danger that Wayne might bruise and break it made her emotions throb. What if his obvious affection for her turned out to be based on the fact she was rich?

Wayne joked, "We have to learn this job well and help Uncle William make his millions."

Uncle William's voice rumbled from a few feet away. "I heard that."

Miriam swallowed hard but didn't say anything. Millions of dollars . . .

Wayne continued. "We must be close to those millions with all the sales we rang up today."

Uncle William grinned. "In my day and time it won't happen. Who needs that much money anyway? We have the Lord's grace, do we not?"

"I agree." Wayne turned back to Miriam. "There, that's about it. Easy, just like I said."

She had no time to argue because another customer walked up. She punched in the numbers like Wayne had done, and it really was easy. It was good that Uncle William didn't take credit cards. That would have made it harder, and every sale would remind Miriam of her own debit card hidden in her pocket.

Wayne smiled his encouragement as he walked out the door with the purchases a young man had made. By the time he returned, Miriam had another customer rung up.

"Now who's slow?" Miriam's voice trembled with the tease, but it was the best she could do.

Wayne's grin was broad. "I supply quality service to Uncle William's customers, and that includes conversation. And we can't rush about and drop plants now, can we?"

"You said none of that about me!" Miriam reminded him with a chuckle as he disappeared out the door with another customer.

When he returned, Miriam continued.

"Slow people always make excuses, I've heard." It was a clumsy joke, Miriam knew, but Wayne didn't seem to mind.

He stepped closer and whispered, "You don't need excuses. I'm sure you have *gut* reasons for everything you do."

Her face turned crimson. Did Wayne understand her that well? The thought took her breath away.

Wayne continued as if he hadn't noticed her flustered condition. "I think you and your sister are adjusting really well to our ways out here on the prairie. It's not everyone who could fit in so easily."

"I don't know about that," Miriam responded. "But I did come out here looking for the promise of a different kind of life."

"Have you found it?"

Miriam lowered her head shyly. "Maybe."

"Serious troubles at home, then?"

"Oh!" Miriam pulled in her breath before exhaling. "Nothing like that. *Mamm* and *Daett* are *wunderbah.* It was just time to get away for a bit . . . and help Aunt Fannie, of course."

Wayne didn't appear convinced, but he still smiled. "Well, I'm glad you came. I'm sure you and Shirley will be a blessing to our community."

What would Wayne say if he knew the

truth? Miriam wondered. Would she still be a blessing in his eyes? Already her resolve to trust him was being tested! Miriam glanced at his face. The kindness was still there. She gave him a warm smile. She wasn't about to blurt out her problems. Not yet and not for a long, long time. After Ivan's shenanigans, trust didn't come easy to her. Thankfully Uncle William walked up again, so no further talk was necessary.

"Well!" Uncle William exclaimed. "Things are wrapping up nicely on this Saturday afternoon. Thanks so much to both of you for your help."

"I was glad to," Miriam replied.

"And I'm getting paid!" Wayne laughed. "And spending a few moments with . . ." Wayne glanced at Uncle William as he let the sentence hang.

Unspoken words passed between the two, Miriam was certain. Something about her. But they were surely *gut* thoughts, she figured with comfort. And for that she was very thankful. Uncle William approved of Wayne and his interest in her. That helped build her ability to trust the young man. Wayne wasn't Ivan Mast. She'd have to remember that. *Wayne wasn't Ivan Mast.* She found her voice again. "I'll head back to the house if that's all you have for me to do."

"Yep, that's all," Uncle William said. "Thanks again."

Wayne didn't say anything, but he waved as Miriam walked out the door.

CHAPTER THIRTY-TWO

Sunday afternoon after the morning service, Shirley was sitting on a long bench in Bishop Wengerd's yard listening to the chatter around her. The service had been held in the bishop's home this morning, and after the noon meal the youth had taken benches out to the yard to sit on as they relaxed and swapped stories. The unmarried young men were sitting on a bench near the unmarried young women. Mahlon Troyer was in the middle of a story of some sort. Shirley leaned forward to pick out his voice from the happy chatter around her. Mahlon hadn't even glanced at her all day, but she still wanted to hear what he had to say. Just because he ignored her didn't mean she would act stuck-up. *Nee,* she would learn from these new circumstances and not grow bitter.

"You should have seen that old cow." Mahlon gestured with his arms. "Never have I seen such a fast track made for the back forty as when one of our cats came out of the haymow and landed on her back. You'd think a sensible cat would let go, but not this one. She must have been scared to death — the cat, that is. The cow just wanted to leave everything behind."

The men around Mahlon roared with laughter.

"A really *gut* life lesson, I would say. You should have seen Bert Weaver run away from his milking one evening. He got swatted on the face with a manure-loaded tail. He hightailed it for the water tank and dove in. His *frau* had to lead him back to the barn!" another man shared.

The men exaggerated, Shirley knew. Both about the cow's escapades and Bert Weaver, whoever he was. She laughed along with the rest of them.

"Mighty tall tales they're telling," Mahlon's sister said as she came up and sat beside Shirley.

"Are they always like this?" Shirley chuckled as a new joke began.

"Usually." Betty rolled her eyes. "But I think you and your sister being here stirs them up."

Shirley gave a short laugh. This might be true in Miriam's case. Miriam was sitting closer to the men's bench listening with rapt attention. Shirley leaned forward again. Wayne Yutzy, who hadn't been able to keep his gaze off Miriam all day, was in the middle of a tale.

"And so I said, 'Why don't we stop for a drink of water?' The threshing day was hot enough for September, and we'd been working hard trying to keep up with the best of us."

Here chuckles and glances passed between the men. They all tried to outdo each other in the fields. In this there was little difference between the Oklahoma men and the ones back home in Possum Valley, Shirley decided.

Wayne continued. "My sisters had told me what they had up their sleeve, so I knew this was coming. One of the lemonade glasses would be spiked with extra salt." Wayne paused for emphasis. "Like a *lot* of extra salt. Of course, a little salt makes for *gut* lemonade, but too much . . ." Wayne chuckled. "Let's say a little harmless choking happens. And that day poor Emery Yoder got the glass. What a sputtering and fuming!" Laughter rolled down the line of men, including Emery.

Mahlon joined in. " 'What's wrong with you?' I asked Emery — as if I couldn't figure it out. Poor fellow."

"I'll sure never forget it," Emery said.

Wayne continued. "My sisters finally jumped to the poor man's rescue, unable to endure his sad cries any longer. They offered him cold water and a fresh glass of lemonade. But his trust was shattered for the day. Emery took small sips of both before he gulped them down. Right, Emery?"

Emery looked sheepish but admitted, "*Yah,* I did."

"Can't say I blame him," another of the men spoke up. "I wouldn't trust you or your sisters in the first place."

Another round of laughter followed. Shirley glanced again at her sister. Oddly, she was sure she'd seen a frown flash across Miriam's face. What could be bothering Miriam? Shirley wondered. Whatever it was, Miriam was trying to keep a tight lid on it. Hmmm . . . Miriam was receiving attention from Wayne and some of the other men, but she still seemed distant. Was Miriam homesick for Possum Valley? Maybe even for Ivan?

If so, Shirley could understand. Sometimes out of nowhere she sorrowed for Jonas despite her best efforts not to. Oh, if only things could have been different for them.

What if Jonas's parents hadn't left the Amish faith and community? Or what if she'd been born *Englisha* or at least Mennonite? Then she might someday say marriage vows with Jonas. But that was impossible the way things stood. Still, she could imagine Jonas sitting among the men and laughing. They were worlds apart in their faith, yet he would fit in here. She and Jonas were more one in heart than they were different. Shirley sighed at thoughts that could never be. Her thoughts drifted back to her sister.

Was Miriam perhaps thinking similar thoughts about Ivan? Did she wonder what would have happened if Ivan had never looked at Laura Swartz? What if he had stayed true to his earlier love for her? What if Miriam had been given the farm by Mr. Bland a few weeks earlier — before Ivan had given in to Laura's charms? Miriam would have taken him on those terms, *yah.* But now the inheritance of the farm had changed everything. Shirley glanced again at Miriam. She was her old self now, joining in the laughter, her dark mood apparently gone.

Now it was Emery Yoder's turn to tell a tale. He'd apparently taken it upon himself to poke fun at the former storytellers. He lifted his chin high as the story unfolded.

"And then the *daett* asked his son, 'Now what was it you saw?'

" 'A snake,' the son said. 'A big snake. Thick as your arm and over eight feet long. It wiggled in the grass. I stood frozen to the ground. I couldn't even scream.'

"The *daett* laughed. 'We don't have such big snakes in Oklahoma. Now in Texas maybe, but not here.' "

Soft chuckles went around the benches as Emery continued. " 'Well,' the son said as he contemplated his *daett*'s words. 'Maybe it was only six feet long — but it was big.'

"The *daett* regarded his son with a stern face. 'Are you sure?'

"The son blinked. 'Well, maybe it was as thick as my hand and four feet long.'

" 'You shouldn't tell tall tales,' the *daett* reminded his son.

"The son pondered his story again. 'Okay. Maybe it was a little one. But he looked big!'

"The *daett* slapped his son on the back. 'Are you sure the grass didn't blow in the wind and that was what you saw?'

" 'Maybe.' The son backed down from his tale even more. 'It might have been something like that.' "

Wry grins and cheerful laughter spread around the circle.

"So maybe you didn't choke on that salty

lemonade?" another man added.

"Just keep that story in mind whenever you hear tales about me." Emery tried to look really wise, but he ended up laughing at himself. "I suppose I did have a rough time of it that hot workday."

"At least he 'fesses up!" Wayne slapped Emery on the back before standing up. "Time for me to head on down the road, fellows. You take care of the young women now."

"Isn't it about time you took care of one yourself?" one of the men teased.

Wayne glanced at Miriam, who turned all colors of red. He grinned. "I've been thinking about it, but let's not go there today, okay?"

Laughter followed Wayne as he left to retrieve his horse from the barn. Several of the other men also rose and headed for the barn. Shirley stood too. She reached over to nudge Miriam on the arm. "Isn't it time for us to go too?"

Miriam jumped, and her face got even redder. She'd been lost in thought — whatever those thoughts were. Her sister had it bad for Wayne whether she wanted to admit the fact or not. Shirley was glad. Miriam deserved a break.

Betty spoke close to Shirley's ear as Miriam turned to talk to the Kuntz sisters. "I'll tell Wayne you're ready to leave. He'll want to help with the horse."

"Sounds good," Shirley said. Why not help Miriam along in her relationship with Wayne?

Betty hurried away, and minutes later she was waving from the barn door, a look of triumph on her face. Wayne must have agreed to help. Shirley nudged Miriam again. "Come on. Our buggy will soon be ready."

Turning from her conversation with Naomi, Miriam said, "What?"

"Time to go," Shirley told her. "Wayne's getting Sally ready for us."

Miriam gasped. "Oh!"

The Kuntz sisters smiled. "Goodbye for now. We'll see you tonight at the hymn singing."

Shirley and Miriam picked up their things and walked to the barn. They greeted Betty and Wayne cheerfully. "Thank you, Wayne!" Miriam said. "But you really didn't have to help us. We're not the helpless Yoder sisters from Possum Valley."

Wayne looked at Miriam and smiled. "I was more than glad to help you."

Miriam smiled in return. "Thank you, Wayne. I appreciate this."

Chapter Thirty-Three

On a Sunday evening two weeks later, Ivan was sitting on the couch in the living room at the Swartz home. Outside, the late-summer sun hung low on the horizon. Ivan drew his gaze away from the window and forced himself to focus. Sitting beside him, Laura was fidgeting with a fold in her dress. She'd been tense all day, even when her usual sunny smile was thrown his way. He could tell from clear across the room at the church service that she had an extra crease in her jawline and wariness in her eyes. But when she climbed into his buggy after the hymn singing, she chattered nonstop all the way home and was continuing to do so even now.

"You should have been there. Aunt Martha stopped by to visit this week. She stayed for two whole hours right in the middle of corn-cutting time. At least she helped while we talked, although I'm not sure we got any more done than we would have without her. We talked about everything and anything. Aunt Martha thinks there will be plenty of weddings again this fall. She even dropped a hint about us, Ivan, although we haven't been seeing each other that long. Aunt Martha knows that full well and understands perfectly . . ."

And Ivan listened. Mostly because he expected the moment to arrive when she stopped so they could face whatever was bothering Laura. He didn't have to think long to imagine what that might be. They had never quite settled the Miriam Yoder issue to Laura's satisfaction.

Ivan returned his gaze out the living room window. He could ask what was wrong, but why do that? He didn't really want to know, and he figured Laura would get there sooner or later. Had she found out about the letter he'd written to Miriam? Miriam had never answered, so how would Laura find out? Miriam wasn't the type of girl who would blab that kind of thing around. Or maybe Laura had learned of his visits to the Yoder place in the weeks before the two young women had left for Oklahoma. Someone might have seen him and mentioned it.

Ivan stiffened when Laura cleared her throat. He was up to none of this. He'd bolt the house if she started in with questions about Miriam. What kept him here was Laura's charm and her kisses, though there had been fewer of those lately. Ivan didn't want to talk about Miriam. Surely Laura understood that.

Her voice cut through his thoughts. "I'm sorry I talked so much on the way home."

"I liked it." He looked at her. In a way it was true. Maybe not for the reasons Laura might think. He liked the sound of her voice. Also, as long as she chattered, he didn't have to worry that she'd bring up Miriam.

"Really?" Her face brightened.

"Of course!" Ivan smiled. "You're beautiful, Laura, and your voice is charming. What's not to like about you?"

She colored considerably. Her voice carried an edge when she spoke again. "Please don't lie to me, Ivan. I couldn't handle that right now."

"I'm not lying!" He stared out the window. The sky had darkened completely. Now would come the questions. And now he would leave — beautiful and charming though Laura was.

"You're not lying?"

He heard the hesitation in her voice. "No!" He turned to face her. "Why do you

346

think I'm still here?"

She flinched but rallied her nerve. "Do you like the person I am? Even though I'm shallow and immature and not like Miriam?"

"Miriam!" He made a face. "What has Miriam to do with you and me? She's not even in Possum Valley."

"What if she was?" The question came quickly. "Would you still be here . . . with me?"

Ivan sighed. "*Yah,* Laura, I would. I like you. Now can we talk about something else?"

"Then why don't you kiss me anymore?"

Her face was turned up to his endearingly, he thought. "Because I've been trying to behave myself." He looked away. "We have been going pretty fast, you know."

Her lips trembled. "Is that the only reason?"

"Of course!" He didn't try to keep the irritation out of his voice.

"Then you *do* love me?" Her arm slipped into his.

He forced himself to relax. "More than you'll ever know, Laura."

She beamed and drew closer. "Oh, Ivan! You don't know what it does to me to hear you say it. I was beginning to think you . . .

you . . ." She stopped mid-sentence. "But I won't think such things! Not about you. I can trust you, right?"

"I'll always like you, Laura." His arm tightened on hers. "There's no question about that."

She frowned. "Even though I'm not like Miriam?"

"I'm not talking about Miriam." The edge was back in his voice.

She sighed and leaned against him. "And neither do I want to talk about Miriam. I'm going to forget about her completely and only think of us."

"Suits me fine." His hand sought hers.

She looked up at him. "Did you hear what I said about what Aunt Martha said about us?"

His smile widened. "About our wedding this fall?"

The words rushed out. "Of course Aunt Martha wasn't serious, and there really isn't a wedding yet."

He reached over to touch her lips. "That's why we have to take it slow, Laura. I'd love to kiss you . . . even right now . . . but we'd better not."

The heat burned on her cheeks. "You're so noble and true, Ivan. How can I ever be worthy of you? I'll never be in a million years."

He smiled wryly. "I'm no saint, dear."

"Oh, Ivan!" She clung to his arm. "You've never called me 'dear' before! Will you always call me 'dear'? Even when I get all old and wrinkled and have borne a dozen children?"

His laugh rang through the room. "That's getting a little ahead of ourselves, isn't it?"

She snuggled against him. "I can't help thinking about such things. You'll be such a *wunderbah daett* to our children. I can't imagine one of them ever leaving the faith, or even going astray slightly. You might even be a minister someday, Ivan. I'm sure Aunt Martha would cast her vote for you."

Now his face had turned bright red. Yet her praise and confidence comforted him. Miriam would never say such things, not in a hundred years.

Her fingers stroked his face. "You'll look so *gut* in a beard, Ivan. You're handsome now, but the maturity of a beard will add so much. Every girl in the community will wish then they had put forth more effort to snag you."

He chuckled. "I'm sure you have to look long and hard to see much *gut* in me."

Her laugh was soft. "You're so modest and

humble, Ivan. And so sweet. I can't imagine what was wrong with Miriam that she couldn't see it."

He stiffened beside her. "Who says I care about what Miriam thinks?"

Her fingers stroked his arm. "You don't have to deny your admiration for Miriam, Ivan. I'm just glad you picked me. I feel honored you changed your mind."

"It's not what you think," he managed. Words rose to his lips, but he held them in. There would be no benefit in a disclosure of where his wanderings had taken him with Miriam, and from the sound of things Laura already suspected. And why should he mention that Miriam had rejected his advances?

Her voice interrupted his thoughts. "You don't have to be worried about me. I understand. I want you to love me, and I want to love you. We're made for each other. We've always been. It just took a while for you to see it."

He glanced away. "You're much too nice, Laura. You really are."

"Then we're perfectly suited for each other." She pulled his arm tight into hers. "Kiss me, Ivan. Just once tonight."

He hesitated only a moment before he pulled her close. She lifted her face to his and threw her arms around his neck. Long seconds later he pulled back for a breath as she clung to him. He whispered, "We shouldn't kiss anymore, Laura. We really shouldn't."

"But I love Ivan. I love him so much." She pulled his head down so she could kiss him again.

Ivan gave in for a moment, but he sat up straight when a door hinge squeaked somewhere. How embarrassing if Laura's parents came in. It was no scandal to be kissing, but still he knew it would bother him. They'd gone far enough, and Laura knew it. That was why she was keeping on, no doubt. The girl wanted to extract a proposal of marriage from him.

"There's no one around," Laura whispered in his ear. "Don't stop now."

"*Nee*, that's enough." He pulled away as her suggestion burned through his mind. Why couldn't they marry this fall? Laura had dropped many hints, but she couldn't come right out and ask the question herself. He needed to do it, and this was probably her way of helping him do so.

"Oh, Ivan!" She held his arm and put her head against his shoulder. "I can never get enough of you or your kisses."

In the silence Ivan's mind continued to spin. Perhaps this was a blessing in disguise.

He didn't deserve Laura's love, but here it was offered to him on a silver platter. Sure, there would be great responsibilities that came with marriage — a house to find and a wedding to plan. But Laura would do most of that. All that was required of him was to ask the question. Laura was clearly leading him in that direction . . . and had been for a long time. She knew he would give in. She wouldn't have thrown herself at him so freely otherwise. He would ask her tonight. He saw the matter with the clarity of bright daylight. She was waiting even now with her head tightly against his shoulder. She waited with confidence because she knew him well. What more could he ask for or expect in a *frau*?

Was this not the Lord's will? He'd done much in the past months he shouldn't have. What better way to cleanse his soul than to accept the responsibility of marriage. He would be a *daett* soon after, no doubt. Laura would bear him many children, and they would grow old together with love in their hearts. How could things be otherwise with the way they understood each other? Laura would always love him, and he would never tire of her affections. There was no doubt in his mind on that subject.

This would also be his way of atoning for

his dishonesty with Miriam. How had he even dared think he could marry a girl just to get a farm — even if it was the best one in the county? The corruption that had been in his heart took his breath away. Laura must have known this, yet still she loved him.

He had arrived at the moment. He reached over to stroke a wisp of hair that had escaped from under her *kapp.* "Will you marry me, Laura? Even this fall?"

Her face turned up as she looked into his eyes. "You know the answer, my love. My heart would have no greater joy."

"But how can you love me? I'm not a *gut* man. I have many flaws." His fingers moved the hair across her forehead.

Her gaze burned into his face. "*Yah,* I know you, Ivan. And I have always loved you from the moment our family moved back to Possum Valley. I know your failings, but I also know your strengths. I love you."

He lowered his head for a kiss, but she sat up. "We have lots of plans to make, so we'd better get started."

"I thought I'd get a few kisses after proposing," he said as his hand reached for hers.

A smile played on her face. "You've already had kisses tonight, my Ivan. But don't worry — there will be many more. Right now I want to think about the plans we must make. Oh, I can hardly believe it! You did ask me, didn't you? I can't believe it!"

"*Yah,* I did!" He smiled. "I did. And I still want your acceptance kiss."

"Just one." She moved closer. "And then we must plan things."

He held her for a long time, and she didn't object.

"We must invite Miriam to the wedding," she whispered when he let her go.

His face fell. "Why? I don't want her near my wedding."

"She might not even come." Her hand stroked his. "But we have to invite her. She's part of our young people's group, and it wouldn't be right not to. And if we don't, the community will talk. There's no reason not to invite her."

"I guess there isn't," he said hesitantly.

Her hand touched his face, and he pulled her close again.

CHAPTER THIRTY-FOUR

The following Monday evening Miriam was in her room upstairs with a letter from *Mamm* in her hands. There was nothing secret about the letter — both Shirley and Aunt Fannie had read it when it arrived earlier in the day. Miriam just wanted to be alone while she wrote her response. Shirley could write letters with people around her, but Miriam needed privacy.

She unfolded the letter and read the first paragraph again.

Greetings, my dear girls.

I was so glad to hear that things are going well with both of you in Oklahoma. Not that I expected otherwise, but the place seems so far away. I think of you so often. We are all doing well here in Possum Valley. Today Daett and boys worked on Mr. Bland's farm. They'll be back soon for supper . . .

Miriam laid the letter on the bed. The news that followed brought back the warmth of home. She should be homesick about now, but she wasn't. That was the surprising part. Yesterday had been another *wunderbah* day with the Clarita community's young people. The joy in her heart was still fresh. Wayne had given her the nicest smile yet, if such a thing was possible. All of his smiles were so *wunderbah.* Whether she wanted to accept them — that had always been the question. But now she knew she wanted to. That was the amazing thing. The Lord had opened up the path, but how it had all happened, she wasn't sure. She still had Ivan's letter in the bottom of her dresser drawer, right beside the five hundred and twenty dollars in cash.

Miriam squeezed her eyes shut. She wouldn't think of either Ivan or the money right now. Ivan was in the past, and she still couldn't figure out what she should do with the money. She couldn't spend it here without questions being raised, and there had been no opportunity so far to give the money away. So she would wait and trust the Lord to lead her. He always had before, and there was no reason to think He wouldn't now. Hadn't He brought her to a community in which she could find peace and the promise of new life — perhaps even true and lasting love?

The image of Wayne rose in Miriam's mind, and she allowed a smile to cross her face. The man loved her. There was no doubt about that. She would never think to question his heart now. Not after she'd been here these weeks and had been exposed to his sincerity and honesty. Wayne was the real thing. This time she wasn't mistaken. Not like she'd been with Ivan. Wayne would soon ask her home from the hymn singing for a Sunday evening date. She was sure of that. He'd almost asked her yesterday afternoon.

Wayne had asked instead, "So how do you like Oklahoma by now? And what of our community here?"

"Shirley and I both love it out here. And the people too," she'd replied.

"I'm glad to hear that." Wayne's smile had been full of his usual warmth. "I hope you'll be staying for a while yet." Then he'd cast his gaze toward the ground. "Well, see you at the hymn singing tonight then."

"Sure. I'll look forward to seeing you," she answered.

And they had parted ways.

Miriam pulled her thoughts away from what had happened yesterday and focused on the letter from *Mamm.* With quick movements she rose and gathered up pen and paper from the dresser top. With a chair pulled in front of her for a desk, she sat on the bed and wrote.

Dear Mamm,

Greetings again. Both Shirley and I send you our regards and great affection. We read your letter with joy in our hearts. It's often that we think of home and everyone there. I suppose Shirley is downstairs right now writing her own letter. I'm ensconced in my room for privacy. Seems like my thoughts come better when no one is around. I guess we were made differently.

I hope *Daett* is finding the new farm a blessing. I know you didn't mention much about this in your letter, and perhaps I shouldn't either, but the subject is never far from my mind. I sometimes wish Mr. Bland hadn't done what he did, but I know it can't be helped. And would I really want that part of my life changed? I wonder sometimes if my heart has betrayed me. Maybe I chafed under *Daett*'s lectures about the evils of money. Maybe I even desired wealth. I hope none of this is true. I've talked to the Lord about it. If it is true, I ask you and Daett for forgiveness. Now that I have experienced a little of what the world calls success, I know for sure that Daett was absolutely right. We should be content with what we have and never want more.

I don't wish to speak ill of Shirley, but I think she's struggled with that lesson, though she has learned much out here. The people here are so *wunderbah.* They teach us things without saying much. That's another reason why we're enjoying our stay so much, to say nothing of the great benefits they have been to us.

Miriam paused and put the pen down. She stared at the wall. There was so much she wished to write but couldn't. She wanted to spill her thoughts out on paper — the joy of Wayne's attention and her sorrow over how money had affected her. But what would follow would not be beneficial, especially since she hadn't told anyone about the cash inheritance. *Mamm* would never understand why Miriam had the two million dollars in the bank — if she even believed it was true. And then *Mamm* would wonder why Miriam hadn't gotten rid of it by now. Someday she hoped to find someone she could talk to about anything and even confess the turmoil in her heart. Maybe it would be Wayne . . . if he asked her on a date or to be his *frau*. She certainly couldn't marry a man and keep such a secret.

Miriam sat up and grabbed the pen. Wayne hadn't asked for a date, so she was being foolish in having such thoughts about him. Yet, she couldn't help herself. And Wayne would make a *wunderbah* husband. She was convinced of the fact the more she saw of the man. Wayne would know what she should do about her money problem. Already a measure of trust welled up in her heart, which she considered a miracle. That she could even think about trusting another man with such a secret after Ivan Mast was the Lord's doing.

Miriam pushed the thoughts of Wayne and Ivan away and wrote rapidly. When she finished she signed the letter with a flourish: "With much love, Miriam." There, that was done. Now for the other letter — the one to Ivan. She'd decided she needed to respond. She hadn't planned to, and Shirley had advised against it, but Miriam knew she had to. It wasn't decent not to let Ivan know her answer was no, she wasn't interested.

Miriam sighed. Someday she wouldn't have to sneak around — once this money problem was solved. But for now anything that it touched seemed to produce ungodly fruit. Confession was what she needed most. Miriam squirmed and stared out the window. Her face softened moments later as she breathed a quick prayer: "Help me, please, dear Lord." He will supply what she needed and guide her, Miriam reminded herself. And hopefully soon. She wrote with quick strokes on a fresh page.

Dear Ivan,

I don't want a misunderstanding to remain between us. The truth is that I will never return your affection. I don't hold anything against you. There was a time when I would have rejoiced to hear such words from you, but that time has passed. Any chance of a relationship between the two of us is over. I hope you understand.

Miriam

P.S. Hopefully there are no hard feelings between us.

She shouldn't have added that last line, Miriam thought, but it was too late now. Ivan would see the scribbles if she crossed out the words, and she didn't want to rewrite the whole letter. Let Ivan think what he would. He should be thankful she'd even responded to such a letter as his was. But she was glad she had. It was the right thing to do. Now to get the letter out to the mailbox without the household knowing about it.

Miriam jumped when Aunt Fannie called up the stairs. "There's someone here to see you, Miriam."

Had Wayne arrived to ask her home on a Sunday evening date? How appropriate that would be after writing to Ivan. Maybe this was what the Lord had waited on — the moment when she made things right in her past. How else could this coincidence be explained? She'd only written the final words to Ivan just seconds before. Miriam drew in a deep breath, gathered up the correspondence, and headed downstairs.

Aunt Fannie met her at the bottom of the stairs. "Deacon Phillip is here. He's waiting for you out on the front porch."

"Deacon Phillip?" The living room swam before Miriam's eyes. "I haven't done anything wrong that I know of."

Aunt Fannie laughed. "Silly you. Nobody said you did anything wrong."

But I was expecting Wayne. The words

almost slipped out.

Aunt Fannie pointed toward the front door as if Miriam didn't know which way to go.

Shirley, sitting at a desk and writing a letter, gave Miriam a sympathetic glance as she walked past. Did Shirley know what was going on? Miriam pasted on a smile as she stepped outside. She barely knew the deacon. She'd seen him sitting on the ministers' bench each Sunday, of course. He was a young man, recently married. He now turned toward her with a friendly look.

"I hope I'm not disturbing you tonight, Miriam."

"Of course not." Miriam steadied herself against the porch railing with one hand.

"Maybe you want to sit?" The deacon motioned toward one of the rocking chairs.

Miriam shook her head. She felt better on her feet at the moment — whatever this visit was about.

Deacon Phillip coughed. "I'll keep this short. I hope I don't shock you with our request. You may find it unexpected."

"Request?"

"*Yah.* The school board met last week, and they asked if I would come and speak with you." Deacon Phillip let a small grin creep across his face. "The others said they were too busy this week to come, so here I am."

"What would they want from me?" Miriam asked.

"I know this is short notice, but . . ." Deacon Phillip smiled. "Well, we'd like you to consider teaching our community's school this term. It starts in a few weeks." A nervous laugh escaped his lips. "I don't know what we'll do if you say no, but I'll say this much. The school board thought of asking you the first week you arrived, but we didn't want to rush into anything. And we wished to observe your life. I did write Bishop Wagler in Possum Valley for his recommendation of you." Deacon Phillip lowered his head. "I hope you're not offended."

"No, not in the least, but . . ." Miriam groped for what to say. "This is . . . such a surprise . . . and . . . well, an honor." She paused. "I'm curious as to what Bishop Wagler had to say. I know I'm not perfect . . ."

Deacon Phillip chuckled. "You don't have to worry on that matter. Bishop Wagler had only glowing praise for you, Miriam. He seemed to think highly of your *daett* and your entire family. So what do you think? Will you teach for us?"

Miriam clutched the handrail. "I've never taught before."

"You seem to have the maturity the job needs." Deacon Phillip's tone was encouraging. "You would have to commit to staying a year out here, at least until next May."

"I understand." Miriam paused again. "I never expected this. I've never thought about me as a teacher."

Deacon Phillip said, "Sometimes that attitude makes for the best teachers, Miriam. Pride is an awful thing to have in one's heart."

Pride. What would the deacon say if he knew she had a secret bank account with two million dollars in it? And that she'd not even told her family about it. Miriam pushed those thoughts away. She wouldn't pass up this chance to work.

"I need to pray about this, but I think I'll do it." The words came out a whisper. "And thank you for asking."

"I think we owe you thanks." Deacon Phillip chuckled. "You'll make a great teacher, Miriam. A really great one!"

Chapter Thirty-Five

Shirley stared out the window at Deacon Phillip's retreating buggy. "What on earth did he want?" she asked Miriam, who was back inside and sitting on the couch.

"She's probably excommunicated already," Uncle William teased. He laid his copy of *The Budget* on his lap with a smile on his face.

"Don't joke about such things!" Aunt Fannie scolded mildly from the kitchen doorway. Baby Jonathon was in her arms, and at that moment he released a loud wail.

"See, there's trouble in the air." Shirley went over to sit beside Miriam. "Now, tell us all about it."

"I'm sure there was only *gut* news," Uncle William offered, although he appeared puzzled by the visit as well.

"Are you going to tell us?" Shirley prompted.

"They want me to teach at the school this term."

"Teach?" Comprehension slowly dawned on Shirley.

"That is *wunderbah* news!" Aunt Fannie said, taking her seat in her rocker with a now-quiet Jonathon on her lap.

Uncle William glowed. "Seems the community has accepted you just fine — and you too, Shirley." He nodded in Shirley's direction before turning again to Miriam. "I'd say this is quite an honor."

Shirley still stood by the window. "Miriam hasn't said whether she accepted."

Miriam stood up. "I told them I'd pray about it but likely accept. But I can change my answer if you object."

Shirley's smile was a bit forced. "I don't want to teach, if that's what you're asking. And this is a great honor for you. Why would I object?"

"There's no reason to object," Uncle William spoke up. "This is a great compliment."

"And it speaks well of you too," Miriam said to Shirley, Aunt Fannie, and Uncle William.

Shirley didn't seem to hear as she turned her attention to the window again. "Another buggy just pulled into the driveway," she announced. "I wonder who it is? Oh, Wayne Yutzy, of all people."

"What could he want?" Aunt Fannie asked, patting the baby on his back.

Miriam knew what Wayne wanted. And now that the moment had arrived, her body felt numb. Hadn't she expected and looked forward to this visit?

"I expect I know what he wants," Uncle William said with a little grin on his face.

Aunt Fannie glanced at him. "Of course! What's wrong with me. And the house such a mess. What are we going to do?"

"Well, I guess I'm not needed for the evening." Shirley turned and headed for the upstairs.

Miriam stood and stopped Shirley with a touch on her arm. "Please, Shirley. I don't want you to be upset."

Shirley met Miriam's gaze. "I know. And I didn't mean that remark to sound as short as it did. Just give me some time, and I'll be okay."

Miriam hesitated.

Shirley smiled and gave Miriam a gentle push toward the front door. "Don't pass up your chance at happiness, Miriam." Then Shirley went up the stairs with quick steps.

Miriam watched her until she disappeared through her bedroom doorway. Shirley would be okay. They would talk more later. Right now she needed to focus on Wayne. She went out the front door and stood on the porch. She noticed Wayne already had his horse tied and was halfway to the house. She stepped out and met him at the bottom of the steps. With a bright smile she said, "*Gut* evening, Wayne. What a surprise."

"I like surprises," Wayne answered, matching Miriam's smile. "I hope you do."

Miriam retreated a step. "We can sit on the front porch, if you'd like."

Wayne didn't answer as he glanced down the road. "Did I just pass Deacon Phillip's buggy?"

Miriam didn't hesitate. "He was here. I'm to be excommunicated next Sunday."

Wayne blinked twice. "Say again?"

Miriam laughed. "That was Uncle William's joke. Sorry."

"Now you're trying to scare me." A grin spread slowly across his face. "So what did the deacon want? Is Uncle William in trouble?"

"*Nee.*" Miriam took a seat on a front porch rocker. "He came with an offer for me to teach school here this term."

Wayne's face lit up. "That's great! An excellent idea, if I must say so myself. You'll be awesome."

"Awesome? Don't you think that's a bit too much? I'll settle for *gut.*"

"Not from what I know of you and your sister." Wayne settled into the other chair. "I'd say you're being taken right into the community. I think Oklahoma has been waiting for you."

Miriam lowered her head. Praise and attention were still so new to her. And now Wayne Yutzy was sitting on the front porch with her. If pride hadn't already crept into her heart, it might arrive now.

Wayne continued as if he hadn't noticed her reaction. "People have been saying so many nice things about you. I'm not surprised that the school board has asked you to teach."

"They probably didn't have anyone else."

Wayne laughed. "It is a little late in the summer, so maybe that's partly true. But don't let that deceive you. We don't just settle for anyone, especially when it comes to teaching our children."

"That's a comfort to know." Miriam heard the thrill in her voice because his words brought comfort . . . great comfort.

Wayne glanced her way. "I'm sure you passed the interview with flying colors."

"Not everything is always like it seems," Miriam said, as thoughts of her inheritance flashed through her mind.

As if he understood her thoughts, Wayne said, "I have to give you credit. You haven't flaunted your financial status either. We've all heard about the farm you inherited and gave to your parents."

Miriam took a deep breath. "*Yah.* Mr. Bland's farm." Hopefully her face hadn't gone red. "I figured people knew, but I try not to think about it."

Wayne nodded. "That speaks to your *gut* character, I'm sure. Would you mind sharing a little of the experience with me? I hope you don't think that's forward, but I'd like to know."

Miriam glanced down at her hands. "I'd be glad to." A measure of relief flooded her. Wayne cared about her. He really did or he wouldn't want to know her history. He wanted to know the details of how things had gone down. He wasn't asking because he wanted her money. Tears stung her eyes. Someday she would tell Wayne the entire truth, but for now she'd answer his questions and see how it felt. The Lord understood her heart and knew she didn't wish to deceive anyone. She just needed to be cautious. She hadn't asked to receive the land and money from Mr. Bland or to walk this road of riches. It was a different path from any she'd ever imagined. Was she to be blamed if she faltered or didn't do everything right?

Miriam found her voice again as Wayne waited patiently. "I liked Mr. Bland a lot. I worked for him as his caregiver for a few years before he died . . . during the daytime, of course. He was a kind old man, and I enjoyed working for him. I had no idea he planned to leave me anything when he passed on. In fact, *Mamm* and I expected him to live for many more years. It wasn't like he was sick or couldn't take care of himself. He was alone at night, and his sister, Rose, took care of him on the weekends. Well, most weekends. I primarily cleaned the house, fixed meals, and visited with him." Miriam paused to catch her breath. "And then he died one morning. Unexpectedly . . . on the front porch. I'd taken him out for a breath of fresh air and then went into the kitchen to fix breakfast. We were the only people there at the time." Miriam hesitated. "Mr. Bland dreamed of his wife the night before. She'd passed on years earlier, but he told me he'd seen her again. Maybe she came for him . . . with the angels. He was *Englisha*. He was also a *gut* man, so I'm sure the Lord took care of him."

Wayne was listening intently. "I'm sure the Lord did if He sent you to care for him."

"You shouldn't say that." Miriam felt the blood rush up her neck. Why did Wayne say such nice things? Should she be blunt and just ask the question on her heart? *Yah,* she should and just get it over with. She gave Wayne a searching look. "I know you like me, and I like you. We haven't dated, but I know you're interested. I have to ask because I've discovered it does make a difference to some people. Although I've given the farm to my *daett,* he intends to give it back to me when I marry. You're not here because I will have a farm someday . . . are you?"

Wayne smiled and didn't look offended. He chuckled before saying, "I haven't really thought about such things, but I guess I can see where that might be an advantage to the man who manages to win your hand in marriage." He colored slightly. "Do I have to solidify my intentions this early in the game? We don't know each other that well, and I haven't even said yet what I came for."

Miriam smiled although her face was still red. This *gut* man was blameless, and she'd done nothing more than stick her foot in her mouth.

Wayne obviously relaxed as he cleared his

throat. "I'm sorry if I've given you cause to suspect my character."

Miriam looked at him. "I think I'm the one to apologize. You haven't given me cause. Back home I ran into that problem, so I guess I'm a little hesitant."

Wayne's voice was gentle. "Maybe you'd best move on with your story." He shifted on his chair. "So did you attend this Mr. Bland's funeral?"

Miriam nodded. "With his sister, Rose. She picked me up."

"That was nice of you." Silence fell again, until Wayne reached for her hand and gave a quick squeeze. "I'm glad you found your way out here to Oklahoma, Miriam."

Miriam's heart pounded. "So am I."

A smile spread across Wayne's face. "Then our feelings are mutual."

Miriam choked a bit as she admitted, "To be completely honest, I guess my motives for coming to Oklahoma weren't all that pure. I was running away from problems at home." She wanted to tell him why she'd been so reluctant.

Wayne shrugged. "I suppose we all have them."

Words continued to spill out. "Did you ever have an old girlfriend who rejected you, and then she wanted to start over when she found out you'd inherited a nice farm?"

Wayne grimaced. "No. Is that what happened to you?"

Miriam held back her tears. "*Yah.* Ivan began dating someone else. But when Mr. Bland died and left me the farm, he wanted me back."

"Do you still care for him? Do you want him back?"

"*Nee!*" Miriam exclaimed. "I don't. Really, I don't. But he was . . ." She paused. This talk was getting more serious than she was ready for. She tried again. "Anyway, I thought it would be *gut* to come here for a fresh start. The Lord opened the doors for us to help Aunt Fannie with her new baby. It's been good for Shirley too. I don't wish myself back in Possum Valley at all. Not for one moment. I like everything about Oklahoma, about the community, about . . ." Miriam stopped suddenly. Wayne knew what she'd almost said. She could tell by the look on his face. And his response was all she could have hoped for.

His hand reached across the space between them and touched her arm again. This time his hand rested on hers and stayed there.

She felt the gentleness in his touch. She didn't move or even dare to breathe.

His gaze sought hers, and she met his look. "I didn't come over here tonight to talk about farms and former flames." His voice revealed sweet tenderness. "I'd like to bring you home from the hymn singing on Sunday night, if that's all right with you." His look was open and expectant. "The Lord has brought you out here, Miriam. And He's opened my heart to you. All these years I've never dated or even asked a girl home from a hymn singing. But now I feel He's telling me the time has come. So, please, Miriam, don't say no."

Like she could do that! Miriam almost laughed at the thought. She would never say no to dating this man. Not in a million years. And her secrets would be safe with him. Someday she'd tell him everything — when the right time came. Until then, the love budding within her heart for Wayne would continue to grow.

"Yah," Miriam whispered. "I would be greatly honored to have you bring me home on Sunday evening."

CHAPTER THIRTY-SIX

Thursday morning Miriam awoke before the first signs of dawn had broken through the eastern sky. Uncle William had asked her to help in the greenhouse today. That meant she would see Wayne, and they might have a chance for a few words together — in between their work, of course. Work couldn't suffer because that wouldn't be right. The chairman of the school board, Ezra Mullet, planned to stop early this morning with more details on the teaching job. Miriam hurried to dress and then rushed down to the kitchen where the kerosene lamp had been lit and set on the table.

Aunt Fannie glanced up at her. "What are you doing up so early?"

Miriam groaned. "I couldn't sleep, so I thought I might as well make breakfast. I'm sure you have plenty of things to do, so you won't mind."

"You're still all atwitter over Wayne asking to bring you home after the hymn singing. That's what this is about, isn't it?" Aunt Fannie asked knowingly.

"I guess so," Miriam agreed. If her aunt only knew how atwitter she was! She was looking forward to this morning and to the planned Sunday evening with Wayne.

Aunt Fannie regarded Miriam for a moment. "You *are* atwitter . . . or troubled. I can't tell which. Surely you and Wayne didn't have a falling out all ready."

"Oh, no. It's not that!"

Aunt Fannie appeared relieved. "Confusion comes and goes when you're in love, so don't worry about how it will go."

"I'll try not to," Miriam agreed.

"Gut!" Aunt Fannie touched Miriam on the shoulder as if to give her courage before leaving the kitchen. "And thank you for making breakfast."

Miriam smiled. Aunt Fannie didn't understand the full extent of her predicament, but she was supportive. Wayne had offered Miriam love with an open and honest hand, and Miriam was accepting it — but also keeping a huge secret from him. When should she tell Wayne about the money? It was still early in their relationship. She didn't have the courage to confess because she was afraid the love and adoration in his eyes might vanish or be tainted by the knowledge. So the miserable secret would have to remain that way until Wayne had asked to wed her — if he did. And maybe she'd even wait until they'd said the sacred vows together. She would surprise him then. What a wedding present! Wouldn't any husband appreciate waking up the morning after his wedding and finding out his *frau* had substantial funds in a bank account?

Miriam placed a pan on the stove for the eggs. There was no hurry to get started on breakfast, but at the moment she wanted the distraction. If she didn't slow down, breakfast would be ready and cold long before the family's usual time to eat. Indeed, she was all atwitter, she decided. She'd have to trust the Lord and leave romance plans in His capable hands.

"What are you up to?" Shirley's voice broke into Miriam's thoughts.

Miriam jumped before whispering, "Hush, you'll wake the house."

Shirley came into the kitchen. "What's gotten into you anyway?"

"What does it look like I'm doing? I'm getting ready to fix breakfast."

"I can see that." Shirley frowned. "But it's early — even for you."

I've been thinking of Wayne, Miriam almost admitted. She stopped herself. Shirley had spoken very little about Wayne since Monday night. Miriam had tried several times to share about him, but Shirley always changed the subject. Was this quiet time in the early morning hours an opportunity for a sisterly heart-to-heart? She took a quick breath. "Shirley, can we talk about . . . about what we've been avoiding since Monday? About what's bothering you?"

Shirley paused by the kitchen sink. "I've been struggling with how much the community has accepted you, including Wayne, and now they've offered you the teaching position. I'm glad for you. I'm sure you've sensed that, haven't you?"

"Yah." Miriam waited.

"I *am* glad for you. I think it's *wunderbah.* I just feel left out." Shirley fiddled with the empty dish-drainer rack. "I would take the chance you're being given in a heartbeat. I told you Monday night not to pass this up. But in my heart I wonder why I'm not receiving blessings from the Lord too."

"But you are! You are blessed. You've always been."

"That's what I used to think. But look at my state now." Shirley's tone was mournful. "And right in the middle of a community that is so *gut.* I can't seem to become part of things here. I want to, but I don't seem to really fit."

"Maybe it's not your fault. Maybe . . ." Miriam searched for the right words. What she wanted to say was, *Maybe the Lord is bringing correction to your life.* But that didn't sound kind and wouldn't be encouraging. It might even come across as prideful since everything was going so well regarding her situation.

"I want to live a godly life." Shirley stared out the window at the dark horizon. "I've always wanted to. I knew that running around with Jonas wasn't right, but still I did it because it was so fun, and enjoyable, and exciting. I broke it off to come here and hopefully find God's blessing on my life. But what I've found is . . . well, it's boring. No eligible men seem interested in me, especially not like Wayne does to you. Even Mahlon Troyer, who doesn't have a fraction of the money Jonas has, thinks me worthy of a mere hello. Do you understand what I'm saying, Miriam?"

"I do, but I'm at a loss regarding what advice to offer," Miriam admitted. "I don't know what to say. I'm no saint, and I never expected to be blessed this way."

"I am thrilled for you." Shirley gave Miriam a quick hug. "It's just hard to watch when I feel like I'm standing outside in the cold, that's all. And now you're going to be a schoolteacher. I wish some excitement would come along in my life."

"You'd better not wish for my troubles, sister. You don't know the half of what I'm dealing with."

Shirley's smile was weak. "I suppose I don't. But thanks for listening and trying to understand, at least."

"I wish I could do more for you," Miriam said as she turned back to the stove.

There were faint noises coming from the downstairs bedroom, so Uncle William would be out soon to eat an early breakfast. Shirley set the table. Uncle William's cheerful face soon appeared in the kitchen doorway, followed by the rest of his body as he came in. "What kind of service have we got here? Breakfast already?"

Miriam wrinkled her face. "*Yah,* it's a little early, I know."

"The better to begin the day!" Uncle William didn't appear disappointed. He vanished, only to reappear with his Bible. With a flourish he pulled out a kitchen chair and sat down. His lips moved as he scanned some of the pages. Aunt Fannie entered the kitchen. She squeezed his shoulders, and the two exchanged loving smiles.

Miriam transferred the skillet of bacon to the table, along with the eggs. "Everybody sit down, and we can eat."

Aunt Fannie's face beamed. "My, my, I feel like a queen in my own house!"

"You don't mind an early breakfast then?" Miriam asked.

"Not at all," Aunt Fannie assured her. "But that doesn't mean you have to do this every morning."

Uncle William laughed. "It would be nice though."

Aunt Fannie playfully slapped him on the arm. "You'll have the girls believing that, so quit it."

They were all laughing as Miriam and Shirley took their seats. Uncle William led out in prayer:

Now unto You, oh God, the great Creator of heaven and earth, be glory and honor and praise. Mighty are Your works, and everlasting is the strength of Your arm. Remember now Your children and the creation of Your hands as we forget not Your lovingkindness toward us. Give us power this day to walk in Your will and wisdom to understand the guiding of Your Holy Spirit. Forsake us not and then call us home to the glories of Your heaven.

Bless also the food that Miriam and Shirley have prepared. Bless their willing hands and hearts. Remember them with favor and grace. Do likewise to those of our families who stand in need today. Give us of Your abundance, for which we give You deep and heartfelt thanks. Amen.

"Amen," the others echoed. Shirley helped Miriam pass the food as silence settled over the table. The quiet moments of the early morning hour gave one a peace and tranquility in the midst of the rush of the day that would soon be upon them.

When they finished eating, Uncle William opened the Bible and began to read from Psalm 8: "O LORD our Lord, how excellent is thy name in all the earth! . . . When I consider the heavens, the work of thy fingers, the moon and the stars, which thou hast ordained; what is man, that thou art mindful of him? and the son of man, that thou visitest him?"

Miriam could understand that sentiment. Why was she experiencing all these blessings from the Lord? Why wasn't Shirley? Was there something she could do to help and encourage her sister?

"O LORD our Lord, how excellent is thy

name in all the earth!" Uncle William concluded and closed his Bible. A hush settled over the table.

It was broken when Aunt Fannie bounced to her feet. "No sense in daylight a'wasting."

"I'll do the dishes," Miriam offered.

"You'll do no such thing." Aunt Fannie sent Miriam off with a wave of her hand. "Shirley will help me because you're helping in the greenhouse. Get on outside and start your day."

Uncle William grinned from the kitchen doorway. "I'll put her to work, don't worry about that."

"Not too much work," Aunt Fannie said as she shook her finger at him.

He laughed.

Uncle William would do nothing of the sort, Miriam thought as she followed him out the front door. As she suspected, they were only a few feet away from the house when he told her, "Take five or ten minutes and enjoy the beautiful morning. I'll be in the greenhouse getting things started."

Miriam cleared her throat. "Those were *wunderbah* words you read this morning. Thank you."

"They also spoke to me." Uncle William gave Miriam a kind look before he turned, walked to the greenhouse, and then disappeared inside.

Miriam had returned his look and now continued to stroll. Her uncle knew more than he let on, she decided. He might even have chosen those words especially for her this morning. The thought sent warmth through her heart. She didn't deserve any of the blessings God was raining down on her life right now. But then she supposed no one really did. They were blessed by God because of His great mercy and grace.

With slow steps Miriam moved among the greenery lined up along the side of the greenhouse. The sun had peeked over the horizon, but the dew still lay heavy on everything. She touched the wetness with her fingers and tasted the moisture. This was water from heaven that the Lord gave. Her soul had been blessed this morning with the Word of God and His creation. Like the thirsty ground and water, she'd soaked in the Word's sweetness. Surely before long there would be answers to her problems. Eventually, if they continued dating, she would tell Wayne about the money. And after that, even if Wayne was the saint she expected him to be and said the money didn't mean a lot to him and wouldn't change his plans — there was still . . . well, what to do with the money. What would they do with such a large sum? She hadn't forgotten her *daett*'s many warnings about the corrupt influence money had on people's souls.

Miriam lifted her face toward the sun and shielded her eyes from its brightness. She didn't know the answers to her questions . . . and perhaps she didn't wish to know because then she'd have to make some difficult decisions.

CHAPTER THIRTY-SEVEN

Thirty minutes later Miriam was watching from inside the greenhouse as Wayne's buggy pulled into the driveway. She shouldn't hide here like a sneaky child, Miriam told herself. But the thought of her secret and telling Wayne about it had caused her heartbeat to accelerate. If Wayne saw her with this flushed face, he'd think she was ill.

Thankfully Uncle William was at the other end of the building and hadn't seen this acute tension attack that had gripped her. Perhaps if she hurried out and helped Wayne unhitch he would attribute her appearance to her rush to lend a hand. She forced herself to run outside, but slowed down when Wayne caught sight of her. His face lit up with a cheerful smile. "*Gut* morning, teacher!" he hollered from where he'd parked by the barn.

"*Gut* morning!" she called.

As she approached, Wayne was busy with a stubborn tug. He didn't seem to notice anything different about her.

"Stuck!" he muttered. Seconds later the leather piece came off with a jerk. Wayne laughed. "See? You fixed the problem just by walking up. Your grace flowed right over me and solved the problem."

"I did no such thing!" Miriam retorted with a half smile. "And you embarrassed me with that teacher stuff. I haven't even taught my first class."

Wayne grinned. "Maybe, but that's still my opinion. So let's not quarrel this early in the morning, seeing as we get to work together all day."

"Suits me."

Miriam waited while Wayne took his horse into the barn. She should get busy before he returned, but she was rooted to the ground. What if she followed Wayne around all day unable to think of anything except telling him about the money? But really, she shouldn't tell Wayne on Uncle William's time while they were at work. Such a startling revelation needed time to be absorbed and responded to, all of which couldn't be done while Wayne focused on work. But how could she look forward to Sunday evening with Wayne with this cloud of secrecy still over her head? Or even getting through today. She wanted to enjoy Wayne's teases and light chatter. And she would! The Lord would help her. She must forget about the money for now.

Wayne appeared again. He closed the barn door and walked toward her with quick steps. Miriam rubbed her face with both hands and smiled. "Got your horse all tucked in and tidy for the day?"

Wayne gave her a quick grin. "Yep. I'm ready for work. You didn't have to wait for me."

"I wanted to." Together they walked toward the greenhouse. She couldn't seem to stem her voice around Wayne. She chattered away, the words coming out in what seemed to her a torrent. She didn't dare glance at his face as she continued on about the weather, the morning, and anything else that popped into her mind. *Be quiet!* she told herself to no avail.

As they neared the doorway, Miriam finally stemmed the flow of words.

Wayne paused, and his words stopped her short.

"I'm looking forward to Sunday evening," he said.

Miriam reached for the doorframe with one hand to steady herself. "So am I,

390

Wayne. But there's something I have to tell you then. Something important."

"Deep, dark secrets." His grin was broad.

Obviously he had no idea how deep and dark her secrets were. "Maybe," Miriam managed. "I'm sorry for bringing it up here. I know we have work to do."

"Don't worry about it." His hand reached out to brush her arm. "I just want to spend time with you, Miriam. You don't have to talk about anything you don't want to. Just serve me pie and ice cream and cheesecake and I'll go home happy."

"All of that?"

His grip was firm as he held her arm this time. "I'm teasing. You don't have to serve anything. I'm just thankful to have learned to know you the little that I have. And I'll be thankful for a few more hours spent with you. Don't take your troubles — whatever they are, too seriously. We all have our imperfections and flaws, you know."

"You have flaws?" She steadied herself with both hands.

He laughed. "*Yah,* but I'm not telling you them. At least not on the first date, so don't think you have to spill your secrets either. I'm hoping we'll have many more chances to get to know each other in a deeper way."

"Oh, Wayne!" Miriam let go of the doorframe. "Thank you for understanding. But I still think I should tell you what's on my mind before we get much deeper into this relationship."

His smile was warm. "I'm touched how serious you're taking this. It's a *gut* sign to me. I hope the Lord blesses you for it — as I know He will."

Miriam nodded. "The Lord wants us to be honest. That's what *Daett* taught me."

"And he's done that well, I'm sure." Wayne slipped past her as Uncle William appeared from around some potted plants. "I'd better get to work."

"I know," Miriam whispered after him. "Me too."

"No dating on my time now!" Uncle William teased. "There's work to be done."

"Just a few looks and whispers here and there, I promise," Wayne shot back. They both laughed.

Uncle William gave instructions to Wayne as a buggy pulled into the driveway, right after an *Englisha* car parked in front of the greenhouse.

From a distance, it looked like Ezra Mullet, the school-board chairman, but Miriam wasn't sure. The Lord knew she needed a distraction right now and timed this so perfectly. After a long, serious talk about school matters surely her mind would be in a much better state. She'd be ready to concentrate on work.

Although Wayne said they didn't have to spill secrets until they got to know each other more, she really wanted to tell him. She counted on him to understand and help her. Well, at least he'd understand *why* she felt she had to tell him. The thought of what Wayne would do beyond that sent a shiver up her spine. If he rejected her for keeping such a secret from everyone, that would have repercussions far and wide. Ezra Mullet might even reconsider her qualification as the community's schoolteacher.

With steady steps Miriam approached the buggy. Ezra peered out with a pleased look on his face. His voice boomed in the morning air. "Just the girl I want to see! And I didn't even have to go looking for you."

Miriam paused near the buggy. "Uncle William told me you might be by this morning."

Ezra glanced toward the greenhouse. "I hope I'm not interrupting your work. I tried to get here right after chore time, but the morning is getting on, I know."

"It's okay," Miriam assured him. "We're not busy yet." Wayne appeared briefly in the greenhouse doorway. He waved and disappeared again.

"Nice young man there," Ezra said. "Not that it's any of my business, but that's one of the questions we must ask our prospective teachers. Are you dating at this time?"

Miriam felt her neck getting warm. "Wayne has asked if he can bring me home Sunday evening after the next hymn singing."

Ezra appeared quite pleased. "There's nothing wrong with that. Wayne's an up-building member of the community. I see you're fitting right in. That's what we like to see in our teachers. Oklahoma isn't for everyone, and we don't want you to hightail it back to Possum Valley in the middle of the term."

"Oh, I wouldn't do that," Miriam said firmly. But what would she do if it didn't work out with Wayne? Would she still be willing to stay in the Clarita community? Her head pounded. She couldn't approach Ezra later next week and tell him that she did, indeed, plan to return to Possum Valley after all — and in total disgrace. She had to clear this matter up with Wayne as soon as possible.

"Is something wrong?" Ezra scrutinized her face.

"I was just thinking through the responsibilities," Miriam shared. "You really don't know that much about me. Perhaps I'm not the best person for the position?"

A slight smile crept across Ezra's face. "So that's what's wrong? Thinking about us, are you? Well . . . we know enough, I would say. But we appreciate your concern. It speaks well for your character, as has everything else I've heard. I confess that Deacon Phillip wrote to your bishop back in Holmes County . . . a Bishop Wagler. He had only *gut* things to say. I'm sure there are no complaints the bishop doesn't know about."

He meant that as a question, Miriam was sure. She met Ezra's gaze. "I've behaved myself. I mean, how many *ordnung* rules can a girl break? I'm done with *rumspringa,* and I joined the church a year ago already."

Ezra nodded. "I'm glad to hear that. We don't practice *rumspringa* here. It's refreshing to see a young person from somewhere else make up her mind at such a young age." Ezra paused. "How old are you?"

"Twenty." Miriam glanced at him. "I thought that would be the first question you'd ask."

Ezra grinned. "Never ask a woman's age — at least not at first. I wasn't too far off. I guessed twenty-one."

"Thank you," Miriam said with a smile.

She decided she'd take his guess as a compliment.

Ezra continued. "As you probably know, our school isn't a large one. You will teach all eight grades, and there are a few pupils in every class this term. Will that be a problem?" He studied her carefully.

Miriam hesitated. "I haven't taught before, so I'm not sure." But her answer seemed to satisfy him.

"It'll be a learning experience, I'm sure. You'll be pleased to know that our teacher from last year, Sarah Mullet, my niece, has agreed to help you. She married last fall and is expecting her first child. That's why she's not teaching this year."

"I'm sure I'll have plenty of questions, although I can't think of any right now. I hope she'll meet with me before school starts."

Ezra laughed. "First-term jitters, *yah*. Well, that's *gut* too. Overconfidence isn't the best approach, I say. In life or anywhere else."

"I agree," Miriam said at once. "And thank you for this chance. I can't say how grateful and honored I am."

"You are more than welcome." Ezra jiggled the buggy lines. "I guess I'd best be going then so you can get to work. I'm sure you'll be an outstanding teacher for us." He clucked to his horse and said, "See you later" as the horse turned to head back down the driveway.

Miriam waited a few moments and watched until Ezra was gone from the driveway. The parking lot had begun to fill up with cars while she spoke with him. Uncle William and Wayne probably had their hands full, but they'd survived so far, she thought. A few more minutes wouldn't hurt. She needed to slow down the thoughts buzzing through her head. A quick trip to the mailbox would be just the thing. There might even be a letter from *Mamm.* That would bring a much-needed sense of familiarity with all the new things happening around her.

Miriam put her thought into action. She walked to the mailbox and found a pile of mail inside. She flipped through the items on the walk back to the house. There was a letter postmarked Berlin, Ohio, but the handwriting was unfamiliar. Shirley met Miriam at the front door, and she handed her the letter since it was addressed to both of them.

Shirley wasted no time ripping the envelope open. She scanned the page, and her face lit up. "It's another girl, Miriam! *Mamm* and *Daett* named her Anna, after our great-aunt on *Mamm*'s side. Naomi's the one who's written to us about it."

"Isn't it a little early for the baby?" Miriam took a deep breath. "I didn't think it would be this soon."

Shirley read on. "Naomi doesn't say anything about that. Just that all went well. Oh, this is so exciting. We have a new sister!"

So the letter contained *gut* news. Miriam heaved a sigh of relief. Now, it was time to get to work.

CHAPTER THIRTY-EIGHT

On Sunday evening after the hymn singing, Miriam waited beside Wayne's buggy as he disappeared into the Byler barn with his horse. Soft moonlight flooded the countryside. Miriam took in a deep breath of the summer air. Tonight had been a wonderful evening so far, and she was confident it would continue. She'd baked a cherry pie yesterday, and Uncle William had helped her make homemade vanilla ice cream last night. They'd eaten some for supper, and Aunt Fannie had declared the effort perfect. The rest was in the freezer for tonight. Everything was ready.

Now, if her heart would cease its heavy pounding she might be able to relax. There was no reason to be anxious, Miriam told herself. Wayne had been his usual kind and gentle self on the way home from Deacon Phillip's place, where the hymn singing had been held.

She took another deep breath. Silence hung heavy in the air, and she took in ghostly shapes formed by the plants outside the greenhouse. Aunt Fannie and Uncle William would be asleep now, along with baby Jonathon — or so she hoped. Even if they weren't, no one would hang around since this was her first date with Wayne. The living room would be theirs for the evening.

That thought brought a tinge of sadness. Shirley wouldn't be around either. She'd hurriedly headed home to Possum Valley right after the news of baby Anna's birth. In fact, Miriam guessed that about now *Mamm* and *Daett* would be on their way to the bus station with a hired driver to pick her up. Shirley was scheduled to arrive a little before midnight, Ohio time.

The whole thing had been so sudden — the arrival of the letter with the news of baby Anna's birth and Shirley's sudden announcement that she would return home immediately. She used the excuse that she needed to help *Mamm* now that the baby had arrived. Miriam knew this wasn't the real reason. Shirley had given up on finding happiness in Oklahoma. In a way, Miriam felt like she'd failed her sister.

But Shirley's problems paled right now in comparison to her own, Miriam decided.

She feared how this evening would end despite her prayers and her trust in Wayne. Her faith was weak, but surely the Lord understood. He would carry her onward.

She might never have another moment like this, Miriam reminded herself as Wayne came toward her in the moonlight. She had a *wunderbah* boyfriend in hand — someone who loved her. She would risk all to tell him the truth. It must be done.

Wayne's face broke into a broad smile as he walked up to her. His hand moved forward for a moment, as if he meant to reach for hers.

Miriam trembled. She didn't dare reach for him, although Wayne's hand in hers would be heaven on earth.

"Nice evening," Wayne said as he gestured toward the house. "Are you ready to go inside?"

"Maybe we can stay out here a few more minutes." Miriam clutched the buggy wheel. "It's so lovely in the moonlight."

Wayne grinned. "Anywhere with you is fine with me, Miriam. And I must agree it's lovely. These prairie nights with a full moon have their own special glory."

Miriam laughed nervously. "It's my first summer here, so I want to enjoy it to the fullest."

"Hopefully there will be many more." Wayne gave her a quick glance before he turned his gaze at the full moon.

The light that flooded his face showed a hint of stubble. Once Wayne had a *frau,* his beard would grow full and long. Miriam turned the thought away at once. This was not for her to think about. Not until she'd made her confession. And wouldn't out here in the moonlight be a better place to tell him than on the couch in the living room? She couldn't see Wayne's face as easily out here, but then neither could he see hers.

"Wayne?" Miriam gathered herself together. "Do you remember I said I had something important I wanted to tell you?"

He seemed to think for a moment. "Yah, I remember, but you don't have to." His voice was quiet. "Whatever it is, Miriam, I'm fine with it."

She searched his face. "What if I've committed a grave sin? Wouldn't you want to know that?"

His voice was confident as he said, "You haven't. I know it."

Her heart beat faster. What confidence this man had in her. It took her breath away.

"I'm sure you haven't done anything extraordinarily wrong, Miriam. No one is perfect, but I'm sure you come close." He reached over and squeezed her hand.

She held on for a moment before she let go. "There's more to the story of my inheritance from Mr. Bland, Wayne. I want to share something with you that I haven't told anyone else — not even my family."

He waited calmly and patiently.

When Wayne didn't say anything, Miriam continued. "Mr. Bland left me the farm, which is now set up in a trust to benefit my family. None of us can sell it without the consent of the others. But Mr. Bland didn't just leave me his farm. He left me enough money to operate it — and much more. He bequeathed two million dollars to me. The money is in a bank account under my name."

He stared at her, and then looked back at the moon.

Minutes that seemed like hours ticked by.

"Please say something, Wayne," she whispered.

He shrugged. "What am I supposed to say? Do you think that changes anything in my mind? That I might be impressed with that amount of money instead of you? None of that's possible . . . unless it's that my feelings for you increase because of your integrity."

"Higher?" Miriam choked on the word.

"How about lower?"

Wayne didn't hesitate. "No way, Miriam. There is no negative side of this. You didn't ask the man to leave you his farm and money."

"I could have refused it. I could have at least given the money away . . ." Her voice trailed off.

Wayne shrugged. "You were right in not doing any of those things. If the Lord allowed you to have that kind of money, then He must have a plan for your life that will require those assets."

Miriam gasped. "Like what, Wayne? *Daett* says money is a terrible corruptor. What could I possibly need such an amount for? What kind of trials would the Lord send that would require two million dollars to fix?"

Wayne's smile was gentle. "Don't look on the dark side of things, Miriam. I didn't mean it that way. Money can be used for *gut*. The Lord might desire for you to do much *gut* with that money. We don't know what He has planned. Obviously you didn't go out and spend it like many people would. Isn't that wisdom to your credit?"

Miriam took a deep breath. This was more than she'd hoped for. It seemed too good to be true. Wayne saw that the Lord's hand must be in her situation! And Wayne seemed unimpressed with the amount of money involved. Had he not heard correctly?

Miriam repeated the information. "It's two million dollars, Wayne. A two followed by six zeroes."

His laugh was soft. "I heard you, Miriam. And I suppose you're worried that I might want my hand in the cookie jar, so to speak. I'm not concerned, Miriam, and I don't desire your money. This information doesn't change anything between us, Miriam. I don't want or need the money. Things are different out here. Can't you feel and see it? Not that any one of us is perfect, but we think differently. I know for myself that I would have felt the same way about you even if I'd known you had two million dollars stashed away. When I first laid eyes on you, I told myself, 'Now here is a woman of character I want to know better.' And I've not changed my mind. I feel blessed to be interested in a woman like you, Miriam. I do care about you a lot, and I'm grateful that you seem interested in knowing me better too."

"Oh, Wayne!" Miriam was so relieved that she could hardly talk.

Wayne's hand found hers and squeezed it gently.

She clutched both his hands. She wanted to lean on his shoulder, but that wouldn't be seemly. She felt the Lord had orchestrated this moment.

"I'm glad you told me," Wayne said, interrupting her thoughts. "That must have been a great weight on your shoulders to carry alone."

"*Yah,* it was." Her voice was a whisper. How perceptive of him to see her heart and need so plainly. "I thought at times you'd leave once you knew I had so much. Even though my heart told me it wouldn't matter to you, my fear kept reminding me that it might."

"Why, Miriam?" His hand tightened on hers. "I'd never think less of you, Miriam. Not for something like that. I mean, what's money?"

"Maybe it does signify too much to me," Miriam confessed. "For as long as I can remember *Daett* told us about the evils of money — how it corrupts and the power it holds over people. I guess I was afraid more than anything else. An experience back home has left me a bit . . . confused about how to handle all of this."

She decided that was all she needed to tell Wayne about Ivan at this point. One confession was enough for tonight. Maybe sometime in the future, but right now Ivan's fake attention felt cheesy and out of place. She wouldn't even honor him with a mention. And what she used to feel for Ivan — or imagined she felt for him — seemed small and insignificant compared to her feelings for Wayne. The moonlight and the relief from sharing her secret was probably accentuating her feelings, but they were real enough in their own right.

Miriam knew now she could trust Wayne with her heart. He would know what needed to be done — if and when they said the wedding vows together. Her heart beat faster at the thought, but her fingers slipped from his grasp when a new one took its place. "Do you think I need to share this news with someone else right away?" She glanced up at him.

Wayne didn't hesitate. "I don't think that would be the Lord's will. He's given *you* the money to handle. And I'd say you've shown yourself worthy of the task. So there's no reason to create a problem or give fodder for rumors. Not that there is anything to be ashamed of, but your *daett* was correct on one point. Money can do strange things to people."

"But it won't change us?"

In the moonlight his smile was genuine.

"We'll have to pray that it doesn't. And we can ask for the Lord's grace each and every day."

"Thank you, Wayne," Miriam whispered. If he'd given her wild assurances that nothing would change, she would have doubted him — but he hadn't. She smiled. "Now, I'd best entertain you inside the house before you starve to death. Let's go in."

Wayne chuckled. "I was about ready to think I'd never get to eat pie tonight."

Miriam took a quick step forward. "Come inside then!"

His hand found hers. "Miriam, I was teasing, but pie does sound good."

She clung to his hand on the short walk. They let go only when they reached the front door. Her heart right now could barely be contained. Floods of relief and joy, happiness and love were rushing through her. She thought she might be in danger of floating away for all the *wunderbah* emotions she was experiencing. And Wayne must be feeling some of the same things because his face was glowing!

She left him seated on the living room couch while she went into the kitchen. Minutes later she returned with two bowls of homemade vanilla ice cream on two slices of cherry pie, the delicious fruit oozing out the sides exactly like cherry pie was supposed to. Wayne took all of it in and smiled his approval. "It looks like you're quite some cook."

"How do you know I made it?" she teased.

His smile didn't dim. "Because I know you."

"Sounds like you have me all figured out." Miriam sat beside him and offered a silent prayer: "Thank You, dear Lord. Just thank You."

Chapter Thirty-Nine

Miriam set a brisk pace as she walked toward the community's little one-room schoolhouse. The sun had barely peeked above the horizon, and the cool morning air hung low to the ground. What a *wunderbah* day this Saturday was! The morning felt fashioned just for her and this blessed time in her life. She was so unworthy of all the Lord was bestowing on her.

Ezra Mullet's niece, Sarah, had shown her the schoolhouse on Wednesday. And Miriam now had a special dress — a dark-blue one she'd finished last week — for the opening day of school hanging in her closet at home. Her thoughts should be on focused on schoolbooks and lesson plans, Miriam reminded herself, but this morning Wayne was the brightest thing on her mind. Thoughts of him crept in everywhere she went. They'd had two official dates now, and she'd seen glimpses of him all week at the greenhouse. During work hours they'd spoken only briefly — mostly "*gut* mornings" shared with warm smiles. Wayne had stayed true to his word these past two weeks and hadn't once brought up the matter of the inheritance.

It was still hard not to doubt the man at times — the possibility that he really was like he said he was so boggled her mind. And yet it seemed to be true. Wayne wasn't influenced in any way by her wealth, and his attitude fit perfectly with his *wunderbah* character. Thoughts of him towered over her head like Mount Everest in those stories of faraway lands she enjoyed. She had to admit that Wayne loved her for herself, even though she found it hard to believe.

The memory of Wayne's words from last Sunday evening stirred in her mind. "I really want to make it clear, Miriam, how blessed I am that the Lord has brought you into my life. I mean, what were the chances that you'd find your way out to Oklahoma from Possum Valley? And that you'd like it here once you arrived?" His smile had lit up his whole face. She hadn't known what to say so she'd murmured something that she couldn't remember now.

She'd accept all this eventually, Miriam told herself. Wayne was no Ivan Mast. She mustn't allow the negative character of one man to color her perceptions of all the others who touched her life.

Sunday evening she'd wanted desperately to give Wayne a kiss. That was a thought that took her breath away. Why had such a desire risen up inside of her? Never had she felt that way with Ivan, even with all the smiles and glances they'd shared.

Miriam turned onto the side road leading to the schoolhouse and began to walk even faster. She must not think about kissing Wayne. With his quality character, he probably wouldn't kiss her until after they'd said wedding vows. And here she was with thoughts of her wedding this morning when they'd only had two dates! They would have another one tomorrow evening, but that was still only three. Miriam slowed her quick steps. Just because Wayne was the perfect man didn't mean she should think of kisses and saying wedding vows with him without due consideration.

She knew Shirley had kissed a man — Jonas. But Miriam wouldn't cheapen her relationship with Wayne by giving in to hasty kisses. She would enjoy each step of the way, savoring each moment. Things would progress fast enough.

Miriam slowed down even more as she

approached the front door. She entered the schoolhouse and paused for a moment to catch her breath. Her gaze took in the high ceiling, the rows of desks, and the smell of books and ink. This was her schoolhouse for the term. The community's children would be entrusted to her care. What a great honor this was, and one she hadn't looked for or even expected in her wildest dreams. What a *wunderbah* work the Lord had done for her — not only in Wayne's heart, but in the community as well. Coming to Oklahoma had certainly been the right choice for her. It was true that things were always the darkest before dawn. She would have to remember that in the future when trouble knocked on her door.

Miriam frowned as she thought of Shirley. There had been no letter or any news beyond a brief call to the phone shack to let them know Shirley had arrived safely home. No doubt Shirley was still struggling to find her place in life. She was probably still disappointed she hadn't found her happiness in Oklahoma.

Miriam stared out one of the schoolhouse windows. Was Shirley back with Jonas? The question had come to her last night, but she'd pushed it away. Shirley knew better than to give in to that temptation. Hadn't she said emphatically that she knew Jonas wasn't the right man for her? Hadn't she made a serious effort to change the course of her life? *Yah,* Shirley had. Perhaps those attempts wouldn't all be in vain. But how easily one could slip back into the old ways. Shirley had always struggled to keep her promises, even though she usually had the best of intentions.

A rattle of buggy wheels interrupted Miriam's thoughts. She walked to the window, pushed aside the drapes, and peered into the yard. She exhaled suddenly when she saw Wayne climbing out of his buggy. She heard his clear voice calling to his horse, "Steady, boy. Stay right here."

The reins hung straight down as Wayne walked toward the schoolhouse door with sure steps.

Why was he here? Miriam wondered. Surely, there wasn't trouble at Uncle William and Aunt Fannie's place. And how did Wayne even know she was here? He was supposed to be at work getting ready for another busy Saturday morning.

His knock on the door pulled her out of her thoughts. She rushed forward, watching Wayne's face as he peered through the door window. Miriam paused to catch her breath before she opened the door.

"I figured you'd be here." A smile lit up Wayne's handsome features.

"Surely there's nothing wrong?" Miriam clung to the doorknob.

"Nee." He glanced at her white knuckles. "I'm sorry. I didn't mean to scare you."

Miriam heaved a sigh of relief. "I'm glad everything is okay. I wasn't expecting you, so I wasn't sure what to think."

"I won't stay long," he said. "May I come in?"

Miriam opened the door wider. "Of course!"

Wayne entered and glanced around. "You have quite a responsibility here — molding the minds of the community's young children. I'd swoon if I had to do this."

"You wouldn't!" Miriam giggled. "I'm sure you'd be much better at this than I will be."

"Don't underestimate yourself." His smile was warm. "May I sit at one of the desks?"

He's so cute, Miriam thought as she watched Wayne squeeze his lengthy frame on the small bench behind a desk that was looking smaller and smaller. His legs stuck out into the aisle. Miriam laughed.

Wayne gave her a mock glare. "Is that the proper attitude for a teacher to show one of her students?"

"You're not a student," Miriam corrected and laughed even louder. She slid into the desk chair next to him.

Wayne looked approvingly her way. "Now that's how a teacher should act."

Miriam let the moment wash over her. She felt almost giddy — something that seemed more like Shirley than her. It was a delicious feeling all the same.

"Ah, the times of a youngster." Wayne leaned back as much as he could in the little school seat. "So innocent and with the entire world in front of you. How great those days were."

"You make it sound like you're absolutely ancient," Miriam chided.

He grinned. "Old and withered before my time. That's me and mine."

"Don't include me in the old part!" Miriam teasingly snapped at him. She felt goose bumps come as his gaze settled on her.

Nervous now, Miriam stood and was about to say something when a pile of books on the front desk toppled to the floor. She rushed to retrieve them, but Wayne stopped her with an upraised hand.

"Allow me, please." He unwrapped himself from the desk.

"I'm such a klutz!" Miriam's words came out a shriek.

His look said everything she needed to hear. *No you're not. I understand why you acted like that, and I love it.*

Her knees were weak, so Miriam sank back into another chair so she wouldn't fall into a heap on the schoolhouse floor.

After Wayne picked up the last book and placed it back on the desk, he said, "I think I'd better get to work."

Miriam rose and followed him to the door.

Wayne turned back, gave her hand a quick squeeze, and then turned and headed to his buggy.

Miriam watched him go as her heart pounded. The place on her arm where he'd touched her seemed deliciously warm and stayed that way long after Wayne's buggy was out of sight. It took a few minutes for her to get down to business. What a *wunderbah* surprise, Wayne's visit. They were two people in love . . .

The desk where Wayne had sat stood askew, so Miriam straightened it. Her hand moved over the surface where moments before his arms had rested. Wayne, the man of her dreams. And what a man he was — able to handle her secret and still focus on and love only her. What a great gift the Lord had given her! In a thousand years she'd never be able to thank Him enough.

If Wayne asked her to marry him on any Sunday evening, she would say *yah* without hesitation. It was a little too soon to expect that, and Wayne would do what was appropriate. She could wait. She could wait for a year, or two years, or three years. She'd wait until Wayne thought the time was right. And then she would wed him back in Possum Valley. They would live together for whatever time the Lord saw fit to give them, and they would be thankful the whole time — in sickness, in health, in the *gut* times and the bad.

Miriam took a deep breath and focused. She had to stop thinking about Wayne so she could prepare the school lessons. With great effort Miriam forced herself to get out the tablet she'd found in a desk drawer and start writing. She wrote the first sentence in bold letters: "Lesson plans for the new term." But where to go from here? What she needed was something fresh and imaginative to grab the students' attention. She'd want their full cooperation, and that meant not having any boring, dull moments. Already she could envision the students with their heads bent over their desks busily doing their schoolwork. She'd teach like Alma Beachy had done back in Possum Valley. How Miriam had loved those student days. Now she was the teacher!

With a sigh, Miriam swiveled in the teacher's chair behind the front desk. The truth was that she was sure she wouldn't be half the teacher Alma Beachy had been or even Sarah Mullet. Maybe after many years she could be, but the first year she shouldn't expect to do too much innovation. In fact, she would primarily use the outline Sarah had left her. She retrieved Sarah's lesson plan and schedule from the bottom desk drawer and scanned the pages. *Yah,* this would work fine.

Now she could finish and go home to catch another glimpse of Wayne out in the greenhouse. There might even be time this afternoon to help out a little. Perhaps they could speak a few words together. She was hopelessly in love, Miriam admitted with a smile. And she was so very happy about it.

CHAPTER FORTY

Aunt Fannie came into the living room with baby Jonathon in her arms. "Any news from Possum Valley I should know about?"

Miriam glanced up from the letter that had come this morning. "Not really, but you're welcome to read it when I'm done. And you could have opened the envelope when it arrived, you know. You didn't have to wait for me to get home from teaching school." She handed over the handwritten pages from *Mamm*.

Aunt Fannie placed Jonathon on his blanket on the floor and settled in her rocker, but not before giving Miriam a stern look. "One should never open anyone else's mail. You know that."

"But it's okay with me," Miriam protested. "*Mamm* is your sister, and I'm staying at your place."

Aunt Fannie just shook her head and then read the letter silently. *Mamm* had written news about baby Anna. The baby had developed colic, which *Mamm* hadn't expected. Colic mostly occurred in first or second born, she said. Not an eleventh child. Aunt Fannie nodded. She was of the same opinion. Amish women generally agreed on such common ideas. Yet here was baby Jonathon, their first child, sleeping through the night with hardly a peep, while *Mamm* wrote of hours spent walking the floor with baby Anna. *Mamm* also mentioned she was thrilled to have Shirley home — that the Lord must have moved on Shirley's heart to return.

Miriam wasn't so sure about that. Still, *Mamm* wouldn't say something she didn't believe. So perhaps it had been for the best. Maybe Shirley had retained the lessons she learned here in the Clarita community. Hopefully she was now putting them to *gut* use at home. From what *Mamm* wrote, Shirley was taking her turns caring for Anna right along with fourteen-year-old Naomi.

Miriam turned her attention to the other letter that had arrived in the day's mail. It was from Shirley and would likely be more forthcoming about news than *Mamm*'s letter had been. But did Miriam really want to know what troubles Shirley might be in already? There might be news of her renewing contact with Jonas Beachy. That would definitely put a damper on Miriam's good mood.

So far the day had been a good one — as had all three days of the new school term. That left only one more day this week, and what could go wrong in that amount of time? Didn't the rough things come to pass on the first day of school or maybe the following one? Friday should be a breeze. She'd survived so far with no calamities. Teaching school suited her much more than she'd imagined.

Only Wayne brought her more happiness right now — and the Lord, of course. She couldn't live without Him and His blessings. She wouldn't even be in Oklahoma to experience Wayne's love and the community's acceptance if the Lord hadn't led her here. Wayne was going to pick her up later tonight for a young folks' gathering — sweet-corn husking at Deacon Phillip's place. She didn't want anything to spoil her evening. Especially something Shirley might have written in her letter. Perhaps she should put the letter away until she got home tonight? *Nee,* Shirley might have *gut* news to share. Miriam mentally shook herself. Why did she always expect the worst? She glanced at Aunt Fannie, who still had her head bent over *Mamm*'s letter. Miriam picked up the envelope. A quick cut with the letter opener was all it took, and the letter was in her hand. She unfolded the first of two pages.

Dear Miriam,

I know you already know I'm at home, and that we are in the midst of dealing with a colicky baby Anna. She's the sweetest thing, but I sometimes have serious doubts at midnight when she's crying full bore on my shoulder. I suppose it's for the best, and trials come as we need to grow. I know I need plenty, as they say, since temptations abound on all sides of me.

I snuck out to call Jonas the other evening. I suspect you already figured I would, so there's no sense in keeping it from you. I also trust that you won't tell anyone. I know I shouldn't keep secrets from Mamm and Daett, but I can't seem to help myself. And I've told you now.

All the gut things I learned in Oklahoma now seem faraway and unreal. Why I didn't stay out there, I don't know. Well, that's not entirely true. I intended to stick it out there, and many things had been going so well. Maybe that's why it caught me by surprise — the sudden urge to go home. So when the face-saving opportunity of baby Anna's birth came, I jumped at the chance. I probably shouldn't have left, but that's always been one of my problems — wanting to look good to others and win their praise, which wasn't going so well in Clarita.

So now I'm back in Possum Valley, and everything's the same again. I still have "the touch," shall we say? Is it my fault that unmarried Ohio men pay me attention? I don't think so. They're supposed to, and I like it. But I'm not the happiest, to tell you the truth. Sure, while I'm with the Possum Valley youth group and everyone's having a good time, I'm happy, but afterward I feel kind of empty inside. The trial of baby Anna's health is my saving grace, I think. It keeps me occupied and tired out. I sure hope I didn't bring this on the family because of faults and sins. Maybe they need cleansing? I wonder sometimes, and I feel horrible about it. But what can I do? I had my chance in Oklahoma but couldn't stick it out. Oh, for resolutions that could be kept! I think I'd be in heaven itself if such a thing would happen. Truthfully, though, I think at times it will never happen until I get there . . . which I'm hoping to make it to after a very long life lived with this sorrow and pain.

But I suppose you're busting with impatience on how the phone call went with Jonas. He was sweet like usual, but he didn't invite me over or anything. I didn't bring it up either. I didn't want to stoop that low. Jonas wasn't offended that I called out of the blue. I wonder if he's dating someone else? There was a girl's voice in the background, but he has sisters so I'm hoping it was one of them. Why I care, I don't know. I realize I can't date him again. We're not made for each other. I don't fit into his world. Not really. Nor do I want to. I will just have to do better and remember the lessons I learned in Oklahoma.

Oh, here's some news you might find interesting since things are going well with Wayne and you. And speaking of Wayne, let me say this first. I don't know for sure, but I'm going to take a guess. And not a big one I suppose from how things had been going before I left. Has Wayne asked you to be his frau yet? I don't know why I brought that up, but . . .

Anyway, Ivan and Laura are quite serious about each other. Laura hangs on to Ivan at every youth gathering like she's afraid he'll get away from her. All they do is smile and gaze into each other's eyes all evening. It's sickening, if you ask me. I wouldn't be surprised if there's a wedding this fall for those two. Laura's a little young, but why not? From the way she acts, a wedding seems quite probable.

I was curious enough to hint at the matter with Laura's older sister Esther. The girl sputtered around, so I'm sure it's the truth. Why should I care about them — other than the connection with you? I'm not sure. I still think Ivan was mighty stupid to let you get away from him. But then again, I have to admit again that you were probably right.

So pray for me, Miriam. I want so to do what is right, but temptations are strong around me. Daett prayed for each of us children last night in such tender tones. He broke my heart all over again. I told the Lord I was so sorry for calling Jonas, but you know how that goes. I still want to talk to Jonas, and probably would if I ran into him downtown. That's why, I think, Mamm hasn't mentioned anything about me looking for a job in Berlin. I know the family could use the money. Things aren't quite as poverty stricken around here what with the income from your farm, but a little extra cash is always welcome in the Yoder family.

But on to happier subjects . . .

There are whispers of other weddings in the area this fall. Our cousin Ben Yoder and his girlfriend, Sharon . . .

Miriam looked up when Aunt Fannie interrupted her.

"Does Shirley have any *gut* news?"

Miriam smiled. "Cousin Ben and Sharon might have a wedding planned."

Aunt Fannie laughed. "Now that's gossip of the first order. I thought it was going to happen this fall, but, on the other hand, what would I know way out here?"

"Your guess is probably as *gut* as Shirley's." Miriam lay the letter down and stood up. "It's about time to prepare supper, isn't it?"

She'd finish the letter later in the evening, perhaps after Wayne dropped her off after the youth gathering. Shirley probably didn't have much else of importance to share, and there was supper to prepare and eat before

Wayne picked her up. Thankfully Aunt Fannie didn't ask to read Shirley's letter. She must understand that sisters tell each other things not meant for their older relatives' ears.

Aunt Fannie left Jonathon squirming on the rug in front of the stove and joined her in the kitchen. That wouldn't be possible once the baby learned how to crawl, Miriam knew. But for now Aunt Fannie could help because she could watch him through the kitchen doorway. When they finished dinner preparations thirty minutes later, Aunt Fannie pointed toward the upstairs. "Go get ready for your evening. Then you can eat before we do, so you'll be finished before your beau arrives."

Miriam didn't protest. This had become their routine on the evenings when the community's young folks had planned activities. Miriam hurried to her room. She paused in front of the closet. What should she wear? The work in the cornfield tonight would get dirt all over her dress, but everyday clothes didn't feel quite right. Better to wash the stains out later than be uncomfortable. Why not wear the dark-blue dress she'd made for the opening day of school? The dress had been a little present to herself in celebration of the great honor the community had given her. Still, she must not hold any occasion or the dress too highly. A corn husking would keep her estimation of the dress in its proper place.

With the dark-blue dress on, Miriam returned to the kitchen and ate supper. Before she finished, she heard buggy wheels rattle down the driveway. Aunt Fannie waved her back down when Miriam leaped to her feet. "Wayne can wait. He's way early."

"But maybe there's a reason," Miriam protested.

"Not anything more than he wants to see you." Aunt Fannie smiled even as she directed Miriam back to her chair. "That's not reason enough to skip part of your supper."

"But . . ." Miriam tried again.

Aunt Fannie cut her off. "It's *gut* for a man to wait sometimes. And you're not running out to explain. He can figure it out for himself."

Miriam took a deep breath and sat down. She finished eating, but the food went down in gulps. What Aunt Fannie said was no doubt true, but she wanted to see Wayne probably more than he wanted to see her! And certainly more than she wanted to eat. She finished and bolted from the table.

Aunt Fannie's look reminded Miriam to slow down and act dignified. Miriam did so with great effort. She went out the front door after garnering Aunt Fannie's smile of approval.

Wayne leaped down from his buggy when she approached. "*Gut* evening! I hope I didn't interrupt your supper."

She smiled. "I was almost finished. I tried to hurry."

He didn't offer her his hand up into the buggy, and neither did she expect him to. That wasn't a custom in their communities like it was in the *Englisha* world.

Wayne appeared pleased as he climbed in after her and sat down. "Well, here we are again!"

"*Yah.*"

"Are you ready for the evening?" He didn't wait for an answer before clucking to his horse and driving down the lane. They were already comfortable in each other's presence.

How quickly they'd come to feel at home around each other, Miriam thought. Soon she would even dare to lean against his shoulder. Miriam almost shocked herself at the very thought. They hadn't even been holding hands for long, and here she was imagining such intimacy! It wasn't even her place to begin such a practice. Already the Lord had given her gifts too great for what she deserved. She shouldn't desire any more than He chose to give, and she needed to be patient and wait for His timing.

They settled into peaceful silence with only the steady sounds of horse hooves hitting the blacktop.

CHAPTER FORTY-ONE

Later that evening the soft rustle of corn-stalks filled the air as the youth group moved down the lengthy rows of Deacon Phillip's sweet-corn patch. A late-phase moon hung low on the horizon, its glow interrupted on the ground by the light of gas lanterns set on the wagon racks.

Deacon Phillip had pulled in three of his wagons soon after Miriam and Wayne had arrived, and now happy chatter filled the night air. Miriam had lost sight of Wayne for the moment. Everyone had a basket near him or her to throw the corn in after taking them off the stalks. Then the baskets of corn ears were emptied into one of the wagons. Miriam tossed an ear into her basket and searched again for Wayne's form in the dim light. He'd be close by, she knew. Wayne seldom left her side at youth gatherings these days. She wanted to make sure she didn't get all clingy like Laura Swartz was with Ivan, according to Shirley.

"How are things going at the Byler house?" Betty Troyer asked, breaking into Miriam's thoughts.

Miriam smiled in the soft light. "Okay. Baby Jonathon is practically taking care of himself these days. It's hard to believe he's almost eleven weeks old."

Betty's gaze swept the length of the cornfield and rested on Wayne. "Things are going well in another department, it looks like."

Miriam couldn't stop her huge smile as she said, *"Yah,* Wayne is *wunderbah."*

"Wayne's a nice fellow, there's no doubt about that," Betty said. "We're glad you moved here. We need as many young couples for our community as we can find. Especially after we lost the Swartz family a while back. I thought at one time Wayne might fall for their daughter Esther. I think he's done much better with you."

"Thank you," Miriam said. That Wayne might have been attracted to Esther Swartz didn't surprise her. She was as *gut* looking as her sister Laura and probably had a boyfriend back in Possum Valley by now. Miriam hadn't expected such plain talk tonight. Still, Betty obviously thought she fit in the community, which was another

433

great blessing.

"I like it here," Miriam said.

"Shirley must not have," Betty probed.

What should she say? Miriam wondered. And how much did Betty know about Shirley? News travels fast in the communities, and Shirley's relationship with Jonas Beachy might well have reached Betty's ears.

"I guess Shirley didn't find what I did in Oklahoma."

"We're not all the same." Betty's voice was gentle. "So how's she doing?"

"She's taking care of baby Anna mostly." That wasn't quite what Betty wanted to know, but Miriam didn't want to speak of Jonas and lessons not heeded. Miriam hurried on. "It turns out that Anna's quite colicky, so *Mamm,* Shirley, and my sister Naomi have been pacing the floor with her all hours of the night. I'm glad baby Jonathon sleeps like an angel at night."

"Like I said, we're all different." Betty glanced up as Wayne neared. "Now look who's finally here."

"At least you're not some handsome dude trying to steal Miriam from me," Wayne retorted.

Betty's laughter rang through the cornfield. "I think you have things pretty tightly sewn up on that score."

Wayne smiled at Miriam. "I like to think so, but all things in the Lord's *gut* time."

Miriam shyly smiled at Wayne, who was chuckling at Betty, who pretended she was rushed off. She "hollered" over her shoulder, "I'd best get out of here. I don't want to interfere with the Lord's workings, you know."

"Are we that obvious?" Miriam asked Wayne when no one was within earshot.

Wayne studied Miriam's face. "Betty is just teasing, but if talk about us bothers you, I can leave."

"Don't you dare!" The words burst out of Miriam's mouth.

Wayne laughed out loud. "That's *gut* to hear. I was beginning to wonder."

That was also a tease, Miriam knew. Wayne surely had to be certain about how she felt about him. On that matter she'd been plain enough — perhaps even too plain. Miriam looked around. What a perfect night and place for a kiss in a cornfield. Miriam drew in a sharp breath at the thought. Thankfully Wayne was busy with a stubborn cornstalk and didn't hear her sudden intake of breath. Here she was — twenty years of age and never been kissed.

What with the charm of the moon and the emotions swirling around inside of her, it was no surprise she was thinking such things. She glanced toward Wayne. Would he kiss her if she wanted him to? She removed another ear from a stalk. Wayne was too honorable. He wouldn't kiss her tonight because he was being careful not to advance too rapidly in their relationship. Look where throwing caution to the wind had gotten Shirley with Jonas Beachy. Miriam shivered, glad she wasn't Shirley. She didn't have to sneak around to see Wayne, and from the looks of things, the entire community approved of their budding relationship. So Miriam decided she would wait for her kiss, and once it came she would probably faint with joy. *Yah,* someday she would kiss Wayne. Soon — hopefully. Miriam shivered again at the provocative thought.

"You cold?" Wayne asked as he moved closer.

"Nee," Miriam said. She was embarrassed. What if Wayne knew what her thoughts had been. He'd think her indecent. She'd better get to work, she decided.

Miriam and Wayne continued to work, and they soon reached the end of the row. He stood tall to straighten his back. "Now for the really hard part — getting the husks off."

Miriam glanced at the others who were finishing up their rows and moving out of the cornfield. "At least we can sit down."

Wayne picked up their basket and dumped the corn in the nearest wagon. Miriam stayed close beside him as the huddle of young people gathered on the lawn. Chairs were brought out, and a bonfire lit. By the time the wagons were brought up, the fire was leaping high into the night air. Chairs had been set up in a circle around the fire pit. Everyone filled their baskets and got started.

"This isn't the easiest, is it?" Miriam asked as she tugged on an ear of corn. She glanced up at Wayne's face and thought the flames casting flickering shadows on his features made him appear even more handsome.

"I told you so." Wayne lifted a piece of the green corn husk into the air. Playfully he allowed the end to drag across Miriam's arm.

Miriam batted it away so Wayne couldn't see how much the teasing meant to her. Wayne could see she was pleased, but he didn't have to see how pleased.

"There's Mahlon Troyer and my sister Joy over there," Wayne whispered moments later. "They sure have their chairs close together."

Miriam looked up and stared across the

flames. "I didn't know the two of them were. . . ."

Wayne gave her a quick glance. "Do you approve?"

"I hardly know them." Miriam hesitated. "But from what I do know, I think they'd be great together."

"Joy has liked him for a while now, but Mahlon has taken his time, as any decent man should."

Miriam leaned toward Wayne. "You are perfect with your timing."

A broad smile spread over Wayne's face. So Miriam had been correct in her assumption that Wayne was carefully pacing their relationship. That was why he hadn't kissed her yet. She watched him staring into the fire, glad he couldn't see how much her face was turning red. He'd probably attribute it to the warmth of the fire, but it was really from Miriam's desire to lean over and kiss him. Finally she focused on the corn. For now she'd have to settle for the sound of his voice murmuring softly next to her.

"It's so peaceful out here. I've experienced this so many times before, yet tonight seems extra special. I'm glad you're here with me, Miriam. Very glad."

Miriam spoke softly, "It's a special night for me too."

Comfortable silence fell between them broken only by the sounds of corn being husked and the people around them happily chattering.

Wayne finally cleared his throat and looked at her. "Any news from home lately?"

Miriam pulled off a corn husk with a quick rip. "*Mamm* wrote, and Shirley too. Everything's going normally, except for baby Anna's colic. That's unusual, everyone agrees. But what can anyone do about it? The Lord decides what each person goes through, I suppose."

"He does." Wayne's gaze drifted her way again. "About the time you think everything is figured out, something new comes down the road. That can be *gut* or bad. Take the two of us." Wayne paused for a moment. "I had about given up hope I'd ever find someone who would fit all of my expectations and hopes. Then you came along!"

"Wayne," Miriam kept her voice low, "we're in the middle of lots of people so please don't say such things. Actually don't say it anytime." Now her face probably was the color of the fiery flames. "I'm not worthy of them. You don't know all my faults yet."

He didn't appear convinced. "You can't have too many faults — if any."

"That's what you think!" she whispered back. "I have plenty. Now please keep your voice down."

"I will holler your lovely characteristics to the moon if I want to." He pointed toward the moon's glow on the horizon. "See, it grows brighter by the minute."

Miriam forced herself to relax. Wayne's gaze soon settled on her face again, and she seized the moment and enough courage to whisper, "Thank you for liking me, Wayne. Even with the problem of how to deal with the inheritance, I . . ." Miriam stopped. She hadn't thought of the money in a while, and it seemed inappropriate to bring it up at a time like this.

Wayne seemed to understand. He reached across the space between them and touched her arm for only a second. "It doesn't matter. I already told you that. And it wasn't your choosing anyway."

"You are so kind! You don't know how much I appreciate you."

"I couldn't be otherwise when it comes to you," he said.

Companionable silence fell between them again. The fire crackled softly as the flames gradually decreased. The embers glowed deep-red and orange. If this time together became any more lovely, Miriam thought, she might burst into tears. Even then she believed Wayne would understand. He would also know when the best time arrived for their first kiss.

Deacon Phillip appeared holding packages of hot dogs. "Time to eat, everybody! But you have to cook your own food. That is, those of you hardy enough to face the fire's heat. And, by the way, there's homemade ice cream in the basement that I turned myself."

Laughter rose around the circle as most of the men bounced to their feet. Wayne was among them. He grabbed one of the pointed sticks the deacon's eldest son, Michael, had toted in from somewhere.

"Don't let that hot dog get away from you now," Mahlon teased Wayne. They both held sticks close to the coals and shielded their faces from the fire's heat. Wayne's sister Joy stood and moved closer to Mahlon. Already she was responding deeply to Mahlon's attention, Miriam thought. Just as I did to Wayne's. Perhaps in a year or two they would be sisters-in-law by marriage. That was a thought too *wunderbah* to think about. Even this moment of joy and possibility was almost more than she could bear. She ought to get up and stand near Wayne like Joy was with Mahlon, but her legs likely wouldn't hold her up. She sent her love to Wayne from the chair. She'd do it by the pounding of her heart if nothing else. Wayne might even feel the power of her love across the distance.

Miriam shifted on her chair so she could watch Wayne. He was so handsome . . . so very handsome. And she was so blessed.

CHAPTER FORTY-TWO

The dreamy September sky filled the schoolhouse windows, as Miriam settled in behind her teacher's desk. Outside, the last of the children's voices lingered in the afternoon air. She'd waved goodbye to the last buggies moments ago. How she adored each and every one of her little scholars! She loved her school-teaching job — all of it. But she loved Wayne even more. They had planned a special afternoon together. Uncle William must have felt generous because he gave Wayne extra time off. Still, Miriam shouldn't be too surprised. Uncle William approved fully of her relationship with Wayne Yutzy. She figured Wayne only had to mention what his intention was — a special, late-summer afternoon stroll with Miriam down by the creek — to obtain Uncle William's full cooperation.

How Wayne came up with such a romantic notion, she had no idea. Likely he was up to something. In fact, she was sure he was, and she didn't have to think too hard to imagine what. Miriam's heart beat faster at the thought. Would Wayne ask her to be his *frau* this afternoon? It still seemed a little early in their relationship, but, on the other hand, it felt like they'd known each other forever.

Miriam's chair squeaked as she reached for pen and paper. There was still time to finish her lesson plan for tomorrow. Wayne said he'd be here by four-thirty, and that was still an hour and a half away. If she hurried, she might even have time to write *Mamm* and Shirley the letters she owed them. In her last letter, Shirley hadn't said anything about Jonas Beachy. Miriam guessed that Shirley didn't wish to write more about the matter. Still, she hoped Shirley was keeping her resolution to stay away from the young man.

Miriam sighed. She definitely needed to write Shirley today, perhaps after her time with Wayne, even if that went late. Wayne had been invited to the Byler home for supper after their afternoon stroll. That had been Aunt Fannie's idea after Miriam had shared the afternoon plans with her. Likely Aunt Fannie had gotten her head together with Uncle William and coordinated the event. Miriam wondered if they knew what Wayne's plans were for this afternoon. If he was going to propose, would he have shared it with her uncle and aunt?

That wasn't likely. Uncle William and Aunt Fannie were probably guessing the same as she was. And they might all be wrong for all she knew. Her relationship with Wayne was still in its infancy when compared to most community courtships. Hope was a tricky thing. It could soar easily when one was in love. And right now her hope was soaring . . . maybe she'd finally get kissed by the man she loved! Miriam allowed a smile to creep across her face. If a kiss was forthcoming, maybe she would detail the experience for Shirley. That shocking thought caused Miriam to blush. She would do no such thing! A kiss from Wayne was private and intimate and between just the two of them. And it would remain so.

Miriam forced herself to focus on her lesson plans for over an hour. When she glanced at the clock, she'd finished planning and decided to begin a letter to Shirley. She opened her tablet to a fresh page and began.

Dear Shirley,

Greetings of love, dear sister. I hope this finds you well and in good spirits. I'm sitting here enthroned in my swivel chair at the schoolhouse. It's after four o'clock, and the children have been gone for a while. I feel lonesome for them already, even though I'll see them tomorrow. I wonder how I'll feel when the school term is complete. Likely I'll weep buckets of tears, although I'll try to hide them on the last day of school. How quickly the little munchkins have thrown their heart strings around mine.

You didn't mention Jonas in your last letter, so I hope you haven't been seeing him . . . or spoken with him, for that matter. Keeping in touch with him is not for the best, Shirley. You know that. I want to encourage you to go down the right path. There's so much of your life and mine that lies before us. We don't want to spoil it with bad choices. Stay strong, Shirley. Safety and happiness are found on the straight and narrow way. That certainly has been true for Wayne and me.

Miriam tapped her pen on the desk as her thoughts drifted. Had she said too much?

Surely her sister would understand where she was coming from. But still this was probably enough heavy advice for now. Breezy news would be best for the rest of the letter. She'd add that later. Miriam slipped the tablet into her book bag and grabbed her lunch bucket. She'd wait outside on the lawn for Wayne.

Miriam had just locked the door when Wayne's buggy appeared in the distance. He was right on time. But then Wayne usually was. He was close to perfect — at least in her eyes. Miriam ran the short distance to the road, arriving just as Wayne drove up.

He pulled on the lines and leaned out of the buggy. "Whoa, there! What a welcome!"

Miriam hopped in on the other side of the buggy. "Only what you deserve for being on time. I knew you would be, so don't get all swelled up about it."

Wayne grinned as he turned the buggy around. "Nice afternoon. Just what I ordered, you know."

"You *are* swelled up," Miriam said with a fake glare.

He laughed. "I think the Lord is on my side today."

Wayne *is* up to something special. She was sure of it. And now she'd overreacted and he'd think she'd guessed something. She

447

believed a man should be allowed his secrets until he chose to reveal them.

Wayne didn't seem to notice or be fazed. "Our creeks around here aren't anything glamorous, but it's all Oklahoma has to offer."

Miriam wanted to slip her arm around his, but she didn't. It wasn't time yet, but hopefully that would be soon. Instead she glanced at his face. "I'm just happy to spend time with you."

Wayne's grin returned. "The same goes for me with you."

He was occupied with his plan, Miriam told herself as they drove in silence. Wayne would ask her to be his *frau* this afternoon. She was sure of it now.

"Whoa!" Wayne called out as they approached the small creek. Miriam waited while Wayne tied up his horse before she climbed down. He flashed her a bright smile, but then he looked away at once. A serious look lay just beneath the surface, and she liked that. Wayne wasn't taking their future together lightly. This was an important time, and he was taking the necessary steps like a man should — with honor and sincerity.

Wayne's hand briefly touched Miriam's arm as they climbed down the gently sloping bank of the stream. An easy flow of water filled the bed. Upstream a fish flipped out of the water with a small splash.

"Not much in the way of fish around here." Wayne's laugh was nervous.

"Is that why you didn't bring your fishing pole?" Miriam teased.

Wayne shifted on his feet.

She shouldn't try that tack today, Miriam decided. She wasn't *gut* at teases.

Wayne became serious. "I've not known you for that long, Miriam." He glanced at her. "What has it been — a few months or so?"

"Just since the middle of July," Miriam whispered. Wayne just wanted her to reassure him, she thought. Perhaps she should wrap her arms around his neck right now and give him a big hug. But she'd wait. Wayne needed to say what he had to say in his own time. The hugs could come later.

"It's like I've always known you." Wayne's smile was thin. "I hope you don't think I've been too forward — that I've rushed things between us. It's just that . . ." Wayne stopped and gazed at the water in the creek bed.

"You've been none of those things, Wayne." Miriam reached over to touch his arm. "I think I've loved you since we

449

climbed out of Mr. Whitehorse's car."

"Really?" Relief filled his voice. "I think I felt the same way. Do you think . . ." He paused again.

"I think so." Miriam met his gaze. "I think so with all my heart."

He took a deep breath. "Then you will be . . . you feel what I do?"

Miriam moved closer. "*Yah,* I do, Wayne."

His fingers found hers. "Then you agree to be my *frau* . . . sometime in the near future? Maybe next fall already?"

"*Yah!*" She whispered the words. "You know I will!"

He touched her face. "The wonder of you, Miriam. How am I so blessed?"

Miriam reached for Wayne with both hands, and he responded in kind. Her face burned like fire as Wayne's lips touched hers for the first time. Her mind was a blur of emotion. Wayne's presence overwhelmed her as his fingers pressed softly on her neck.

"Miriam . . ." He pulled back.

She trembled and didn't answer.

He pulled her close again and lingered long.

She would soon not be able to breathe, Miriam realized, but she didn't care. Each moment of this should be enjoyed to the fullest and remembered forever.

"Come," Wayne said moments later, with his hand under her arm. "There's a fallen log we can sit on downstream a bit."

Miriam followed him and then sat beside Wayne with their fingers entwined. When she could breathe again, Miriam whispered. "Just hold me tight, Wayne. I don't want this moment to ever stop."

He nodded. "May the Lord continue to guide and keep us as we plan our life together."

"I will always love you, Wayne." She hugged him. "I love you for loving me just the way I am."

Wayne's face filled with a wide smile. "That was the easiest and best thing I've ever done. Believe me! And it will always be so."

She leaned against his shoulder as tears stung her eyes.

DISCUSSION QUESTIONS

1. Does Miriam's care of Amos Bland differ from how an *Englisha* person would care for him? If yes, what are the differences?
2. How well did Miriam handle the news that Ivan Mast had taken Laura Swartz home from the hymn singing?
3. How would you describe Shirley's weakness as she struggles to keep her promises and best intentions? Is there hope for her improvement?
4. When Ivan approached Miriam after discovering she'd inherited a farm, what would you have told him if you were in Miriam's shoes? What would the results have been?
5. Do you think Jonas has Shirley's best interests in mind? Why do you think he wants to continue his relationship with Shirley?

6. What caused Rose to trust Miriam and how she cared for Amos? Why did Rose never ascribe ulterior motives to Miriam even though others did?

7. Is the obsession Miriam's *daett* has about money healthy for himself? For his family?

8. Does moving away from problems in an effort to start anew usually work? Why or why not?

9. How does the birth of baby Jonathon affect Miriam and Shirley? If a tragedy had occurred during his birth, do you think that would have changed the choices the girls made? If yes, how?

10. Do you trust Wayne Yutzy? Why or why not?

11. Was Miriam wise to tell Wayne about her two million dollars so soon in their relationship? If not, when would be the best time to share such information?

12. Do you think Wayne and Miriam are a gut match for each other? Why or why not?

ABOUT THE AUTHOR

Jerry Eicher's Amish fiction has sold more than 700,000 books. After a traditional Amish childhood, Jerry taught for two terms in Amish and Mennonite schools in Ohio and Illinois. Since then he's been involved in church renewal, preaching, and teaching Bible studies. Jerry lives with his wife, Tina, and their four children in Virginia.